BOOK 2 OF THE DARK ILLUSION TRILOGY

I'M BACK

MARION HUGHES

Published in Australia by Sid Harta Books & Print Pty Ltd,
ABN: 34632585293
23 Stirling Crescent, Glen Waverley, Victoria 3150 Australia
Telephone: +61 3 9560 9920, Facsimile: +61 3 9545 1742
E-mail: author@sidharta.com.au

First published in Australia 2022
This edition published 2022
Copyright © Marion Hughes 2022
Cover design, typesetting: WorkingType (www.workingtype.com.au)

Hughes, Marion
I'm Back
ISBN: 978-1-925707-96-0
pp344

About the Author

Marion Hughes lives on the Mornington Peninsula, Victoria, Australia.

Also by Marion Hughes:

The Von Mueller Deception

Watch Your Back

To my sisters

1

It was 4 a.m. Two black-clad figures climbed out of an SUV parked in a narrow back street and crossed the main road onto the esplanade. One carried a medium-sized backpack.

The icy wind swirled as they headed towards the hazy, yellow lights of the marina.

'Shit, it's cold. I'd forgotten how fucking cold this place gets in winter.'

'Not your go, Ava?' There was a pause. 'That's what you want me to call you, isn't it?'

There was a nod.

'Not your real name though, is it?'

His companion stopped and glared at him with an icy expression.

'Let's get one thing straight. Nothing about me is any of your goddamned business. And that's the way I like things kept. Understood?'

There was a shrug. 'Your call.'

Angelina was used to working alone but, like it or not, from here on in she required someone else, someone with the expertise she lacked.

'I'm paying you big money to do this job,' she snapped. 'I could have chosen anyone but Rodriguez said you were the best. Just stick to your job, do as I ask and we'll get along fine.'

She reached for her hoodie and set off once more at a brisker pace.

Nic Drakos said nothing, but inwardly he was seething. He had nothing against women. The ones he'd worked alongside had been nothing short of efficient and reliable. There was no doubt this woman could hold her own, but he was used to calling the shots. *It's only a night's work,* he reminded himself. *You can put up with her crap for that long.*

The fee she offered made it well worth the effort. Nic had checked his online banking account before he left to pick her up. Half the money had already been deposited, with the remainder to follow on completion. Good money for a relatively low-risk job. Nonetheless, he'd already made up his mind on one thing. If she was to seek his services again, he'd be doing it alone and on his terms.

All was quiet as they approached the marina security gates. A brief smile crossed Angelina's face as she pulled her father's red fob out of her pocket. Nic gave the nod, and they pulled black scarves from their pockets, tying them around their faces. It should be a relatively simple procedure. The woman knew the place back to front: the location of the CCTV cameras, and the times the security guards made their rounds. It was the middle of winter, with conditions far from ideal for sailing. Few, if any owners would be staying on their yachts, except the target of course.

What in hell had the poor bastard done? he wondered.

He cast a quick look around the marina and checked his watch. 'It's 4.10 now. I want to be out of here in twenty minutes. Let's go.'

Angelina was surprised at how agile he was for his bulk. Around six-foot-three, he moved alongside her with the stealth of a cat. The yacht was the last on the track, well away from the nearest CCTV camera that they'd passed with heads bowed.

Nic gave a low whistle as they approached the *Jennifer*, a sixty-five metre double-masted Herreshoff schooner. What he'd give to own something like that. *Shit, what was with this woman,* he found himself wondering. Unzipping his backpack, he pulled out what he needed and stepped on board. Taking the lid off the jerry can he splashed petrol over the deck and jumped off as sure footed as an ibex onto the fixed walkway beside her. He lit a match.

'Get back,' he said. 'Be ready to get the hell out of here.'

Angelina's eyes were fixed on the scrolled letters: *Jennifer* on the hull.

'I want to watch, first. Watch him die.'

Nic wondered if he'd heard correctly as he threw the cigarette onto the deck, which was alight within seconds.

As flames shot high into the sky, he was sure he heard a scream above the roar. Below deck, a man's face appeared, terrified, mouth open. Angelina locked her eyes on his, as his hands clawed at the window and slid down. He was gone.

A fireball of orange and black exploded into the night sky.

'Right,' she said. 'Now we can go.'

They ran.

2

Apart from Lee Farrell, the only regulars at the marina that night were a couple and their two children. It was the youngest's fifth birthday, and their father had promised a sleepover on their yacht. The family awoke to the explosion. Scrambling out of their beds, they rushed up on deck, by which time the *Jennifer* was fully engulfed in flames.

'Shit!' The father ducked below the hatch and into the galley to grab his phone.

It took six minutes for the fire brigade to arrive and by that time the Lorenzo family's yacht was destroyed. A team of firefighters quickly set to with their hoses, pumping water over the burnt-out vessel and those nearby. During the ensuing search of the boat, a man's charred body was discovered.

'This could've been a lot worse if we hadn't got here when we did,' the lieutenant remarked to his offsider, a young recruit not long on the job. 'I hate to think how many mills are sitting on the moorings out there.'

'How many boats can this place hold?'

'Around two hundred and fifty.'

'Geez, that many. Do you get many call-outs here?'

'Not really. It'd have to be a year or so since the last.'

'What do you think caused this one?'

There was a shrug. 'Who knows. An insurance job, perhaps. It's often the case with boats. Maybe the poor bugger below botched things. It's not unheard of.'

'So what happens now?'

'This whole area will remain a crime scene until the Arson Investigation Unit has done its job.'

He looked at the crowd of growing people behind the yellow and red police tape.

'Can't help themselves.' His face was grim. 'They seem to come out of the woodwork.'

'Where from at this hour?'

'Local residents probably, or those driving past. Then, there's the boat owners who live close by. It doesn't take long for word to get around these days.'

¶

'You brought your bags, didn't you?' Angelina asked as they headed out of the city.

'Yeah. So where are we going?'

'The Prom.'

'What? You mean Wilson's Prom?'

'Yep.'

He shot her a sideways glance. 'Why there? That's hours from here.'

'Best to get as far away from the city as we can,' she said. 'The Tidal River campsite is all but deserted at this time of year. You do know where it is, I hope.'

'Yeah, we went there sometimes when I was a kid.'

'Good.'

She settled down in her seat. 'I've booked two one-bedroomed apartments. And then in the morning, we split.'

'So, you want me to drop you off somewhere once we've checked out?'

'No. I've organised all that.' There was a pause. 'Can you turn on some music? Right now, I don't feel like talking.'

That suited Nic fine. The last thing he felt like was superficial, small talk to pass the time.

He activated the Bluetooth audio.

Angelina closed her eyes and leaned back against the headrest. 'Let me know when we reach Leongatha,' she said, 'and we can drop by the supermarket for food and supplies. There's not much choice at the campsite.'

As they headed out of town, Nic reflected on the night's events.

Fire. It was the worst way he could think of to die. He would have preferred to prise open the hatch, step down into the galley and shoot the guy while he slept. But she had her reasons. And he had his money.

Right now, that came as little comfort.

If only he hadn't seen the guy's face. If he'd have been

working alone, he'd have been well on the way out once the match was thrown. The target would most likely die of smoke inhalation before the explosion hit, he'd reason …

But what was done was done.

Living with it would be another story …

What disturbed him most was the calm, cold look on the face of the woman sitting beside him, as she watched the guy burn. Unlike him, she'd chosen to stay …

Nic's preferred method was sniping when it came to a contract kill; a simple long-range shot followed by a quick getaway. It made things easier somehow. No face-to-face contact. No close-up images to haunt him later on. Plus, he was damned good at it. One of the best. That's why he got to pick and choose jobs.

Spending time on his uncle's farm as a child, he learned the necessity of killing and, to a certain extent, had become desensitised. At the age of six, he watched a suffering cow being put down. One shot between the eyes and death was instantaneous. It was the kindest way, he was told. The cow wouldn't feel a thing. Although killing a cow was a far cry from contract killing, he approached his job with the same level of expediency and precision. There were no stuff-ups.

Nic only fell into the killing business. At the age of twenty, he took on a partnership in a gym, and when that folded, he became a security guard, drifting from job to job. The pay was lousy. Big money could be made as a hit-man, so he acquainted himself with criminal underworld figures, watching and learning — eventually teaming up with a crack sniper trained in the armed forces. Becoming a part of an organised crime group was another thing. Nic had to earn their trust.

Living with an assassin did not sit well with his young wife, regardless of the money.

One day, she left.

Nic didn't blame her. They were spending more time apart; there was always a chance he would not even make it home at all. But he found the money too hard to resist. Money that was stashed in offshore accounts as soon as it was made. He planned to be out of the game and set up in a foreign country somewhere in the not-too-distant future. A beach villa, perhaps? He rubbed the back of his neck. If only it was that easy. It was one thing to become part of 'The Family'. Leaving was another thing altogether.

He glanced at the sleeping woman beside him. She was beautiful. He wondered why he hadn't noticed this on their first encounter four nights ago. Perhaps it was because they'd met in a small, dark bar, and her expression had been purely business-like and cold. But right now he noticed her long eyelashes, olive complexion, and thick, dark hair that was swept up in a loose bun, enhancing her high cheekbones. *Would have to be of Latin American descent,* he found himself thinking. Could be a member of any of the organised crime gangs he worked for. However, her accent was Australian, with not a hint of Spanish. *She was going to a great deal of trouble not to be traced,* he thought, as he looked at his GPS which showed only thirty kilometres to Leongatha.

Once they reached the main street, he pulled off into the supermarket car park and cut the engine.

He gave Angelina's shoulder a gentle shake. 'We're here.'

'Huh? Already?' Angelina rubbed her eyes as she sat up. 'Must've been tired. It's not like me to sleep like that.'

'How long since you last slept?'

'It'd have to be over twenty-four hours.'

'Yeah, about the same for me.'

'Aren't you stuffed?' she asked.

'You get used to it. Comes with the job,' Nic replied. 'But I could down a coffee, that's for sure.'

'Me too. There's a bakery in the main drag. They make good coffee,' Angelina said. 'We can stop by once we're finished here.'

As they drove the final twenty kilometres to Tidal River, the early morning sun caught the top of Mt Oberon, towering above like a colossus. Clumps of coastal Ti-tree and Banksia stretched for miles, with no sight of human habitation, and an expanse of water glittered in the distance. He'd forgotten how beautiful this place was. Little seemed to have changed over the years.

The previous six months had been spent cooped up in city high-rise apartments owned by The Family. He never stayed in one place for long, moving from one city to another, depending on the job at hand. Each place seemed no different to the last. The moment he stepped out onto the street, he was met by a sea of people, mobiles pressed against their ears, faces strained and drawn. The air always felt thick and oppressive and the towering buildings let in little light. The constant stream of traffic and honking of horns added to the feeling of claustrophobia.

The scene that lay ahead lifted his soul, and despite his weariness, he felt better than he had in months. *God, I'm glad she brought me here,* he thought, *even if it's only for one night.* Extending his stay wasn't worth the risk. He'd managed to go unnoticed so far, and he intended to keep things that way.

The setting gave him a new perspective. A yearning to move on sooner than planned. Get back to the simple things. Fresh air and nature. Another two years, he decided. Then he'd call it quits.

ꝗ

At the Tidal River campsite, they pulled up at the main office. Angelina reached for a pair of dark sunglasses and a baseball cap. 'You wait here,' she said, 'and I'll get our room keys.'

He was glad she'd booked separate units. He was feeling tetchy and could do with a good sleep. He didn't know what he might say if she pushed too far.

They drove around to the car park where the one-bedroom units lay. As he opened the back of the SUV to retrieve their belongings, he observed the small, blue and black backpack in the corner. It made him think of a forgotten overnight bag in a departure lounge. He'd never known a woman to travel with so little luggage, but he held his tongue. He wasn't about to risk an angry response. One more day, he reasoned, and he was out of there. He reached over and pulled it out, along with his sports bag.

'Let's get these in first,' he said, 'and I'll come back for the food.'

She nodded.

Their units were the last two of six set in a clearing, surrounded by native scrub. Mt Bishop looming large in the distance and two bright green and scarlet lorikeets perched on the branch of a nearby tree, could have been a scene in a wildlife calendar. Angelina glanced around and nodded with approval. 'Good. We've got the place to ourselves. I don't know about you, but I'm in need of some sleep.'

He nodded. 'Sounds like a plan.'

'I'll join you for dinner if you want,' she remarked.

'Fine by me. What time?'

'Make it around seven.'

The rooms were spacious, with timber sundecks and barbeque areas, not that they would be spending time outside. Even at this early hour the air was chilly, despite the occasional ray of sunlight peeking through the trees. He reckoned that the split air conditioner on the wall would be welcome at night and the cupboards held ample spare blankets. Right now, all he needed was a hot shower and a good sleep.

It was already 4 p.m. when he awoke. Throwing off the blanket, he rose and changed into his tracksuit and runners. He could hardly wait to get out into the fresh air and hit the track. It had been a long time since he'd had the freedom to go out anywhere without looking over his shoulder. He strained to think of the last time he'd gone on a holiday — enjoying what everyone else enjoyed, leisurely breakfasts, running along the beach, of perhaps taking a dip in the pool. He frowned. It would have been eight years since he'd spent time with Kelly, in the Daintree.

At seven, there was a knock on the door. Angelina stood, dressed in active gear and runners, her pink and white top emphasising her olive skin and exotic looks. Transfixed, Nic stood by to let her pass. But it was the smile that caused his heart to almost stop. The first smile he'd seen.

'Can I sit anywhere?' she asked.

'Go for it.'

She walked gracefully across the room to a sofa and sat, one leg tucked under the other, watching him. 'Oh, man. That sleep was good,' she said, bubbling with exuberance.

He settled in the seat facing hers.

For several minutes, Nic listened in amusement as she chatted on about nothing in particular, barely pausing for breath. He could scarcely believe she was the moody, curt woman of the previous day. She paused as if she had read his mind.

'I was a bitch yesterday, wasn't I,' she remarked.

'No.' His response was guarded. 'It was clear you had things on your mind.'

'Maybe, but I could have behaved better. It wasn't like me, and I apologise.'

'Don't worry about it.'

'Thanks.' Another one of those smiles, and Nic felt his legs go weak.

'I haven't even offered you a drink,' he said too quickly.

'Sounds good.'

'I only bought a six-pack, sorry. I didn't think to ask if you wanted something from the bottle shop.'

'A beer's fine, then let's get the barbeque fired up. I'm starving.'

Nic watched her through the window as she cut up the salad and set the table inside. It had been so long since he'd been in this situation. He'd dated a few women since Kelly, but he was careful not to take them back to his apartment. A tantalising mixture of steak, onions and mushrooms rose from the hotplate, and he smiled. It brought back memories of summer evenings on the farm when neighbours dropped by for a beer and barbeque. *What about her family*, he wondered. *Where had she grown up?*

It was eleven when Angelina rose from the table. The night had gone way too fast for Nic. She extended her hand. It felt cool and soft in his.

'I've enjoyed your company, Nic.' She held his eyes.

'Thanks. I won't be seeing you in the morning. You can drop off the keys at the office before you go.'

He felt like blurting out, 'Can I see you again, sometime?' But he said nothing.

After she'd gone, he took out another beer from the fridge and sat where she'd just been. Closing his eyes for a few moments, he took in the faint trace of her perfume; the nearness of her.

3

Angelina's blinds were still drawn when he rose and packed. He hoped to catch a glimpse; say goodbye, but there was no sign of movement. Intrigued as to who would be picking her up, he decided to stay and watch. At the main office he handed in his key, then drove to where the campsites lay and parked his car amongst some others under the trees. Then edging his way back to her unit, he found a secluded spot and waited. Checkout time was 10 a.m. He glanced at his iPhone. Not long to go.

At 9.45 Angelina appeared in the same clothes as the night before, backpack slung over her shoulders. But this time, she wore hiking shoes. He followed at a distance. She was heading towards the track that led to Sealers Cove, two or so hours away. There was only one way in and out. Someone was picking her up by boat. But who? And where was she being taken?

The track to Sealers Cove was one of the National Park's most popular, particularly during the tourist season when groups of hikers set off, sometimes with camping gear, to stay the night on the sheltered beach and enjoy the picturesque setting. Surrounding the track was a mass of green foliage, native trees and ferns providing a scene of tranquillity and peace. But not Angelina. She didn't notice the shafts of sunlight seeping through the light green canopy or hear the incessant chattering of birds against the stillness. She pressed on, eyes hard, striking the ground in even, fast footfalls, thinking of what lay ahead. A sleeping lizard woke in alarm and managed to scuttle. As she headed down the final section of boardwalk leading to the beach, she hoped the place would be deserted. She didn't feel like facing glib comments from passers-by and the last thing she wanted was to be spotted leaving by boat.

She was in luck.

The vessel was already moored ten metres out. With a quick scan of the beach, she pulled off her hiking boots and socks, rolled up her leggings and waded out.

'Good timing, Seb,' she said as she climbed aboard.

'I knew you'd be early,' he responded, pulling up the anchor and starting the engine.

'Did you organise the car?'

'Yeah. It's been dropped off at the farmhouse.'

Neither spoke during the twenty-minute trip to Port Welshpool. A driver was already waiting in a car by the jetty.

g

Binginwarri is a remote, rural area set amongst rolling green hills, with sweeping views of Wilsons Promontory. Dotted with farmhouses here and there, many deserted, following the collapse of the dairy industry in the nineties, it offers a perfect place for those wishing to get away from it all.

The old farmhouse where she stayed had lain empty for years before it was snapped up at auction by Angelina's connections. Set well back amongst the trees along an isolated road, it was the perfect place to carry out their clandestine operations. Only a hundred and fifty kilometres from Melbourne's CBD, a skip and a jump to Port Welshpool and the vast waterways beyond. Many a shipment of drugs had been stored at the farm, in transit to the city.

No one stayed for long. That was the policy. If the cops came, it appeared like someone's weekender.

¶

It had been three weeks since Angelina's arrival at the farmhouse. She sat, sipping her coffee, deep in thought. The place offered the privacy and isolation she needed. But the deal was a two month's stay only. Her contacts needed the house for other things. She glanced around. The place was crap anyway. Paint peeled off the ceilings, there were large patches of mould on the walls and the floor was worn and cracked.

Winter. She couldn't have picked a worse time to stay. The house was hemmed in by pine trees that let in little light and gave rise to permanent cold dampness. She had to make do with a small open fire, an old heater that she carried from room to room and extra layers of clothes.

It wasn't long before she went in search of the comforts she'd been accustomed to: an occasional night's stay at a city hotel or the apartment of her latest lover. It took some time before she learned the true identity of the handsome, smooth-talking Nigerian who could have stepped out of a movie set. Isamotu Lawai was visiting Australia on a twelve-month tourist visa. In fact, he was a member of an organised crime syndicate in Lagos specialising in weapons trafficking, scamming and the kidnapping of wealthy foreign industrialists. He'd learned that big money was to be made in Sydney trafficking drugs, alongside West African crime gangs with links to Mexican drug cartels. *Why not give it a go?* he thought. There was nothing to lose. Fake passports and papers were not an issue and he had the connections to stay on, should he choose to, once his visa expired.

Isaac, as he was known, had only planned to fly in and out of Melbourne for a weekend's visit but one encounter with Angelina at a city nightclub changed all that. The weekend extended into a week's stay, followed by another. Within a month he'd relocated to Melbourne to be closer to her, and conducted his business online.

Isaac was used to charming and cajoling women. As a

teenager, he'd spent his days in internet cafés as part of a gang scamming wealthy, older women around the world. They were easy pickings until the authorities stepped in and the targets started wising up. He could never understand their stupidity in handing over their money in the first place.

Isaac had long since moved on, but the lessons he'd learned gave him the upper hand with women. Or so he thought.

With Angelina, he'd met his match. She gave little away and he learned not to ask questions. It all added to the intrigue. He was quick to discern a natural cunning in women on the wrong side of the law. His intuition soon proved correct. Within a week she sought help in obtaining a fake passport and papers, no questions asked. And she repaid him with the promise of moving in.

For the first time in his life, Isaac found someone he wanted to settle down with, as had his father, Okafor. Despite the hardships of raising a family of eight in Nigeria's largest city, Okafor remained true to his wife of thirty years and worked tirelessly as a taxi driver to make ends meet. But it was not enough to provide the opportunities he wanted for his large family. Nigeria offered limited career options and jobs were hard to come by.

The only chance of escaping the poverty cycle was to leave the country as a skilled worker with his children. But that took money to arrange. And Isaac had grown sick of waiting. He had no intention of working long hours for a pittance like his father, who'd grown old before his time. There had to be a better way. At sixteen, he ran away from home and it wasn't long before he hooked up with a gang, one of many on Lagos's poorly policed streets. Life was dangerous but big money beckoned. That was twelve years ago and he hadn't looked back.

The twelve months spent in Australia had worked out better than expected but with his visa soon to expire and Angelina on the scene he had serious misgivings. Who was she really? What had she done and who was she hiding from? How could he protect her in a foreign country where the fear of being caught himself one day was always at the back of his mind?

One afternoon when they had just had steamy sex in the bedroom, he leaned over on one elbow and stroked her face.

'There's something I've been meaning to ask.'

'Mm?' she asked, eyes closed.

'Would you consider leaving Australia and come to live with me in Lagos?'

There was a shrug. 'I don't know that I'd like it.'

'You said you needed to go undercover for a while.'

There was no response.

'Try six months and see how you like it,' he said. 'You can always come back.'

There was a pause. And Isaac's pulse quickened.

'I might think about it,' she said.

He would have to be content with that.

'No strings attached, though,' she was quick to add.

Isaac grinned. 'And what if it turns into something else? Just think of the kids we could have. With your looks and my body ...'

Fat chance of that, she thought. Isaac was a good lay but kids were another thing altogether.

¶

Angelina leaned across to get another log from the wooden box near the hearth. Wiping her hands on her jeans, she sat cross-legged, elbows on knees, hands cupping her chin, watching the dry wood catch light. The bright ball of orange brought a smile to her face. It reminded her of the fire she'd lit in the marquee when she was six. The sight of her grandmother's prayer table going up in smoke had mesmerised her. Especially the wooden crucifix. The last thing to burn.

The wind rattled the window and she glanced over her shoulder. Another storm was expected. Best she have an early dinner and get to bed. She had a big day ahead.

4

It was just after 8 a.m. when Angelina arrived in her home town. She drove through the main street, turning left at the petrol station and pulling up outside the red brick cottage she recalled visiting as a child.

The old woman should be up and about by now, she told herself. Old people always got up early, didn't they? But what if the daughter was home? There was no car in the driveway. That was a good sign.

She walked up to the front door and rang the bell. Nothing. She rang again. In the distance, she could hear shuffling footsteps approaching.

'Who is it?' A voice came from the other side of the door.

'Madeleine's granddaughter,' she replied.

The door slowly opened, and an old woman stood, shielding her eyes from the sun with one hand.

At first glance, Ginny Heyes could be anyone's grandmother in her nineties. She was small and hunched over with cropped grey hair, wearing an old dressing gown and slippers. But there was a blankness about her watery eyes as she stepped aside to let Angelina in.

'Who did you say you were?' Ginny peered at her.

'Angelina. Madeleine's granddaughter. My mother was Lucinda. Remember her? She took over your housekeeping duties after you left.'

'Of course, I remember Lucinda. What a beautiful woman she was. You should have seen the way all the young men looked at her.'

Angelina drew breath. This was a start.

'So, what can I do for you?' the old woman continued.

'I've come to ask you about my mother.'

'Oh. Well, take a seat, and I'll make us a cuppa.'

Angelina's jaw hardened. *Stupid old cow*, she thought, *I don't want your fucking tea.*

She flashed the old woman a smile. 'That'd be good.'

'My, those eyes,' Ginny observed. 'You are like her, aren't you?'

Angelina sat on the old sofa and glanced around the cluttered room. The cramped space made her feel claustrophobic. Opposite were two winged chairs with side tables. In the corner was a large shelf that held bric-a-brac and framed photographs. A crucifix hung above the door. It had the smell of an old person's place, of curtains drawn and windows rarely opened. And a dog, perhaps? She could still hear the radio in the kitchen as the old woman fussed about.

'Now, where were we?' Ginny asked as she handed Angelina a cup and saucer.

'My mother.'

'Oh, that's right.' She sat down. 'And how is she?'

Angelina gritted her teeth. 'My mother died while giving birth to me. Don't you remember?'

'Oh, that's right. What a tragedy that was, you poor dear.'

Angelina was beginning to think the six-hour trip had been a waste of time, but she pushed on regardless. At least the old housekeeper could recall some things.

'Do you know anything about her? Where she came from? Why she went to Kilkenny in the first place?'

Ginny scratched her chin. 'Not really. Madeleine never told me much.'

'Can you think of anything, anything at all?'

'Well, I think she came from some convent. That's right. The nuns sent her.'

'Was the convent near here?'

'Oh no, it was a long way away. Up country somewhere. Madeleine spoke of it sometimes. She was one of its benefactors.'

Angelina leaned forward intently. 'Can you think of the place?'

There was a moment's silence. 'Ballarat perhaps, or was it Ararat? All those places sound the same to me. Somewhere up that way.'

Angelina whipped out her mobile and did a quick Google search. There was a number of them. She felt her heartbeat quicken. All had long since closed, but it was a start.

She met the old woman's eyes. 'There's one more question I need to know. Do you have any idea who my father is? Did my mother say?'

'What was that?'

Angelina was losing her patience.

'The father of Lucinda's baby,' her voice rose a notch. 'Do you know who it was?'

No response.

Angelina jumped up and shook the old woman's arm, her eyes blazing. 'Think, for God's sake.'

Ginny pulled her arm away, her eyes wide with fright. 'You're hurting me.'

Angelina stepped back quickly. 'I'm so sorry,' she said. 'It was unforgivable of me.' She wiped the corner of her eye with a fingertip. 'It's just that I've grown up never knowing anything about my parents.'

There was silence. Only the faint blare of the radio could be heard from the kitchen.

'Who did you say you were again?' Ginny asked vaguely.

Angelina looked at the blank eyes in disbelief. *She doesn't remember a thing I just said.*

'Angelina,' she reiterated. 'Lucinda's daughter.'

'Oh, that's right. What time is it, dear?'

Angelina checked her watch. 'Just after nine.'

'Oh, that's good. My daughter should be home any minute. She'll be happy to see you. You remember her, don't you?'

Angelina nodded. She remembered the woman, all right.

Louise Heyes would have to be in her late sixties by now, a thin, dour woman with sharp eyes, whose gossip caused no end of trouble in the town.

'I'd like to stay, but I need to get going,' she found herself saying quickly as she rose. 'Pass on my best wishes to your daughter.'

Ginny rose to see her to the door. Angelina squeezed her hands. 'It's been good seeing you after all these years.'

'And the same goes for you, Lucinda. Please come again.'

I can't believe this, she thought. 'Thanks,' she said with a smile. 'I'll do that.'

As the door closed behind her, Angelina headed to the car with a scowl. Without wasting time, she got in, giving the rear vision mirror a quick glance. All clear. She pulled her hair in a tight ponytail and reached for her baseball cap and dark glasses. Best to get out of there as soon as she could. For a moment she toyed with the idea of heading to Kilkenny, just to check things out. But she thought better of it. The next visit would come around soon enough.

5

It was late afternoon by the time Angelina returned to the old farmhouse. The long drive had given her plenty of time to think. An hour's break at a large trucking stop was spent accessing websites, and by the time she walked out, she had most of the information she needed.

A few follow-up phone calls gave her the answers she'd been seeking. The old convent where her mother had been sent was long closed down. But its records were found at the Ballarat Archdiocese. Lucinda Alvarez was nineteen when she had sought refuge at the convent, and her life was sufficiently in danger for the nuns to move her somewhere safe as soon as arrangements could be made. Lucinda had requested anonymity, and the nuns had honoured her wishes. The only records stated that Lucinda and her family were illegal immigrants from Brazil; and a contact number for her brother, Antonio. Angelina punched in the number with trembling fingers, but as expected, it was no longer in existence. Without hesitation, she rang another number.

'Juan, it's Ava. I've got a job for you. It's urgent. Can you get on to it straight away?'

All Juan needed was a name, estimated age and country of origin. She was confident that she'd have all she needed — her uncle's phone number and a fair bit about him as well.

It was close to midnight before the call came through.

'Hi Juan, yes, of course, I'm still awake,' she said. 'What have you got for me?'

She listened with widened eyes. 'You're kidding me!'

When he'd finished, she said, 'Good job. No, no, that's it for now but expect to hear from me soon.'

Angelina could hardly contain her excitement as she hit the end button. So, her uncle was operating outside of the law, too. She smiled to herself. *Blood ties, hey?* She walked over to the cupboard and pulled out a bottle of red. Already she was planning her next move. Juan's information certainly made things easier. Dealing with a stay at home, family man would have been another thing altogether. She poured a drink, sat on the couch and smiled. This was a call for celebration, all right.

¶

Antonio's phone rang just as he was finishing breakfast.

'Am I speaking with Antonio Alvarez?' The voice was female, educated, polished.

'Who is this?'

'You don't know me, but I have information you may find of interest. It's to do with Lucinda.'

There was a sharp intake of breath. 'What's this all about? How do you know Lucinda?'

'Let's say we meet and discuss it.'

Antonio's heart hammered in his chest. Was this a hoax? The authorities had been after him for ages. But there were unanswered questions about his sister that had been burning deep inside all these years. He had to know if this was genuine.

'When?'

'Tomorrow. Your call where and the time.'

Antonio thought quickly. He needed an open space where she could be spotted from a distance if she was not alone, somewhere they could talk without being overheard. He named a park in the city's top end, close enough to his contacts if things turned for the worse. Late afternoon should do it when most people were on their way home from work and only the occasional jogger or dog walker passed by.

He frowned, pulse racing, as he pressed the end button on his mobile. A call like this was the last thing he expected.

¶

At five the following afternoon, Antonio turned up his coat

collar, dug his hands in his pockets and sat on the weathered park bench. Winter had truly set in. The trees had lost their leaves, and the grass was damp and spongy underfoot. The sky was darkening with the threat of a storm.

From his vantage point, he could see most of the park. It was all but deserted, but in the distance he saw someone cross the road and head up the path.

There was no one following.

As she approached, he rose and waited.

'Antonio?'

He nodded.

'I'm Ava.' She shook his hand.

He gestured to the seat. Antonio was sure he had seen her somewhere. It was difficult to tell. She wore a black hoodie, so it was hard to define her face. But it was those eyes.

'Thank you for agreeing to meet me at short notice,' she said.

He nodded. 'So, let's cut to the chase. Is this a matter of extortion? Are you using my sister as leverage?'

There was a moment's pause.

'No. I'm Lucinda's daughter.'

'Liar!' Antonio's eyes blazed. 'My sister died while giving birth.'

'That's right, she did,' Angelina said. 'But whoever told you neglected to say that her baby lived.'

Antonio was too stunned to speak for a moment.

'Do you have a way of proving it?' he asked.

Angelina reached into her tote bag and produced a small, pink backpack. With one quick movement she pulled her hoodie off, and her thick, dark hair tumbled around her shoulders.

'Do you believe me now?'

Antonio gasped. 'Oh my God!' His heart hammered furiously in his chest. 'Why didn't you come to me before this!'

'I didn't know that I had any relatives until recently.' She paused. 'Look, I won't beat around the bush. I've come to you because I need help.'

'What sort of help? Money?'

'No. I've got my own. There have been some issues, complications with the law.'

'What sort of complications?'

'Arson, money laundering and some other stuff.' Angelina paused for a moment and locked her eyes on his. 'Look, I need to go to ground for a while. And seeing as we're family and in the same game, I'm asking for some protection, 'til I get on my feet.'

There was a moment's silence.

'I'll need to think about it for a while. Talk it over with a few others. I'll get back to you. Where are you staying?'

'The Sheraton.' She rose and glanced down at him. 'Please don't take too long. I value my freedom.'

He watched her walk away, the same walk as his sister's.

¶

The day he received the news of Lucinda's death nearly broke him. He never wanted to send her to the nuns in the first place, but he could no longer protect her. It was the only place he could think of. They'd found her a position with a family of considerable wealth. But it was far away. 'She'll be safe there,' they promised. So much for safety, he thought grimly.

If only he'd known from the beginning where they'd sent her … but the nuns had denied him access. 'It's better this way,' they said.

He'd let her down … wasn't there for her when she needed him the most. And now, the opportunity presented itself all over again. This time it was his niece in need of protection. He couldn't let her down the way he had her mother. He ran his hands down his face and looked up into the gathering darkness. Before he spoke to the others, he needed to know whether her story added up. He knew someone with access to the police database. It was a start.

Two hours later, he had the information he wanted. His niece's real name was Angelina Lorenzo, wanted for suspected arson, attempted murder of her sister and embezzlement from her family's business. Antonio gave a whistle. His niece certainly didn't do things by halves. Lorenzo Wineries were well known. But who were her contacts? He'd look into that later. He quickly made a call.

'Paulo?'

'Yeah, what's up?'

'Can you be at the house by nine in the morning?'

'I can be. Why?'

'There's someone I want you to meet. I won't go into it now. And bring Luca.'

Antonio was deep in thought as he showered and prepared dinner. Where the following morning's meeting would lead, God only knew.

6

The meeting place was an old two-storey Victorian terrace house in Richmond, soon to be demolished. It was one in a row of four, purchased for a song by Antonio and his gang ten years prior.

They'd been happy to hold off selling until it was worth their while to do so. And finally, things were on the improve. Old houses like theirs were being snapped up for property development, with prices booming.

But local residents had been quick to make a protest and were being listened to. If the laws changed and the houses became heritage listed, they'd be worth a fraction of their current value.

Antonio was on to it. They had a buyer and were awaiting the paperwork.

Angelina pulled up in the narrow street and waited. Antonio was yet to be seen. She'd never taken much notice of terrace houses in the past. They shared internal walls, and she wondered how people could tolerate living close to others within such confined spaces. What stood out was the ornate cast ironwork on the balconies and front fences, a stark contrast to the unremarkable red brick houses of a similar vintage further along the street.

A car pulled up behind. Antonio stepped out and walked around to her car door. 'Follow me,' he said, 'the others will be along soon.'

He led the way to the second house from the end. The wooden front door was padlocked, and he produced a key. She noted the original stained-glass surroundings of the door, typical of the era. Both front windows were boarded up, as were those in the adjoining houses.

'Squatters,' he explained, gesturing to the paint tags of local gangs on the walls. 'It's not easy keeping them out.'

She followed him along a narrow passageway. There was a door to each side, both closed. Upstairs, there were just two rooms. One was empty except for a dust-covered wooden table and four old chairs. Faded, patterned tiles covered the floor. She guessed they were originals. There were large cracks in the plaster walls and the unmistakable reek of mould. She glanced at the other room; its door was propped open by a green milk crate. It was empty. The windows were not boarded up like those on the lower level and the deserted street below was visible through the grimy panes. A mouse came from nowhere, scuttled along the skirting board and disappeared through a nearby hole.

Antonio rubbed the dust from the chairs with his hand. They had barely sat down when footsteps could be heard from the passageway downstairs.

His offsiders, Paulo and Luca, appeared in the doorway. Both were tall, thickset creatures with shaved heads. They wore black.

Antonio rose.

'This is my niece.'

Paulo looked suspicious. 'Didn't know you had a niece.'

'I'll fill you in later. It's legit.'

There was silence.

'Don't you worry,' Antonio went on, 'she's done some fancy stuff.'

'What sort of fancy stuff?'

'I'll get to that,' Antonio told him.

He motioned towards the two seats opposite.

Luca took one look. 'Nah, we'll stand.'

The pair leaned against the nearby wall, arms crossed.

'So what's this about?' Paulo asked.

'Let's say my niece is in a spot of bother.'

Luca's expression was wary. 'Oh yeah? What sort of bother.'

'Perhaps she can tell you that herself,' Antonio said.

Angelina gave a brief overview, mentioning only the details she wanted them to know.

Paulo's eyes, amber and unblinking, struck Angelina as those of a predator. His voice was cold when he spoke. 'So, what do you want from us?'

She returned the look. 'I need living quarters and a car, preferably out of the country. Apart from that, I can take care of myself. It's only a short-term arrangement.'

'And what about money, papers, passport?' Luca probed.

'Under control,' she told him.

'Is that so,' Paulo said smoothly. 'And how can we trust you?'

'Do you think I was sent here or something?'

'Well, were you?'

'I work alone,' came the cool response. 'Look, what you do is your business and is of little interest to me. I have my own contacts, my own agenda. You understand?'

There was no response.

'You can check if you want,' she told him.

'Yeah, we'll be doing that, all right. How about a name for starters.'

'Try Nic Drakos,' she said. 'You've heard of him, haven't you?'

'You could say that.'

The room went silent.

'Well, is there anything else?' Angelina asked.

'Nope.' Paulo nodded towards the door. 'You can go. We've got all we need for now.'

Antonio rose and showed her out.

'Cheery bunch, aren't they,' she remarked on the doorstep.

'Did you expect any different?'

'I don't know what I expected. So, the three of you will be having a chat, I imagine.'

He nodded. 'You'll have your answer soon enough.'

Before she turned to leave, he said, 'So what's with the name? Your real one suits you better.'

'So, you've checked me out?'

'What did you expect?'

She shrugged. 'Ava, Angelina, a name's a name. I needed another for my papers and passport. It'll do.' Her eyes locked on his. 'And it's what I want to be known as, okay? Answering to both only complicates things.'

She had a point. He nodded.

Angelina went to give him a hug but thought better of it. It didn't seem right, somehow.

When Antonio returned to the others, Paulo gave a whistle. 'Shit. You're full of surprises, aren't you?'

'Yeah,' Luca added. 'Talk about a looker.'

Antonio nodded. 'So was her mother.'

Paulo crushed his cigarette with the heel of his boot and grinned. 'You sure missed out in the genes department.'

The humour went unnoticed. 'I owe you guys an explanation,' Antonio said. 'To be honest, I didn't know she even existed until yesterday.'

'Wanna talk about it?'

'Maybe, but not now.'

'How about I do the checking up bit,' Paulo said. 'Maybe you're a bit close to it all.'

Antonio nodded. 'Maybe. Text me when you find anything.'

❡

Nic Drakos was surprised to get Paulo's call. He'd worked for the Brazilian's gang from time to time, but it was a while since they'd made contact. The moment Ava's name was mentioned, he was instantly alert. Paulo could be trusted, and Nic told him everything about the night at the marina.

Paulo listened intently. It was clear that Antonio's niece was ruthless and planned things meticulously. The escape route via Wilsons Prom, for starters. She had to have connections, but it appeared she worked alone and on her terms.

'Why are you checking her out?' Nic asked.

'She's Antonio's niece.'

'What! He never told me he had a niece.'

'Yeah, same goes for us. Antonio's about to fill us in.' There was a pause. 'So, how did she get your number?'

'Rodriguez passed it on. She was after a hitman.'

'Rodriguez!' Paulo explained. 'Fuck. The lady's sure full of surprises. Look, I've got to go. I'll be in touch soon.'

Nic placed his mobile on the car seat beside him, his thoughts racing. He hadn't stopped thinking of Ava since the Prom. Maybe, just maybe, there was a chance they'd get to cross paths once again …

¶

Paulo made another phone call. This one lasted an hour.

With much to think about, he went to a local pizza and

grill to sit and reflect. He hadn't eaten all day and was ravenous. Before he rose to pay the bill, he texted the other two: *meet at my place in an hour.*

At three, the other two sat at the table of their shared house while he fetched them a beer.

'Your niece has already had dealings with Rodriguez,' he said to Antonio.

'What?' came the incredulous response.

Rodriguez was head of one of the small but powerful Brazilian gangs in Bangkok. He had provided them with a place to go undercover from time to time.

'Your niece's adopted name is Lorenzo. Right?'

'Yeah. Why?'

'Remember how Dominic Lorenzo was killed at a raid at a hotel in Bangkok not so long ago?'

Antonio nodded. 'Yeah, it was splashed all over the media. A crime gang, the police said. They never caught them.'

'It was a crime gang, all right. Rodriguez masterminded it. Did all right, too, from what I remember. Took off with a load of cash and other stuff.'

'So, what are you getting at?'

'It was no random attack. It was a hit job. Some woman rang Rodriguez from Australia. Wouldn't give her name. She knew every detail about Dominic Lorenzo, though. Paid big money. Straight into Rodrigues's account. No questions asked.'

Antonio was staggered. 'You mean Angelina, Ava whatever, was behind it?'

'Yep. Your niece ordered the contract killing of her father, I mean, stepfather.'

'But how can you know that for sure? The woman wished to remain anonymous, you said.'

'That crossed my mind as well, except a month afterwards, the same woman contacted Rodriguez, asking for a hitman. He recommended Nic. The description of the woman Nic was with when he blew up the Lorenzo yacht matched your niece.'

'Shit. What else has my niece done that we don't know about!' Antonio exclaimed.

'Who knows. We've got enough on her now if she chose to blab. I say we give things a go. With her looks and brains, she could be of use to us. What do you reckon?'

'I'm in,' Luca said.

Antonio nodded his head. 'Okay, I'll get back to her. But let's keep this conversation to ourselves, all right? The less she thinks we have on her, the better. Niece or no niece, she'll need to prove herself.'

As the other two chatted, Antonio sipped his beer, deep in thought. What in the hell had gone on in his niece's life? What would cause her to wreak such havoc on the family that raised her?

§

Angelina had a smile on her face as she texted Isaac:

Considered Nigeria and decided against it. Time to move

on. Hope there's no hard feelings. Don't bother contacting me. Stay safe.

7

Angelina checked out of The Sheraton and made her way down the lift to the underground car park. There was a lot to think about. The previous night's conversation with Antonio changed everything. She could hardly believe her luck. Three weeks, and he'd have her out of the country. That allowed just enough time to vacate the farm and put together what was needed.

She pulled out into the early morning stream of traffic and drove through the outer suburbs towards the freeway, switching the car to cruise control. Two things were on her agenda before she flew out. The rest could wait until things had settled and she felt safe enough to return. Who knew when that would be? Hopefully a year, perhaps two; the wait would be worth it.

¶

At 11.30 p.m. Nic Drakos heard his mobile ring. He

glanced at his watch with a frown as he reached across the kitchen bench.

'Yes?'

'Nic, it's Ava. Interested in another job?'

ℊ

It was 3 a.m. and Nic was still wide awake in his Docklands apartment. He glanced once more at the photo she'd sent through of the fortyish man with fine features, hazel eyes and dark hair flecked with grey, wondering what the guy had done.

He'd passed on the scant information Ava had provided, to his contact, and awaited the response with curiosity.

ℊ

The email came through the following day. The target was Paul Guthrie, who had left a trail of aliases, each beginning with his Christian name. Known to Ava as Paul Anderson, Guthrie had taken on the name Paul Reed since flying into Thailand from Australia six weeks ago. He was believed to be somewhere in the Chiang Rai district. Enjoying the high life. Followed repetitive, rigid routines and was obsessive about time.

Nic lay stretched out on the couch, head propped against the cushions and laptop balanced on his chest. *This guy's sure got some history*, he thought, as he read on.

Money laundering, corruption, links to Asian triads and the Russian mafia, shonky property development deals throughout Asia and third world countries.

It didn't take long to make the connection between the target and Ava. The yacht that he'd set alight belonged to the Lorenzo family. Paul Anderson worked for Dominic Lorenzo before he fled the country. A quick Google search and his suspicions proved to be correct. Ava's true identity was Angelina Lorenzo; currently wanted for questioning by police.

Whatever had gone on in her life, the Lorenzo woman sure bore a grudge or two.

He sent another email to his contact, closed the laptop and placed it on the floor. He felt his heartbeat quicken as he reached for his mobile and tapped her number.

'Ava?'

There was a pause. 'Yes.'

'It's Nic. I've got just about all I need. The guy's in Thailand.'

'Is that so?'

'Yeah. Flew in a few weeks back. Do you still want to go ahead?'

'You bet. Where is he hanging out?'

'Chiang Rai somewhere. When I find out the exact location, I'll let you know.'

'Good. Catch you soon.'

Angelina clicked off with a satisfied smile. If all went well, the hit would be carried out before she left the country.

Angelina would have liked nothing more than to finish Anderson off herself, but she didn't have the resources to hunt him down, and she didn't want to be linked to his death. She may have avoided the Australian Police so far, but the Thai Police were an unknown prospect altogether. She couldn't believe her luck in coming across Nic in the first place. With what she had in mind from here on, she needed someone with his credentials alongside. It was time to make her next move. It wouldn't matter that she'd just returned from town. The trip back would be worth it.

She picked up her mobile once again and tapped his number.

'Yes?'

'It's Ava again. Had a thought. Will you be in town tomorrow night?'

'Yeah.'

'Fancy a drink? Thought you might like to catch up before you head off.'

Nic's heart skipped a beat. 'Sounds good,' he said, doing his best to sound casual. 'Where?'

'I'm booking in at Sofitel on Collins for a few days. There's a bar, The Atrium, on level 35. How about we meet there at eight?'

Nic could barely take in what he'd heard. This was totally unexpected and oh so welcome.

❡

Angelina sat in a club leather chair of the stylish bar watching guests come and go. Most had already left for nearby theatres and shows. When things became too much at the farm, she'd head for the city to spend a night or two at a place like this: Crown, The Sheraton — always a different hotel, a different disguise. Usually, she headed straight to her room, then perhaps hit the gym or went to the CBD for a spot of shopping. She generally avoided the hotel's bars and restaurants. A single woman was likely to create attention. But tonight, she could be just one of any couple out for a drink on a Friday night.

She saw him approach from a distance, and was reminded how good looking he was. Late thirties at a guess, olive complexion, tall and muscular, with brown eyes and dark hair cut short. He wore jeans and a casual shirt over a white t-shirt.

'Hope you haven't been waiting long.' Nic pulled out the chair opposite.

'No, just arrived,' she said with a smile.

He glanced up at the glittering glass canopy that sat like a swirl of ice overhead. 'Quite something, hey,' he remarked.

'Thought you'd like it. One of my favourite places.' She paused. 'A bit brazen of me, wasn't it, asking you here?'

He raised an eyebrow.

'I didn't ask if there was a wife, girlfriend.'

Nic shook his head. 'And if there was?'

'I don't go along with the wives and girlfriend thing.'

'Same.' He paused. 'I'm glad you rang, Ava. It's good to see you again.'

'You too.'

He smiled. 'So, what can I get you to drink?'

As the night wore on, Angelina was bubbly and talkative, much the same as the night she dropped by at the Prom. There was no reference to their pasts or the impending hit job and Nic found conversation surprisingly easy.

And as the evening drew to a close, she reached across the table and placed her hand over his.

'Stay?' she said softly.

The word came out of the blue and caught Nic totally off guard. His breath caught in his throat as he met her eyes.

'Okay.'

They rose, and he slipped his arm around her shoulders as if it was the most natural thing in the world as they headed towards the lift.

Angelina's room was on the seventieth floor; spacious and modern with floor-to-ceiling windows providing expansive views over the city that was ablaze with lights, giving the iconic St Patrick's Cathedral, MCG and Yarra River a magical quality of their own.

Nic followed Angelina into the bedroom and she stopped, turning to face him, unbuttoning his shirt and running her hands under his t-shirt and across his bare skin. For a moment, he closed his eyes, scarcely daring to believe this was really happening. It was a long time since a woman had had this effect. Angelina kicked off her shoes and reached up on tiptoes, her arms slipping around his neck.

'I want you,' she said softly.

He bowed his head and brushed her lips with his until her mouth parted, and he kissed her, gently planting kisses on her face and down her neck. With trembling hands, he unzipped her dress and pulled it to the floor, undid her bra, slipped off her pants and ran his hands slowly over her body.

'You're beautiful, Ava. You're so goddamned beautiful.'

Scooping her up in his arms, he flicked off the light with his elbow as he carried her to the bed. Against the backdrop of city lights, he took off his clothes and lay over her, lowering his face into the soft skin of her breasts. Strong hands stroked her thighs, gently parting them with his knee. She pressed back with a moan as he slid deep inside, aching and burning for her, his breath quick and fast. Their lovemaking was fierce and urgent, and when they were done, he rolled to one side and held her to him, gently tracing her face with his fingers, his eyes never leaving hers.

He awoke early, not daring to move in case he woke her, gazing at her smooth brown skin, long lashes and curved lips as she slept. He lay in bed for another hour, but he had a meeting in the city at nine; enough time to make it across town to his apartment to change. Gently, he eased his arm from under her shoulders, swung his legs around to the floor, rose and dressed. He was sipping coffee on the sofa when she appeared in the doorway, fastening the belt to her white bathrobe.

'What time is it?' she said sleepily.

'Eight. I have a meeting. Remember?'

'Oh yeah.'

She walked over and sat on his knee, wrapping her arms around his neck. 'So, you're off soon.'

The scent of expensive perfume, still faint on her skin and the softness of her hair against his cheek caused his body to react. The night had passed way too fast.

'Yeah, once I've had my coffee,' he said.

'Was it good last night?'

So many things he wanted to say but didn't. 'Yeah, it was good. And you?'

She pressed one finger teasingly against his groin. 'Yeah. Good.'

He smiled, but his mind was in turmoil. It had taken years to get over his divorce, and he'd become accustomed to a single lifestyle, with the occasional fling on the side: no ties, no complications.

Having another woman on his mind was the last thing he needed.

Neither spoke for some time. All that could be heard was the faint hum of the air conditioner in the corner.

When it was time to go, he kissed the top of her head, and they rose. At the door, he took her chin in his hands and looked into her eyes. He went to speak but stopped himself.

'What?' she said.

'I don't want to think of last night as a one-night stand, that's all.'

'Who said anything about it being a one-night stand?' she said. 'Tonight's my last night here. Will you share it with me?'

¶

Nic arrived at seven. On Ava's suggestion, they stayed in, watched a movie or two on the large plasma screen and ordered room service dinner. Sitting alongside Ava, arm draped around her shoulders, eating popcorn and watching old movies, he felt like a teenager on his first date, excited about the promise of things to come.

It was 1 a.m. when they polished off the last of the French champagne, and then had sex on the lounge room floor. He remembered little afterwards. A hazy recollection of carrying her into the bedroom, crisp linen sheets against bare skin and moonlight streaming through the window.

Check-out was at ten. At eight, Angelina went to reception with the key, and they took the lift to the restaurant for breakfast. Nic was unusually hungry; he put it down to nervous energy. She'd given no indication of what was to follow. Chances of a relationship were slim, but he didn't want to think about that right now. She'd asked him back the second time. He had to be content with that.

The tables were laden with fresh juices, cereals, fresh fruit platters, assorted meats and cheeses and baskets of bread. Nic ordered a large cooked breakfast, and Angelina helped herself to a healthy one.

They found a seat in a quiet corner, away from the hub of diners.

'So where to from here for you?' he asked as he buttered another piece of toast.

'Some loose ends to tie up and a few things to attend to.'

About as much as he expected.

Nic nodded. 'Expect to hear from me in a day or two. Once I have the final details, I'll be pretty much flying out straight away.'

He hesitated. 'Can I ask you something?'

She met his eyes without answering.

'The guy, the one I'm finishing off in Thailand. What's he done to you?'

The look of cold hatred on her face sent a shiver down his spine.

'Because of Paul Anderson, I lost everything. Everything!' she snapped. 'He corrupted my father, tore our family apart. Is that enough for you?'

'Yeah, that's enough,' he said.

'However you choose to do it, I hope you make the bastard suffer.'

g

Angelina's words came to mind as he buckled his seatbelt on the Thai Airways 727 and waited for the engines to fire up. He felt his skin prickle.

8

Angelina was making an early morning coffee when she received a text from Antonio: *Change of plans. Leaving now on November 7th not the 14th. Details to follow.*

Shit, that's only a week away! she thought.

Where to? she tapped back.

Brazil, came the reply.

Angelina jumped up with excitement. 'Yes!' she shrieked. Since she was a small child, she'd yearned to return to her country of origin to uncover her roots. She'd hoped that's where Antonio intended to take her, but thought better of asking. Her uncle and his gang didn't take lightly to being questioned. About anything.

Angelina's mind was in a spin. Everything she'd known about her Brazilian mother was shrouded in secrecy. She thought of her grandmother's evasiveness, the secrets she took to the grave.

Now was the time for some answers of her own.

One week to finalise things. A rush, but manageable. By

tomorrow she'd have packed, and in two days be cleared out and on her way to Melbourne for the remaining few nights. There'd be no telling Nic she was leaving the country until the Bangkok deal was done. She wasn't about to risk him abandoning everything to return home and persuade her to stay.

Just one more thing to be done.

9

The following afternoon Angelina headed to her car parked in the tight garage adjoining the house. Careful to duck her head to avoid the cobwebs, she squeezed past the wall. Snail shells crunched underfoot, and the place reeked of dampness.

'God, I'll be glad to get out of this dump,' she muttered as she pulled the car door as far as it would go and wedged behind the steering wheel. At least the car was well hidden. At a distance, the place looked deserted, and that was how she'd wanted things.

She could have left the hired black Audi in the driveway to face the elements, but the car was in pristine condition when she collected it, and that was how she planned to return it. There were to be no questions over a dent from a fallen branch or hailstones, not uncommon at that time of year. She'd been cautious not to drive with her usual abandon. Being pulled over for speeding was the last thing she needed.

As she headed through the rolling green hills towards

the main road leading to the freeway, she reflected on the weeks just past, satisfied with the region in which she'd chosen to stay. Close enough to the city but sufficiently isolated to avoid suspicion.

She had no idea how long she'd be abroad, but it was a safe bet there'd still be cheap, isolated properties within the area, given its slow rate of progress over the years. However, shops that had stood empty for years were beginning to make way for trendy coffee shops, delis, galleries, local produce and crafts. Perhaps Western Australia or a remote part of Queensland would be safer options.

She reached for her iPhone, selected a playlist, and settled back in her seat for the three-hour journey to her hometown. Twenty kilometres out, she glanced at her petrol gauge. It was under a quarter full. 'Damn it!' Angelina blew a stray lock from her face. Should have checked hours ago. There were two or three service stations before she reached town. She hadn't planned to stop until she got to Kilkenny. Best to pull in at the one least frequented.

Up ahead was a trucking stop, and she veered over. With the motor still running, she reached into her backpack for her beanie. Piling her long hair high on her head, she pulled it on and wrapped her scarf around her neck. With her dark jacket and jeans, she could be any passer-by dropping in for fuel and a coffee. Nonetheless, she felt on edge when she filled her car up at the bowser and headed inside to pay her bill. She had never set eyes upon the young man at the cash register. So far, so good. But it didn't stop her eyes from scanning the faces of those around her. It was a small town.

There was a long queue at the café. Angelina placed her order, then browsed amongst the souvenirs, books and postcards nearby as she waited, purchasing several local postcards. As she was heading out the door a young man, not much older than herself, remarked, 'Hey, don't I know you?'

'No, you don't,' she snapped.

He held up his hands. 'Sorry, okay? You look a lot like a chick from town, that's all.'

With an icy glare, she brushed past and strode towards the car.

Reefing the door open, she climbed in and sat, fuming, as she removed her coffee lid.

Once her breathing had slowed and she collected her thoughts, she wondered if she was simply being paranoid. There'd been no mention of her attempt on Cara's life in the media. The Lorenzo family always kept their affairs private. Nonetheless, she was cutting things fine. It was only a matter of time before the cops nailed her for the murder of Lee Farrell, perhaps even that of her father. Her face was grim. The opportunity to skip the country couldn't have come at a better time.

It was 8 p.m. by the time she reached Kilkenny. The imposing wrought iron gates were wide open. *Perfect,* she thought with a satisfied smile as she did a U-turn and headed down the road to park. She knew that she was taking a risk. One wrong move could blow everything. But she couldn't leave the country without stepping inside Kilkenny one more time. She had to know how much had changed since she left.

Turning into the familiar dirt track, she cut the engine and turned off the lights. Grabbing her backpack from the backseat and a small torch from the glovebox, she stepped out into the darkness. The ocean wind was frigid as she set out along the road. She'd forgotten what a godforsaken, bleak place this could be in winter.

As she passed through Kilkenny's gates and cut across the front yard towards the house, she was consumed by a rage not felt since the failed attempt on her sister's life. She'd come so close to pulling things off. So damned close. This should all belong to her and her mother — the house, the estate. And here she was, sneaking around the perimeter like some thief.

There was a light on in the lounge room, and music wafted across the lawn. The curtains were open, and Angelina crept closer for a look. Remaining well hidden in the shadows of the trees, she observed Cara seated at the piano, playing, while her mother looked on nearby. To Cara's side stood a tall, lean man who watched intently. *Who in the hell's that?* she wondered.

She crept around the path and onto the back veranda. No doubt the locks would have been changed. But that accounted for little. The back door would be accessible, secured once the dog came in from its nightly run. Only then would the alarm be switched on. *Old habits die hard, don't they, Mum,* she thought as she turned the door handle and stepped inside.

All was in darkness except for the distant, faint pool of light spilling under the music room door at the far end of the passage. She could hear voices and edged closer to listen.

'You played that well, Cara, but more crescendo was called for,' a man's soft voice said, followed by the sound of a page turning. 'Start the section again.'

Suddenly, there was a low growl, and the playing ceased. Instinctively, Angelina pressed her back to the wall.

'Oscar, what is it, boy?' Jennifer rose quickly and headed to where the dog lay cowering on the floor. Stroking the-soft coat, she looked up at David, her heart pumping. 'You don't think there's anyone out there?'

He went across to the window and looked out onto the well-lit garden.

'Not that I can see,' he said. 'He's probably picked up on the storm that's coming. I can take a look around though if you wish.'

'No, you're probably right,' Jennifer responded. 'Last time there was a storm, he took off. It took us ages to find him.'

The playing resumed.

Angelina smiled. With a renewed sense of daring, she stepped away from the door and crept along the passageway. Ascending the familiar stairs, careful to avoid the creaking steps, she turned left at the landing and headed towards her room. She had a burning desire to see if things were as she'd left them, and it was her final opportunity to grab what she needed for Brazil.

But things never got to that point. The room had been locked.

Angelina reefed at the unyielding door handle, her face contorted in fury. 'This was my room. Mine!' she muttered furiously. 'How dare you!'

Stepping back from the door, she paused for a moment, reminding herself that now was not the time nor place to get even. That would come. For now, time was running out. One hand on the wall, she crept along the passageway in the darkness to her mother's room, quietly closing the door behind her as she entered. It was only then that she turned on her small LED torch and walked towards the ensuite.

Years ago, she and Cara had stood by as her mother unlocked the safe on the shelf and pulled out several boxes. 'What's inside means more to me than you'll ever know, girls, and one day when you grow up, it'll all be yours,' she'd said.

Angelina stood before the safe and closed her eyes, running her hands over the cool metal in small circles, a slight smile on her face. She'd discovered the code from a passing comment made by her father as they shared a drink after work one evening. The birthdate of her grandmother.

Opening her eyes, she pressed in the numbers and

smiled triumphantly at the click as the lock released. She turned the handle and pulled out the contents. The faded blue box was the thing she reached for first. The one her mother cared about the most — the one containing her grandmother's engagement, wedding and eternity rings, a locket of Cara's baby hair and a silver christening bracelet.

'Yes!' Angelina whispered softly, hardly able to contain her excitement as she grabbed the remaining contents and stuffed them into her backpack.

Leaving the safe ajar, she zipped up her backpack, slung it over her shoulders and checked the time. She had intended to head to Cara's room, but she was already cutting things fine. And she'd little idea how long the music lesson would last. Best to be safe. As she walked past her parents' bed, she stopped. Something was missing. She shone her torchlight on the wall. The photo, her father's favourite, taken of her as a twelve-year-old on the catwalk in her fuchsia pink dress, had been taken down.

Furious, she moved over to her mother's desk and scribbled a note, which she ripped off the notepad and placed in the safe.

Just one more thing to do before she left.

The music was still playing when she crept down the stairs and along the passageway to the lounge room. Quietly opening the door, she entered the room and headed to the coffee table upon which sat the family photo album. Too large to put in her backpack, she clutched it to her chest as she made her way out of the room towards the back entrance.

Silently, she edged around the side of the house and cut across the lawn towards the side gate. The fog was setting in, and she turned on her torch. The rage she'd felt at finding her room locked was long gone. In its place was a sense of satisfaction. She'd achieved what she'd intended and was now ready to leave the country.

❡

'That's odd,' David remarked as the three stepped out of the music room an hour later.

'What?' Jennifer asked.

He pointed to the lounge room. 'I thought the door was closed when we came in.'

Jennifer frowned. 'I thought so as well. Did you go in there for anything, Cara?'

'No.' She peered over Jennifer's shoulder.

'I probably just imagined it, don't worry.' David was quick to reassure. Since the attempt on Cara's life, he'd watched Jennifer with concern. She appeared to be coping well enough, but her eyes betrayed the strain she was under. He knew that the thought of Angelina lurking nearby was always at the back of her mind, recalling the fear in her eyes when the dog growled earlier in the evening. None of them would be at peace while Angelina was on the loose.

He frowned. Even when the police eventually nailed

Angelina, bringing her to justice would be another matter. Although Cara had come out unscathed from the attempt on her life, it was her word against Angelina's that it had taken place at all, apart from Lee Farrell, who was no longer alive to testify.

David and Jennifer strongly believed that Angelina was at the marina when Dominic's yacht burned to the ground. The fire was proven to be deliberate, yet there was no evidence to convict her. The two black-clad figures passing the marina's CCTV cameras with heads bowed could be anyone. At this stage, the only things Angelina could be prosecuted for was embezzlement and money laundering.

Angelina had returned once if only to pay a visit to the housekeeper in town. That was brazen enough. What was to say there hadn't been other times they were unaware of or that she wouldn't be back again? Had she been in the house just now? A cold chill went down his back.

'Would you like me to stay?' he offered.

'No, no, we'll be fine, thanks,' Jennifer said. 'Best we get an early night. I'm taking Cara to the city in the morning. I thought we'd pay a visit to Dom's office. It's time to get back into things again.'

'That's good,' he said. The more Jennifer had to occupy her mind, the better.

'Are you staying in town?'

'Just for a night or two. Now that Kate and Peter have headed to Sydney for a few weeks, the apartment's free. Might as well make use of it.'

David nodded. A change of scenery would do them both good.

'Would you like a coffee before you head off?' Jennifer asked.

He glanced at his watch. 'No, it's getting late. Next time perhaps.'

'When's that, Dad?'

The words caused a rush of warmth. It was only in the past few weeks that she'd started calling him that. He'd doubted that she ever would.

He slid an arm around her shoulders and gave her a hug. 'Let me know when you're back, and we'll arrange a time.'

¶

Jennifer sat on the floor, her face buried in her hands, sobbing.

'Mum!' Cara rushed over and knelt down beside her. 'What's wrong. What happened?'

Jennifer raised her head, tears sliding down her face and pointed.

Cara headed quickly to the open safe and pulled out the piece of paper. On it was scribbled two messages: *It didn't take you long to find a new lover did it, Mum,* and *Your playing's still as lousy as ever, Cara. Don't know why you still bother.*

¶

It was midnight when Angelina arrived back at the farmhouse, but she was still wide awake. Within minutes, she was sitting crossed-legged on the floor by the heater, the contents of her backpack sprawled around her.

Like an impatient child at Christmas, she grabbed one item and then the next, barely able to control her excitement. The value of the goods was immaterial; it was the damage she'd caused that brought most satisfaction. Nonetheless, there were items of considerable worth, jewellery for example, given to her mother by her father. Her favourites, an exquisite set of diamond and white gold earrings, matching bracelet and necklace, and a pale blue sapphire ring, she would keep. The rest, along with her grandmother's rings, would be melted down in Rio where gold prices were at a premium.

There was a notebook containing user names and passwords. Angelina flicked through impatiently until she found the page containing Jennifer's online banking details alongside Madeleine's Trust. She cursed, furious that she hadn't thought to look months ago. Well, it was all too late now. The accounts would have been deactivated the moment they discovered her embezzlement of company funds.

A thick envelope containing wads of crisp hundred-dollar notes offered little consolation.

The remaining boxes containing Cara's baby mementos, her father's love letters to her mother and mementos of her mother's childhood, were scooped up and thrown into the rubbish bin; crammed on top was the family photo album. Angelina forced the lid down with a smirk of satisfaction. Wiping her hands on her jeans, she crossed the room to turn off the heater and poured herself a scotch from the bottle on the mantlepiece before heading to bed.

9

Paul Guthrie strolled out onto the private balcony of his room and pulled up a chair. He sat lost in thought for a few moments, gazing across the vast rows of tea fields to the distant mountains shrouded in low lying clouds. Paul never tired of the view. He liked to rise early, sit outside and breathe in the crisp mountain air before he headed down to the dining room for breakfast. At precisely eight, he drove down the winding mountain road to his office in Chang Rai, two hours away. He left the office no later than four, ensuring an easy run home before the traffic built up. The retreat where he'd stayed the past six weeks was set amongst a vast tea plantation in the Doi Mae Salong mountain ranges of Thailand's Chang Rai province. The perfect place to lie low.

Paul was in his office when he learned of Dominic Lorenzo's death. He wasted no time wiping files containing anything that could incriminate him: unscrupulous business deals, underworld contacts, and hidden bank accounts. But it was not enough. He had no way of knowing if the Bangkok authorities had found copies of the deals Dominic was about to sign. If so, as Dominic's business manager he had a lot to answer for. It was the first time Paul had delved into the exploitation of resources in third world countries. The ramifications would be significant should he go to trial.

There'd been no option but to flee Australia. When it was safe to return was anyone's guess.

He booked the next available flight to Bangkok the following morning — time enough to put together what he needed. Over the years, he'd taken careful steps to avoid detection: changing rentals frequently, amassing few possessions and keeping to himself. Clearing out at short notice was nothing new.

A quick call to an associate in Bangkok secured accommodation in a high-rise block of apartments on the city's outskirts until a more suitable option was found.

Five days later, he sat with a Thai businessman in a nearby Bangkok hotel.

'There's a silent partnership up for grabs, Paul. It's with a tour company about to start up in Chang Rai that offers eco-friendly itineraries; hikes to remote areas, glam camping, that sort of thing.'

Paul raised an eyebrow, and the man opposite shot him a wry smile. 'Not your usual thing, I know, but,' he paused, 'there are possibilities.'

'Such as?'

'Try getting your hands on some Akha Hill Tribe land.'

The businessman now had Paul's full attention. Indigenous Akha tribes were still found in parts of the mountains north of Chang Rai, but they were few and far between, and their land was considered gold.

'Go on.'

'The company's close to signing a deal with a remote Akha Village. A generous fee in return for rare access. We're talking the real deal here, Paul. Not the staged one-hour visits conducted by tribes these days. Think of the money tourists would fork out for something like this, especially if homestays were incorporated.' He gave a shrug. 'As for the rest? Well, that'd be up to you.'

Paul was thinking quickly. Four years ago, a group of struggling Akha farmers were coerced into selling tracts of their land for bargain prices. God knows how much it was worth now.

The task was by no means impossible. Right now, Paul needed to be involved in a scheme that was not connected in any way to illicit dealings. One slip, and he could find himself extradited to Australia. The thought left him in a cold sweat. Depending on what they found, he could be put away for a long time. The funds he'd so carefully stashed away over the years wouldn't be much use to him then. If the land deal didn't eventuate, he'd simply move on. Lie low for a while longer until things settled. With his connections, there'd be little trouble picking up where he left off.

Right now, he was glad he'd agreed to the proposition. A new identity, an idyllic existence in a tea plantation hideaway with an easy commute to his office, was a refreshing change. Although one thing he needed right now was sex. He debated on calling Aranya, a Thai girl who worked at his office. She was slender, in her early twenties, with long dark hair that she wore tied back. He began to fantasise what it would look like loose. She was single as far as he knew — not that that made any difference. The thing was, she came from a small village not far from Chang Rai, and word would soon get around. He wanted no ties or connections. Better to head off to Bangkok for a weekend now and then. He had the contacts to find someone clean. Someone who'd be guaranteed to keep their mouth shut for some extra cash. A bit of nightlife and luxury at a five-star hotel wouldn't go astray either, come to think of it.

10

Nic Drakos's flight from Bangkok arrived at Chang Rai airport at 4 p.m. Just enough time to find somewhere to stay before night set in.

Little had changed since he was last here three years ago. The airport was small and clean, and its staff friendly and efficient. Blooms of orchids and photos of lush mountain vistas caught his eye as he moved through the main building, and for a moment he wished he was one of the tourists heading off for a well-earned break.

Thai airport officials had not questioned his identity in the past, and he had little reason to believe things would be different this time. His passport contained Thai stamps dating back several years. He could be one of many businessmen who made regular trips to the country. He was confident there was nothing that Interpol could pin on him. He took great care in covering his tracks once a job was done. But forensics were rolling ahead at an alarming pace and he was finding it harder and harder to keep up.

Chapter 10

These days he stuck to what he knew best, long-range hits. No traces of remaining DNA. No footprint left in blood to follow up.

There were only a handful of passengers in the queue ahead. He was heading towards the luggage carousel in no time, then out past the throng of people awaiting new arrivals, to the hire car he'd already arranged online.

He'd forgotten how steamy the place was as he stepped outside the airport grateful for the car's air conditioner as the late afternoon sun poured through the windscreen. The airport was eight kilometres from the city centre but seemed much further as he crawled along in the afternoon peak traffic.

He chose a small, nondescript guest house on the outskirts of town. The room was small but clean. He dumped his bags on the bed and headed straight for the fridge. 'You beauty,' he said as he reached for one of the three stubbies in the side door, ripped off the top and downed it in a few swigs. A shower was next on the agenda. He peeled off his clothes that felt as if they'd been on for days and stepped in, gasping as the cold jets hit his body. *Just what I needed,* he thought. Moments later he stepped out, refreshed, and vigorously towelled himself.

For the first time that day, he felt hunger kicking in. Not one for airline meals, Nic had waited for his plane to land at Bangkok airport before grabbing a sandwich and coffee. But that was hours ago. The guest house manager recommended a small restaurant frequented by locals. A Thai curry would hit the spot. But not before he'd located the office of Paul Guthrie. Ten minutes' drive, according to Google maps. He inserted a new sim card in his mobile, grabbed his keys from the table and headed out to the car.

He awoke the following day, sweaty and disoriented. Once he'd suffered little from jet lag, but those days were long gone. It was the thing he hated about travel.

The curtains were drawn, and the room was in relative darkness, but the humidity was insufferable. It was only then Nic realised the air conditioner hadn't been switched on. 'Geez, that's a first,' he muttered, pulling his legs to the floor and reaching for the remote. Another cold shower, longer than last night's, a strong coffee, and he was set to go through his emails.

The fifth one down was from his contact, and he gave it a tap. It read:

Guthrie arrives at the Chang Rai office at ten each morning Monday to Friday and leaves at four. No idea where he's hiding out.

Nic opened the attachment, a photo taken of Paul Guthrie three days ago and his eyes lit up in surprise. It was nothing like the one on his files. Now sporting a beard and thick, dark-framed glasses, Guthrie was barely recognisable. The update couldn't have been more timely. Nic decided to wait a while before tailing him. Enough time to recover and source a gun.

9

Angelina left the farmhouse keys under a brick in the garage as instructed, climbed into her car and headed down the darkened driveway with a sigh of relief. The last time she'd have to put up with bitter winds, cold rooms and mildewed walls. But she'd need to keep a low profile in the city. Although she would have preferred to stay at a five-star city hotel until her departure, she couldn't afford the risk of being recognised. Once her note to Jennifer was reported, the police would be out searching. Even now her senses were alert, watching every pair of headlights that came her way, and she frequently activated cruise control, as an extra precaution.

The motel she'd chosen was on the outskirts of Melbourne, en route to the airport. It looked like one of the better ones, according to her web search. She'd planned to spend three nights there but changed it to two so that she could pay this one final visit to Kilkenny.

It was five by the time she arrived at the main gates. They were wide open, but she had no intentions of entering the grounds this time, fully aware that there could well be a security guard on duty or a watchdog roaming the perimeter. A quick U-turn, and she parked the car further back amongst the trees, returning with her binoculars.

All was in darkness.

For a few moments, she paused and closed her eyes. She could hear the familiar crashing of waves against the rocks, could make out a distant fox's high pitched yippy bark, could taste the salt on her tongue. It was as if she'd never left at all.

But she had. And she would never be welcomed back. The thought of her sister possessing all that should be hers caused her blood to boil, but she forced her mind to the task at hand. Cara's time would come soon enough.

Further in from the track was an old tree that she'd climbed many times as a child, and she made her way towards it, her torch on low beam. From her sturdy vantage point on the third branch, she had a clear view over the house and its grounds through her infrared binoculars. A quick scan told her that the place remained unguarded, but she quickly noted two security cameras that had not been there three days prior.

The wind had picked up and a sudden stench of blood and bone hit her nostrils as she climbed down and crossed the road to place the small envelope containing one of her mother's earrings in the letterbox. Ugh! She covered her nose with the back of her hand and jogged back to the car.

It was close to six when she approached the CBD. Check-in time wasn't until ten, allowing time for a decent breakfast at a café somewhere and a return of the hire car.

11

Nic felt refreshed from his two days' rest and rose early. After breakfast in the dining room, he checked out and drove an hour and a half east to a small village in the Thoeng district to collect his gun. Last of six houses along a dead-end dirt road, the shabby dwelling sat behind an overgrown vegetable garden choked by weeds. Apart from a motorbike propped against a pile of junk in a makeshift garage, the place looked deserted. The front shutters were closed as he climbed the five wooden steps to the central porch, knocked and waited.

'Who is it?' came a voice from the other side.

'Jonas,' he said. 'I called last night. I'm here to see Raen.'

The door opened, and a slightly built young man gestured him inside with a nod.

'Raen,' he called over his shoulder, 'it's for you.'

Soon afterwards, a Thai man not much older than thirty appeared from a room at the far end of the house. Through the open doorway, Nic could see pots and pans hanging from hooks on a distant wall, and the sudden waft of lemongrass, spices and cooked chicken caused his mouth to water.

It was dark and cold inside, and he wondered how they managed to keep warm. *Probably don't hang around long enough to find out*, he thought. Illegal gun dealers were constantly on the move in Thailand. This place would be one of many.

'You're early,' Raen said.

'Yeah, well, I've got things to do.'

There was a nod. 'You've got the money?'

Nic pulled a wad of crisp thousand-dollar baht notes from his pocket, and Raen grabbed it from him, flicking through to check its accuracy.

Satisfied, he disappeared behind a nearby curtain, returning with a 308-bit action Winchester sniper rifle and a medium-sized backpack.

'There won't be any issues,' Raen remarked.

'My contact said that'd be the case,' Nic said as he slipped on a pair of gloves, took the gun and gave it a quick look over. With a nod, he handed over the envelope and watched as the notes were counted. He'd only get a fraction when the rifle was returned. It would be dismantled, the barrel replaced to ensure it was no longer traceable and ready for the next buyer.

Raen disassembled the gun and placed the parts in the canvas bag. 'There's enough ammunition.'

'Good. I'll contact you when I'm ready to return it.'

'How long will that be?'

'I can't say at this point. Five, six days maybe.'

'Drop off point won't be here, you understand. I'll arrange for someone to meet you at Ban Mon Hin Kaeo. It's a small village thirty minutes' drive from here.'

'I'd prefer somewhere closer to Chiang Rai if you don't mind.'

The man flashed a grin of stained teeth. 'It can be arranged. At a cost.'

Nic pulled cash from his pocket and peeled off more notes. 'This'll cover it.'

Raen nodded and snatched the money from the table, and Nic turned and headed towards the door.

Clouds were gathering as he drove through the village. Apart from the odd motorbike passing by and a group of children playing in the dirt at the roadside, few were about. Chickens roamed freely, and more than once Nic found himself frequently swerving to avoid a dog or cat. Half an hour later, he turned off the main road and onto a dirt road when he stopped, where it was safe to swap number plates.

It was three by the time he reached Chang Rai. Enough time to snatch a bite to eat before Paul Guthrie left his office for home, wherever that was. Nic imagined it would not be away. Little did he know how wrong he was.

At 3.45, he parked on the main road near Paul's office and waited. Not long afterwards, a car appeared from a nearby underground car park and turned left. A glimpse of the driver told him it was Guthrie. Keeping his distance,

Nic tailed him north through town for thirty minutes, along the Mai Sai Highway towards Mae Chan, then onto the Highway 1130 turnoff. The road led through rolling hills and open farmland before making its windy ascent into the mountains.

An hour later, Paul's red SUV turned left into a narrow bitumen road, but Nic continued on. He would return later when there was no chance of suspicion that he was trailing Guthrie.

Doi Mae Salong, the nearest town, sat on a ridge high in the Daen Lao Mountain range, not far from the Myanmar border. Another half hour's drive, according to his GPS. There was a sudden steep climb with little visibility in the thickening mist as he manoeuvred the treacherous bends. 'Shit, I didn't know this was coming,' he muttered.

As he approached the town, there was little traffic, but the shops that lined its narrow streets were abuzz with patrons. Nic was surprised to see red lanterns hanging outside shop windows and signs with Chinese characters embossed in gold. He'd forgotten he was in Golden Triangle country, where opium poppies once proliferated, and Chinese soldiers came to make a new life after fleeing a civil war.

Doi May Salong, formerly known as Santikhiri, was relatively unheard of until the 1990s when word got around about a remote mountain village with authentic Chinese customs and cuisine. Although quiet in the rainy season, the town was a popular tourist drawcard from November to February when Thailand was at its hottest and people came for a spot of cool relief.

There'd been a few lodges and villas along the way, and he settled on a small budget guesthouse a kilometre out of town. Just two other cars were parked outside. The place was basic, more like a backpacker hostel than a guest house, which suited him fine. The air reeked of cigarettes as he ascended the six steps and onto the tiled veranda where the main office sat.

No one was about when he entered, so he pressed the bell on the chipped counter. Shortly afterwards, a slightly built man who appeared a mixture of Thai and Chinese emerged wearing jeans and a khaki shirt. He looked to be in his forties, but Nic could never be sure.

'Hi, hope I'm not too late,' he said.

'Not at all. I was just doing a few things out the back.' The man extended a hand, and Nic shook it, surprised at its strength.

'Welcome. I'm the manager here. Anuman.'

'Jonas,' Nic said. 'Pleased to meet you.'

'Are you from Australia?' he asked.

Nic nodded.

'What are you doing this far up?'

'Just passing through. My wife died a year ago and I found myself spending too much time at the office. Thought it was time for a break.'

'I see. Sorry about wife. How many nights you here for?'

'Three, maybe four before I head across the border into Laos.'

'What you want, room upstairs or bungalow out back? Three hundred baht a night for room with shared bathroom or 500 for bungalow.'

'A bungalow will be fine, thanks.'

The manager nodded and reached under the desk for a key card which he activated and handed over. 'Yours last on left. Breakfast seven-thirty till nine-thirty in dining room.'

'Thanks, but I'll probably be up and gone by then most days,' Nic said, then headed out to collect his bags.

A proliferation of shrubs and overhanging trees lined the path that led to his bungalow, one of four with sloped, tiled roofs. The others were vacant. It would be easy to come and go unnoticed.

After he'd showered and dressed, he drove into town for dinner, settling on a dimly lit, crowded noodle shop, then headed to the road that Guthrie's car had turned into. All was in darkness as he continued up a hill that led to a dead-end at the top. A signpost pointed left to a villa retreat, and he turned into the well-lit, gravel driveway. Guthrie's car sat amongst four others in the car park. He would have liked to have waited till it was late to case the place more closely, but already he'd noted two security cameras. There'd undoubtedly be more. Best to keep surveillance at a distance. He'd be back before daybreak. That was just hours away, and he could grab a few hours' sleep.

When he got back to his room, he flicked on the television. The channels were mainly Chinese, so he turned to his iPad and conducted some Google searches instead. The villa retreat was part of the adjoining tea plantation that he'd passed along the way. It offered six thatched, two-storey villas, each set well apart with private balconies boasting uninterrupted views over the tea fields. The remaining twelve single-storey rooms sat amongst gardens close to the main dining room. He'd hedge his bets on Guthrie staying at one of the villas, given what he'd learned of the man's penchant for luxury.

A YouTube clip of the interior revealed contemporary décor in bright colours with a distinctive Thai feel. Not a bad spot to seek refuge. He wouldn't have minded staying there himself. He found himself thinking of Angelina. It was the kind of place he would like to take her. But would she like it? He realised how little he knew of her. He had a sudden urge to call her, but didn't know what he would say. Deep down, he hoped she would have contacted him by now if only to ask how things were going. She could only reach him by message bank on his new sim card, but he feared picking up something in her voice that might indicate indifference.

An image came to his mind of their final night together, her long dark hair spilling over the pillow as she slept and her smooth olive skin contrasted against the ivory sheets in the early morning light.

Truth was, he never wanted the job in the first place.

He'd been about to take a few months' break. The chance to visit his mother in North Queensland, meet his kid brother's two-year-old twins for the first time. But Ava's unexpected call, the chance to meet up again, was all it took to say yes. Suddenly he wished he hadn't.

His jaw clenched. It was too late for regret. He'd committed himself, and from here on in, it was simply a matter of keeping his focus and executing the plan. He had no doubt the demise of Paul Guthrie would make the world a better place.

⁊

It was 2 a.m. when Angelina pulled up in a St Kilda side street and parked the car opposite a set of old detached bungalow houses. All was in darkness except for a dim, yellow street light further along. In the distance, she could hear the faint, rhythmic boom of music from a nightclub still in full swing.

She'd only learned of Theo Samaras at the last minute from Jiang, the contact who'd arranged her fake ID.

'You can trust Theo to keep his mouth shut,' he said.

'How do I know that?'

'Likes to do a bit on the side — things his gang don't know about. Theo's not about to blab. Comes at a cost, though.'

'I just want things done right,' she said.

'They will be. Why don't you see for yourself? Try him out with something small and see what you think.'

'I might just do that.'

'If it helps, I've called on him a few times. Hasn't put a foot wrong.'

From what Jiang had told her, Theo's gang dealt predominantly with stolen goods, illegal gun trafficking and drug deals: a wide range of experience to draw on.

A curtain on the ground floor of the middle house parted slightly, and soon afterwards, the door opened, and a large shadow filled the frame. She assumed it was Theo. Her eyes swept over the street to check there was no one around and then crossed over. Only a small, low wall separated the entrance from the pavement, and she wondered how much if any space was to the rear.

'You're late,' he said, clearly annoyed.

'Yeah, well, I found it hard to find the place,' she shot back as she stepped onto the porch.

The man towered over her. It was hard to make out his features in the darkness, but she could see that his head had been shaved. She handed over a brown bag containing three stamped addressed envelopes and five-hundred-dollar bills. His large hands flicked them quickly and he nodded.

'And that's all, lady?'

She nodded. 'Just make sure it's done.'

'It will be. If you want more jobs done, you know where to come.'

'I'll keep it in mind.'

She turned and left.

Theo watched her go, wondering who put her on to him and wishing every job was this easy.

12

At 5 a.m. Nic returned to the tea fields. Not far along the road that led to the villa retreat, he spotted a cutting to the left, framed by a cluster of dense, broad-leafed trees and long grasses. He pulled in, edging the car as far as it would go under the welcoming canopy. Even in daylight, his dark grey four-wheel drive would be hard to spot from the road. Around twenty metres away, an old shed stood amongst the tea fields. Its close proximity to the main road made it far from ideal, but it was the only place that provided concealment. He'd be back to suss it out once it was dark.

Crouching amongst rows of waist-high tea plants, bin-oculars in hand, he waited, eyes fixed on the retreat, four hundred metres or so in the distance. The air was chilly, and he found himself reaching for his gloves. At 6.40, the sliding door to the middle villa opened, and Guthrie stepped onto the patio wearing dark trousers, a matching jacket and a grey shirt. He pulled up a nearby chair, lit a cigarette, and looked over the tea fields for a while before heading inside.

The villa to the right of Guthrie's appeared unoccupied, but Nic noted a partially open curtain in the one to its left, and he detected movement inside. It didn't bother him too much. At that time of the morning, there shouldn't be too many problems. Maybe the villa would be vacant again by the time he made his move. With a bit of luck, the others would remain so as well. At 7.30, Guthrie appeared in the car park, a black laptop bag slung over one shoulder.

Nic moved quickly to the car and waited until Guthrie's car passed before he tailed him at a safe distance. If Guthrie suspected he was being scrutinised, he was likely to simply vanish.

As expected, Guthrie pulled into the office car park. Nic kept going. Further along, he did a U-turn then headed back to the tea plantation. It was an easy run with little traffic, giving him plenty of time to think. The job was turning out to be more problematic than first thought. Things would have been easier if Guthrie had been holed up at a Bangkok hotel somewhere. He'd find a place nearby where he could come and go with little chance of detection, then sit and wait until the time was right. But Guthrie's Chiang Rai office was a different proposition altogether. There were too many people coming and going, too many risks and uncertainties.

Turning into the tea plantation's main entrance, Nic

headed down the driveway towards the teahouse and pulled up beside a busload of tourists. Pretending to be one of them, he followed the group into the tearooms.

'We'll meet back at the bus at one,' the tour guide told them. 'That'll allow enough time for lunch and a good look around.'

As the group dispersed, Nic headed across to the expansive window. The vista was breathtaking. Terraces covered with rows of tea plants that resembled rolls of emerald carpet stretched as far as the eye could see against the distant mountain backdrop. He could just make out splashes of colour of the tea pickers to the far north as they worked. That was a positive. His plans would be inoperable if they worked close to where he planned to carry out his hit. Still, questions remained. How long before they finished that section and moved on? And where would that be?

But there was another option yet to consider.

After sampling a few teas, he headed to the café for a bite to eat then left the teahouse. At the main entrance, he turned right and drove for another thirty minutes until he reached the scenic lookout. Ten minutes' steady climb, and he reached the spot. No one was about as he parked, and glanced at his watch. 4.30 p.m. He surmised another hour at least, until Guthrie came into view on his way home from work.

Climbing out of his car, he rested against the bonnet, binoculars in hand and surveyed his surroundings to get a feel for the place. To any passer-by, he could be just another tourist in his t-shirt, cargo pants and sandals.

There was little passing traffic as he waited. Immersed in his surroundings, he took a long deep breath. It had been a long time since he'd been able to let his guard down like this. He recognised Guthrie's red car a long way off and glanced once more at his watch. Five-thirty. His reasoning had proved correct.

The lookout provided the perfect vantage point to shoot Guthrie long-range should he so choose. In the distance was a straight stretch of road before its windy ascent to the top. There was no way he'd miss. It was a matter of choosing the day, and the rest would be easy. Another hour and things would be in darkness. He'd be long gone by the time Guthrie's car was discovered. Still, Nic felt uneasy. He'd carried out three hits in similar circumstances but on roads much less travelled than this. There was always the worrisome chance that a vehicle might appear just as he was about to shoot. Or that Guthrie's car might not be the only one on the road. His brow furrowed. Best to run with plan A. Far from ideal but a damned sight less risky. Guthrie's car had already reached the foot of the hill. Time to clear out.

The afternoon light was fast fading as he turned into the cutting and parked, confident its dense foliage would provide sufficient camouflage. Sure enough, Guthrie passed ten minutes later without so much as a sideward glance. Still, Nic was cutting things fine. The more times he returned, the greater risk of being spotted.

Keeping low, he set foot in the tea plantation and moved

quickly towards the old shed. Weeds choked its entrance, and the rusted, padlocked door was wedged into the ground like a stake. Kicking at the dirt around the base until it loosened, Nic turned, ramming one shoulder hard into the door that caved inwards, sending hinges flying.

Stepping inside, he reached for his torch. The shed was roomier than anticipated. To his left was an old tractor draped in dust alongside an array of rusty tools hanging from the wall. There was only the slightest chance of disturbance. One positive, he supposed. On the flip side, the dusty air stifled his nostrils and burned his throat. A memory came to mind of a damp, dust-ridden Moscow attic in winter, where'd he waited four days for his target to show. At least here he'd be in and out within an hour, all being well.

Clearing the immediate area of boxes and old junk, he dragged across a table and bench positioning them under the shed's only window. Well satisfied, he stepped outside, closing the door behind him and bent down, wiping his hands on a nearby clump of grass.

By the time he pulled out of the cutting, it was dark. He headed towards Mae Salong, eyes alert and mind racing. There was so much to be done with so little time. He'd planned to be in and out of Thailand within a week. And he'd already reached the fourth day. He had no intentions of extending his stay. The more people he spoke with, the greater the chances of being remembered. Then there was the possibility of arriving one morning to find Guthrie gone. What if he didn't risk staying in one place for too long. There'd be no choice but to start all over again.

The chilly night air stung his cheeks as he got out of the car for a brief moment; he found it hard to believe he was in Thailand. It was already ten by the time he flicked on the light in his bungalow. He realised he had not eaten since midday, but he wasn't the least bit hungry. A beer and packet of nuts from the minibar would do.

Sleep came easily.

13

By 5 a.m. Nic was showered, dressed and firing up the car outside.

He checked the rear vision on the road leading to the villa retreat, satisfied that all was clear before he pulled into the cutting and parked. Slinging the backpack over one shoulder, he stepped onto the tea fields and crouched amongst the bushes, binoculars in hand. The air was still. Guthrie appeared on his balcony precisely the same time as the day before and sat with a coffee and cigarette. Twenty minutes later, he headed inside. This simplified things. Nic gave a wry grin. Punctuality had its drawbacks.

Once Guthrie was out of sight, Nic headed to the shed. Donning a pair of gloves, he entered and pulled three dust-covered panes from the louvre window. Next, Nic assembled his rifle on the table and presented the muzzle through the gap. He took aim, adjusting the elevation to zero in on the balcony via the Leupold six-three scope. The day was typically, quite still and he would be using

175-grain Federal Gold Medal Match ammunition. He calculated a minimal windage influence, in his mind, already feeling there would be no need for change on action day. It was also the onset of the rainy season, but short of blinding rain making visibility impossible, there was little chance of wet weather affecting his work. He might be forced to postpone if he couldn't see his target but again, the chances of that were minimal. Wasting no time, he disassembled the rifle, placed the parts in his backpack and returned to the car.

Soon he was turning right onto the main road and heading back to the bungalow to fill in time until his late afternoon checkout, stopping along the way at a small, wood-panelled café for a takeaway expresso and a selection of homemade cakes and pastries. A waft of freshly baked bread and coffee beans met his nostrils as he opened the door. It invoked memories of his childhood when he entered his mother's kitchen, as she transferred tray after tray of piping hot buttery, almond kourabiedes (Greek biscuits) from oven to kitchen bench. It smelled damned good.

Nic spent most of the day lying on his bed, propped up by pillows, flicking through TV channels or catching up on world news on his iPad. At 4.30, he packed up, then pulled on some gloves and, using a damp cloth, wiped all surfaces to ensure there were no traces of DNA or other incriminating evidence.

Everything was going according to plan. As far as the

guest house manager was concerned, he was one of many passing tourists. Another night's stay could complicate matters though, especially if his early morning check-out was later cross-referenced with the time of the hit. Nevertheless, the thought of the long night ahead cramped in the front seat of his car was already playing on his mind. He'd done it all before, and every time he vowed it would be the last.

To fill in time he drove around until it was dark, passing many tea plantations similar to where Guthrie was staying. They appeared to be thriving and it was hard to believe that the area had been a proliferation of opium poppy fields not so long ago. At six, he headed back to Mae Salong.

It was Friday night, and the town was busier than usual; the inns, noodle shops and tearooms close to capacity. He couldn't deny the town had a certain charm, with its red lanterns and gold embossed characters, but his mind was on other things. He had to fill in time, and it was causing a sense of anxiety. Every hour felt like four.

A mixture of tantalising smells and freshly roasted tea wafted out from a nearby shop, causing his stomach to rumble. It was time for a decent meal. The next wouldn't be until the following day, after the job had been completed. In the meantime, there'd be jelly beans on hand to re-energise. A legacy of his football days.

He made his way towards a small, busy inn. A good sign.

In his experience, dining amongst the locals guaranteed the best food. Inside, he was approached by a waiter and led to a small table being cleared near the window. The place was abuzz with chatter, Chinese mainly, with a smidgen of Thai. Nic was constantly alert to the movements of those around him and found himself checking the door whenever passers-by drifted in from the street. It came with the territory.

It was past ten, just as he was about to start his main meal, when something caught his eye from a distance. Someone heading his way. Someone familiar. His breath caught in his throat. The man looked different in his casual garb but unquestionably it was Guthrie. Nic hoped he would walk straight past, but he crossed the road, stopped directly outside the window, centimetres from Nic's face, and glanced through the menu on a stand.

Heart thudding, Nic reached in his pocket for his iPhone and lowered his head, his peripheral vision firmly fixed on the pavement outside. He'd been lucky they'd not crossed paths to this point, but the possibility was never far from his mind. He didn't know what the guy got up to at weekends, but Guthrie wasn't the type to stay holed up in his room. He probably ate out frequently. Meals in town were cheap, and there were plenty of places from which to choose. Maybe there was a woman nearby, who knew.

In what seemed minutes but was only a matter of seconds, Guthrie moved on. 'Shit, that was close,' Nic muttered under his breath. The place was busy enough to slip out unobtrusively if Guthrie had chosen to dine there, but even the best of plans had a way of coming unstuck. He pushed such thoughts from his mind, satisfied there was nothing to link him with Guthrie. No associations, phone calls or emails to trace. When the police arrived at the scene, it would be apparent that this was a hit job. Once the authorities delved into Guthrie's past, they'd discover any number of people with the motive and means to get rid of him. It was simply a matter of whether they had the time and concern to follow things through. He doubted it. There were bigger fish to fry.

❡

Sitting alone in the dark under a thin blanket offering little warmth, he willed the morning to come. He wished that he could doze off, even for a little while. A power nap was supposed to work wonders, wasn't it? He wouldn't know. He'd become conditioned to sleeping only at nights and only where it was safe to do so.

14

By the time the sun's first rays appeared, Nic was poised and ready to go. He flung open the car door and quickly climbed out. After a few much-needed stretches and pee, he changed from his jeans and jacket into a pair of dark pants, matching hoodie, and lace-up boots, then jumped back in the car and headed towards the tea fields.

Relieved to see there was little sign of rain, he pulled into the cutting and parked.

On high alert, he swung the backpack on his shoulders, reached for his binoculars, and made his way across the tea fields, acutely aware that someone could appear when least expected. As he approached the shed, he gave the area a last-minute scan. No one.

He donned a pair of gloves, dragged the door open and stepped inside, pulling it closed behind him. Placing his backpack on the table, he unzipped it and took out the parts. In earlier times, he would have purchased several weapons, but since he had first tried the Remington CSR

(Concealable Sniper Rifle), it had become his only choice. Apart from the fact that it weighed less than four kilos, the CSR could be broken down and assembled and still hit the spot without re-zeroing.

The CSR components consisted of the chassis, with fitted scope, folding butt-stock, 35 cm barrel plus the Fast Attack Suppressor. He unfolded the stock before fitting the barrel and suppressor, locking them in place. The magazine was snapped in so there was now nothing to do but wait.

Guthrie appeared around the expected time, and Nic felt the customary surge of adrenaline that came with a hit. He placed the gun on the table, making sure not a millimetre protruded from the window and then held the gun steady against the table, zeroing in on the balcony.

He waited a few moments as Guthrie settled and reached for a cigarette before he fixed the man's face in the crosshairs, finger on the trigger. But just as he was about to fire, he detected a slight movement, and the sliding door behind Guthrie opened, revealing a room service employee with an armful of towels.

'Fuck!' Nic exclaimed in frustration. Guthrie nodded at the young man and said something, pointing inside the villa.

Nic waited a few minutes to ensure the worker was well away from the villa before taking aim once more. The shot was precise. Guthrie's body spasmed, and he crashed back onto the tiles, sending the chair flying. There was a small hole visible in his forehead from which came a slight trickle of blood. But the back of his head would tell a different story. Guthrie lay motionless, in a pool of red, body contorted, eyes wide open and facing upwards.

Nic waited a little longer to make sure Guthrie was dead. His teeth still tingled from the firing as he removed the suppressor and then the rifle barrel. Folding in the stock, Nic quickly placed the parts in the backpack. Next, he replaced the louvre window panes, grabbed the gear and binoculars and dragged the door shut behind him. A quick scan told him no one was about. Wasting no time, he slung the backpack across his shoulders and made a dash for the car.

It was highly likely that someone had heard the crash. The couple in the next villa along perhaps, or the housekeeping returning to the main building. But the possibility didn't concern him. He'd be gone before the alarm was raised, and even then, it would take the Mae Salong police at least half an hour to get there. Tossing his backpack onto the backseat he climbed into the car, fired up the engine and eased out of the cutting, heart hammering against his chest. This was the one time he couldn't afford to be seen.

But all was clear.

On the way to Chang Rai, Nic turned off the main road and found an isolated spot where he swapped the number plates back to the originals and had a quick change of clothes.

Another hour's drive along the main road, he spotted

a large roadhouse. Only then did he realise how hungry he was. After topping up with fuel, he proceeded to the restaurant and filled up on bacon, eggs and hash browns. Only a few diners were present, but it was easy to blend in; just another customer seated in another orange booth, scrolling the screen of his iPhone.

As Nic stepped outside, he could see dark clouds gathering overhead. He made it to the car just before the downpour hit, grateful it hadn't taken place two hours earlier. Before he fired up the ignition, he checked for messages on his mobile. Nothing. Why would there be? Angelina didn't know the day or time of the hit. But underneath he was hoping for something, anything that might indicate he was in her thoughts.

A quick call to the gun dealer secured the gun handover at noon. Drop off point was an abandoned warehouse on the outskirts of Chang Rai. He'd considered calling the airlines to see if an earlier flight home was available, but that could arouse suspicion if the police made enquiries. The last thing he needed was to be accompanied off the plane to Bangkok and taken in for questioning. Best leave things as they stood. His flight departed at midnight the following day. A decent feed and good night's sleep in a comfortable bed at a hotel near the airport would be a bonus.

He returned the hire car at three and took a shuttle bus to a budget hotel three kilometres from the airport. There was a five-star hotel closer to the airport but it was preferable to remain low key. The place looked reasonable enough, a two-storey brick building set amongst well-maintained gardens.

He booked in at the small office inside the main entrance then took the lift to the second floor. Room 209 was at the end of a long, carpeted passageway overlooking the main road. He dumped his bags on the furthest single bed and then placed a "do not disturb" sign on the door. He glanced at his mobile. Four o'clock, 8 p.m. Melbourne time. He expected she'd be home. For a moment, he was filled with self-doubt. Maybe he'd wasted his time. Maybe he'd imagined the look in her eyes that night, mistook the meanings in her words. What if the whole thing had been in vain?

He took a deep breath and reached for the phone.

She answered on the first ring. 'Nic? Where are you? Is everything okay? Why haven't you called?'

Ditto, he thought.

'I don't make calls while I'm working,' he said, doing his best to come across as indifferent. 'Thought you'd be interested to know Guthrie was taken care of early this morning. I'm on my way home, but my flight from Bangkok doesn't depart till tomorrow night. Any chance of meeting up when I get back?'

There was a pause.

'I'm afraid that's not possible.'

His heart began to thud. 'What do you mean?'

Another pause. 'I won't be around, that's all. I'm on my way to Brazil. My plane takes off in an hour.'

Nic felt as if he'd been kicked in the guts.

'And that's it? Shit. You're full of surprises, aren't you? It would have been nice to have known this before.'

'It's not like you think.'

'What in the hell do you expect me to think!'

'Look, just hold on will you until I find somewhere safe to talk.' He heard the squish of her shoes on the polished floor as she walked and the distant roar of a plane taking off.

Then she spoke again. 'You still there?'

'Yeah.'

'This has nothing to do with you — with us. I found out the cops were closing in and had to get out fast. It was no use trying to get hold of you. What could you have done? The only person I could think of was my uncle. His name's Antonio. He has connections. He told me to pack my things and take a taxi to his place. He was making calls when I arrived. There was one seat left on a flight departing for Brazil, and he booked it.'

'How convenient.'

'What's that supposed to mean?'

'Things just don't happen like that, Ava. They take planning.'

For a moment there was silence.

'Perhaps it's about time you came clean,' he said.

'All right, all right. I knew all along I was leaving, okay? I just didn't know when or where I was headed, for that matter. My uncle isn't one to fire questions at.'

There was no response.

'I planned to tell you when you got back, I swear,' she insisted.

Again no response.

'Oh, for God's sake, say something, will you!'

'What do you expect me to say? You did what you had to do and got out. I'm glad you got what you wanted.'

'That's it?'

'Pretty much.'

'You know, after you stayed, I thought there might just be a chance for us,' she said.

Nic's mouth went dry.

'Yeah, well, things happen for a reason, Ava. Maybe it wasn't meant to be. Look, I think we've said everything that needs to be said. It's time I got going.'

'Will you be in touch?'

'Probably not,' he said quietly. 'I'm sure your uncle will have things well in hand. Look after yourself.'

The line went dead. 'Screw you!' Angelina stuffed the phone in her pocket and strode towards the departure lounge.

Initially, she'd no qualms about dumping Nic once he'd served his purpose. She'd found a way out of the country and was looking forward to the sights, sounds and colours of a country she'd waited to see all her life. It was only when Antonio outlined a few things on the way to the airport that the first signs of trepidation crept in. They were to travel separately and act as if they didn't know each other. There was a set of terms and conditions that she was expected to follow once they landed, and after she'd settled in, there'd be a role to fulfil. Like it or not, she was at their bidding.

By the time Nic rang, she'd already changed her mind about letting him go. This was uncharted territory, and she needed protection. A few lies, a few soft well-chosen words, and she expected he'd fly out on the next available flight to join her. Never in a million years did she think he'd knock her back. Not after the two nights they'd spent together.

Angelina gave a defiant toss of her head. He'd change his mind. They always did. Now was not the time to dwell on it. She'd figure something out in good time. Meanwhile, she was well and truly on her own.

All of a sudden she felt uneasy.

As she headed towards the departure gates lounge, by now filled to capacity, she locked eyes on her uncle, who was seated on the furthest aisle. His expression was angry. A beep came through on her message bank.

Who were you talking to just then?

I wasn't. Angelina texted back.

Bullshit. You agreed to speak with no one. Do what you're told.

Angelina was fuming, but she held herself back. With a dark look and toss of her head, she shoved her phone in her bag and stood, arms crossed behind the long queue about to board. If this was a sign of things to come, he'd have a fight on his hands. *It's not as if you're there for long,* she told herself.

Little did she know how wrong she was.

¶

Nic took a shower, shaved, changed and went in search of a strong whisky. Making his way to the bar, he settled at a table overlooking the window and summoned the drinks waiter. He soon lost track of time, watching people come and go as he downed one drink after another. As hoped, the hurt and anger slowly dissipated, and he was left with a welcome sense of nothingness. A couple more, and he should be ready to bomb out for the night and hopefully most of the next day.

At that moment, he spotted a petite, attractive Thai woman in her late twenties, sitting alone on the other side of the room. She glanced back, flicking her hair back as she did so, a slight smile on her lips. She reminded him of a dancer. In the past, he wouldn't have hesitated to ask her to join him for a drink. But right now, he could think of nothing but Angelina.

¶

It was raining. A tropical downpour, typical of this time of year. Outside, guests scrambled for their umbrellas in the car park as they splashed through puddles to reach the hotel entrance. The rain looked refreshing, but it would make the night air even warmer, a stark contrast to Mae Salong's cool mountain rain.

๙

He remembered nothing after turning on the light to his room, and when he awoke with a jolt to the room's shrill alarm, he found himself fully clothed on top of the covers. His head hurt. 3 p.m. Sufficient time to shower, dress and make it to the airport.

As he stepped off the shuttle bus and into the small airport, he felt he'd been hit with an arctic blast, a welcome relief from the thick, steamy air outside. By the time he checked in, downed a coffee, grabbed some Panadol and headed through security, it was time to board.

The flight to Bangkok was delayed, and he knew he'd be cutting things fine if he was to make the connecting flight to Melbourne. He was not wrong. When the plane finally landed at Suvarnabhumi airport, it took twenty minutes to disembark, followed by a lengthy wait at Immigration before a longer than expected hike along the automatic walkway to transit. More delays at security, and he barely had enough time to find his departure gate before the boarding announcement was made. He groaned. His headache showed no signs of abating, and he was dehydrated — drained and in need of water and another coffee. But it was too late to go in search of a café.

There was no choice but to look for a drinking fountain to fill his water bottle and wash down his tablets. Then came the inevitable long wait on a hard plastic seat amongst the throng of passengers.

His section was the last to be summoned.

On board, he squeezed his way along the aisle to his seat near the rear of the plane. Placing his bag in the overhead locker, he sighed inwardly. Being cramped in a small space for nine hours was about as much as than he could deal with right now. *It could be worse,* he thought grimly. There'd be extra fifteen hours flight time if he was returning home from Europe.

There'd be no sleep. The moment he stepped on a plane, he became super vigilant, on high alert for the slightest sight or sound that could spell danger. It came with the territory. He envied those who managed to nod off at will, then sleep for hours, oblivious to the plane's constant hum, the rumble of food trolleys and irksome announcements.

It was bleak and grey at Tullamarine airport when the plane landed. *That'd be right,* he thought. In all his years of travelling, he couldn't recall when he arrived home to blue skies and sunshine. To be fair, it was only just on nine.

There were few holdups at that time of the morning, and he was through customs and downstairs to collect his luggage in no time. He considered crossing the street to where the Sky Bus departed but instead chose to catch a taxi. The quicker he arrived home, the better.

15

Nic remained in his apartment for three days, sleeping in until all hours and wiping himself out on whisky at night. It took just one glance at his bloodshot eyes and dishevelled appearance in the mirror on the fourth to tell him that enough was enough. It was time for a shave, shower and change of clothes, a run in the fresh air followed by a healthy breakfast at one of the cafés in the area. He glanced at the array of takeaway boxes spilling over the bin. No wonder he'd been feeling like crap.

That night laying down on the sofa, head propped against the cushions, reaching for his mobile and making a call.

'Hi, little brother.'

'Hey. About time you rang.'

'Yeah, I know. Been in Thailand for a week or so.'

'Where are you now?'

'Back at the apartment.'

'How long for?'

'Not sure.' He paused. 'Things have changed.'

'What do you mean?'

'Decided to chuck in the job.'

'Fuck, man! Are you for real?'

Nic grinned. 'Yeah, mate. About time I did something different.'

The bond between brothers had remained strong, despite years spent apart. But Nic was well aware that he could have made more of an effort to visit between jobs. And then there was his mother, close by, who wasn't getting any younger. For years she'd believed his story about flitting around the world fitting security devices in hotels. He'd enough knowledge on the subject to string her along.

His brother, Alex, was in fact the only person close who knew of his double life. He never asked questions, never interfered, and Nic loved him for that.

Alex had made it clear how he felt from the very start at his choice of vocation.

'Christ mate, you want to get yourself killed or something?' he said.

'I can look after myself. It's a chance to see places I've always wanted to and bloody good money at that.'

He'd truly believed it then. But over time, things changed. The allure of exotic destinations waned, relationships along the way were dead-end ones, and he lost the adrenaline kick that came with the job. He was good at what he did. One of the best. But his brother was right.

It was only a matter of time before his luck ran out.

Now wasn't the right moment to mention Ava. He didn't know that there ever would be one.

'So, what are you going to do with yourself?'

The words interrupted his thoughts.

'Dunno yet.'

'Well, while you're thinking about it, get your arse up here for a while. I could do with a hand on the property.'

'Might just do that.'

An hour later, he booked a flight to Cairns, knowing that his brother would be angling for him to settle nearby somewhere. But things weren't that straightforward. Although Nic belonged to no gang in particular, he'd been contracted out to several. He knew the whereabouts of too many people, had seen too much to simply head off into the sunset. Once in the game, that was where you were expected to stay. He'd learned that over time. They kept you in work, and in return you kept your mouth shut. If you were one of the fortunate ones to last the distance, there'd be a role higher up somewhere down the track. Those attempting to opt out did so at their peril. They risked a bullet to the head at sea somewhere and cement shoes, sometimes minus their fingertips.

He was willing to take that risk but leaving would require meticulous planning. He'd need to assume a new identity, then make a new start, most likely in another country. With the proceeds from the sale of his apartment and money he'd stashed away over the years, he'd find somewhere half decent. Even so, the truth was he'd be looking over his shoulder for the remainder of his days.

For the time being he'd play the game — hold out on the next job with some excuse or other. A few months' break with his family was looking better all the time.

Nic rose and headed out onto the balcony, surveying the scene before him. The distant Bolte Bridge was bathed in blue and the CBD, ablaze with lights against the night sky, looked closer than it was.

It was Friday night. The night air was particularly chilly for this time of year, but Docklands was in full swing. People were strolling along the water's edge, and music blared from nearby Harbour Town, where cafés and restaurants were alive with patrons. The tenth storey, one-bedroom apartment that he purchased eight years ago had served its purpose. It lay unused for much of the year as he flitted around the world carrying out his hits, but he always looked forward to returning. It was one of the few places he could slip into and remain anonymous. No one, except his brother, knew of the apartment's existence and even he had never been there.

Nic had a car that stood, well covered, in the allotted space below but was rarely used. It was only a short walk to Harbour Town and fifteen minutes to the CBD, with trams and buses passing frequently. The car was peace of mind, if nothing else. If he needed to get out in a hurry, he'd head for the escape exit that led to the underground car park.

The apartment had been purchased at a good time when development was just taking off, with prices relatively low. It had more than tripled in value since, thanks to its waterfront location and close proximity to Harbour Town. He'd have no problems in securing a sale.

He liked the simplicity of his apartment, an open layout flooded with natural light. The kitchen had dark gloss black cupboards, marble benchtops and silver appliances. An island bench with naturally timbered seats was where he mainly sat to eat his meals, and the décor was simple throughout. A typical bachelor pad. Functional and not much more. A large plasma TV dominated the main wall, but there was no photograph, memento, or artwork to be seen.

In a way, he'd miss the place. But with development came change, and the precinct had lost the village appeal that first drew him to the area. New developments were sprouting up to accommodate office workers, young singles, and married couples — a large proportion professionals without children. Work was about to start on a new supermarket and cinema complex, and the old Harbour Town was undergoing significant renovations. There was talk of plans for a Central Park, tree-lined boulevard and protected green spaces in years to come. He hoped so.

Another year, he reckoned, and he'd be gone.

16

It was a seventeen-hour trip from Melbourne to Rio Di Janeiro. Angelina had been looking forward to the four-hour stopover between flights at Doha's International airport. It was cited as one of the world's finest and didn't disappoint. Modern, spacious and luxurious, no expense was spared by its Qatar Airways owners.

Dazzling suspended bronze, silver and gold sculptures were interspersed amongst rows of ceiling lights that reflected luminous pools on the floors below. But it was the expansive shopping precinct she looked forward to seeing the most. Once she'd passed through the main terminal, caught a train to the departure hall and located her departure gate, she wasted no time in heading for the shops. Wandering around lost in time and oblivious to the crowds around her, she passed rows of brightly lit high fashion shops: Armani, Gucci, Harrods … the list seemed endless.

She had the funds, stashed away, to make purchases at any of them. When the time was right …

Stopped at a jewellery shop to scan the array of Cartier watches, she caught a reflection of herself in the window. Her hair swept up in a bun, she wore the emerald drop earrings stolen from her mother, with her stylish outfit. She knew she turned heads. The jet-set life she so craved awaited. So close yet so far.

Two years prior, she accompanied her father on a whirlwind business trip to Italy, her first trip abroad, no expenses spared. They'd stayed at the best hotels with silver service and gourmet cuisine. She wanted more, and her father had promised just that. The night she wore the expensive red dress purchased in Milan to a business meeting was the night he clinched the biggest deal of his life. Trips to Paris, Rome and Cologne, were next on his agenda.

But those trips never came. Angelina had spent years working alongside her father, with the expectation of running the family company one day. But things came crashing down when Paul Anderson entered her father's life, relegating her to outsider in a three-way partnership. Her father swore that having Paul on board would make them richer than she could ever imagine. He promised she'd be let in on their plans when they became formulated. But none of that eventuated. Indeed, she found the pair evasive and secretive.

There had been no option but to take matters into her own hands. She began sourcing contacts of her own and set about learning all she could learn about money laundering, embezzlement and offshore bank accounts. When she did a runner six months later, she was set up financially with the contacts to back her.

It didn't have to turn out the way it did, Dad, she thought. *You only had yourself to blame.* But would things have been different if she'd known that the man that she'd had killed in Bangkok was, in fact, her half-brother and not her adoptive father?

With a frown, she turned away from the window and walked on. In her peripheral vision, she could see Antonio following at a distance. 'Chill,' she muttered under her breath, reminding herself that the short-term sacrifices she was about to make would be worth it in the end.

The nine-hour trip from Doha to Sao Paulo seemed excruciatingly long, especially with a screaming baby on board at the back of the plane. *Will you shut the fuck up, for God's sake,* she thought furiously, *I need some sleep here.* She could see the partly bald head of her uncle seated near the aisle twelve seats in front of hers. He appeared to have dozed off, oblivious to the racket. *How in the hell?* she wondered, grabbing the noise-cancelling earphones from her bag and ramming them on her head.

9

Angelina felt a sense of unease as she made her way towards customs, hoping there'd be no issues with her forged papers. By the time she'd snaked her way along the long trail of passengers to the desk, her hands were clammy, and her chest was tight. But to her relief, she was barely given a second glance by the officer who stamped her passport and summoned the next passenger with a yawn.

She was met in the arrivals area, as arranged, by a stocky man in his thirties who introduced himself as Enzo, and reeked of body odour and stale cigarettes.

'Come,' he said as he took her bags and headed outside towards the car park, to a black car. He opened the back door for her, introduced her to the driver, placed her bags in the back then walked off. In the side mirror, she saw Antonio climb into the car behind.

It was a twenty-minute drive from the airport to downtown Rio, and the driver barely uttered a word. She didn't know whether he was under instructions not to do so or his knowledge of English was scant. It mattered little. She was tired and irritable after the long journey and in no mood for chatter. Lights whizzed by in the darkness, giving her little time to gather her bearings. It was only when they slowed down on the outskirts of Rio that she became instantly alert, eyes peeled. It was 4 a.m. but people were still out and about, bars open, music blaring, and patrons perched on bar stools outside, dressed in summer gear and sandals. She leaned back in the seat with a smile. It was what she'd come to see, and she couldn't wait to become part of it. She hoped that her accommodation was somewhere close.

She wasn't disappointed. A few minutes later the driver stopped at a fourteen-storey apartment block set in a group directly opposite Copacabana Beach. A main road separated the place from the well-lit promenade with its distinctive black and white, wavy pavement stretching for miles in either direction.

Antonio's car pulled up behind hers. He wasted no time getting out and moving across to open her door and usher her inside. The driver followed close behind with her luggage. Inside was a small foyer with a large palm in the corner, a rack containing brochures and pamphlets and a small table, but not much else. Antonio inserted a card in the lift and the doors opened. Once they'd stepped inside, he pressed the button to the twelfth floor, and when the lift glided to a halt, she followed him out and along a carpeted hallway that led to her apartment. He stopped on the last door on the right and withdrew a silver key card from his pocket.

'There's two of them only,' he said. 'This one's yours, and I have the other.'

Angelina bristled but said nothing as he opened the door, and they stepped inside. He nodded to the driver, who put down the bags and left, closing the door behind him.

'All right then, I'll leave you to get settled,' he said. 'You're not to leave this room until we've spoken next. Is that understood?'

'And when will that be?' she snapped.

'Tonight, at seven. I'll be back with dinner. In the meantime, the fridge is well stocked. Any questions?'

Angelina shook her head.

'Good. I'll get going then. I'm in need of some bloody sleep.' He closed the door behind him.

Angelina walked across to the window, fuming. 'You might be tired, but I'm not,' she muttered. The room offered spectacular views across the Atlantic Ocean, and even at that time, patrons were congregated in beach bars along the promenade. She could hear music from a distance, and it took all her willpower not to change into a pair of jeans, t-shirt and sandals and head out to explore. But the veiled threat behind her uncle's words was enough to make her think twice.

The apartment was modern and self-contained. A quick look through the cupboards and drawers showed she had everything she needed. There was little left to do but unpack. After a long soak in the bath, she wrapped herself in the thick, white bathrobe provided and settled on the bed, flicking through the TV channels until she dozed off into a sound sleep.

¶

Antonio arrived at seven with two pizzas.

'That smells damn good,' she said as she opened the door and let him inside.

He nodded, observing the table set up for two and

the bottle of red wine. 'I can see you've found your way around,' he said. 'Are things to your liking?'

'Yeah. Thanks.'

'Well, let's have some dinner, and then we can discuss things.'

They headed across to the table and took a seat. Antonio opened the bottle of wine and poured two glasses, then lifted the pizza lids gesturing her to take the first slice. She took a few bites and gave a nod of approval. 'That's the best I've eaten in a long time. Where did you get them?' she asked.

'The pizza shop, two streets up on the corner. You can't miss it.'

She nodded. 'And the main shops?'

'A couple of blocks back. Any of the side streets will get you there. It won't take long to find your way around.' He paused. 'Do you speak Portuguese?'

Angelina looked surprised. 'No, why should I?'

'It's Brazil's main spoken language.'

'So, you're suggesting I learn Portuguese now,' she raised her chin.

'Enough to get by, that is, if you don't wish to stand out.'

'Hm.'

'Not that you'll find it easy going,' he went on. 'They say it's one of the hardest languages to pick up.'

She rolled her eyes. 'Great!'

'It'll give you something to do.'

She was about to comment but held back.

He closed the lids to the empty boxes, rose and put them in the bin, then sat down again.

'Now, let's get down to business. This is an Airbnb apartment, and being the tourist season, there's a constant flow of visitors in the building, so you'll have no trouble blending in. However, as things quieten down you'll need to take extra measures not to draw attention to yourself. Do I make myself understood?'

She nodded.

'Those acting or behaving suspiciously around here inevitably come to the attention of the authorities. Foreigners in particular. You may be under my protection, but I can only do so much.'

'Look here,' she snapped, 'you've provided me with a place to go, and that's all I need. Forget the protection crap, okay? I'm perfectly able to handle myself.'

'Is that so?' Antonio's voice had a hard edge. 'You don't have a clue what goes on around here. Believe me, you'll need every bit of fucking protection you can get.' He went to rise. 'You do things my way, or you can pack your things right now and get out. Understood?'

'All right, all right. I hear you, okay?'

'I thought so,' he sat down and took a sip of wine, his eyes never leaving hers. 'So don't be surprised to find yourself being watched by one of my men.'

'What!'

'For your security, of course,' he continued coolly.

'That wasn't part of the deal!'

'What deal? We agreed to nothing!' he spat. 'Surely you didn't think this would all be arranged without certain conditions.'

Angelina could feel the anger swell up inside, but she held back. These were early days.

'And my part in all of this? You said I'd be doing something of use in return.'

'Correct. When I give you notice of a deal that's about to take place, all you have to do is dress up, look beautiful and accompany me to dinner. Only the best places. I don't think you'll complain.'

'And that's it? No favours on the side?' she said acidly.

'Don't insult me, girl,' he spat. 'You may be crooked but you are my niece. Don't ever let me hear you speak like that again.' He rose and glared at her. 'I've said all I need to say for now. I'll let myself out.'

'Wait. So where are you staying in case I need to contact you?'

'That's none of your business. An SMS will do.'

Angelina waited until he'd gone before rising. She walked over to the window and watched the place come to life. It was only ten, but the promenade was busy. People were out walking, a floodlit volleyball game was in progress on the beach, and Angelina noticed someone wading out into the water, girlfriend nestled in his arms. She'd planned to head outside there herself the moment Antonio left, but his words had sent her spirits tumbling. She hadn't anticipated being watched. Right now, she needed a drink and time to think. She walked across the room to the table and picked up the bottle and a glass.

Settled on the bed, propped up against a large cushion, she flicked on the TV and selected a movie she hadn't previously seen. She noted her uncle had poured little of the wine. *More for me*, she thought, as she refilled her glass. The wine was exceptionally good, and when she finished the bottle, she had no hesitation in selecting another.

17

Angelina remembered little when she awoke at 7 a.m., fully clothed and feeling violently ill.

'Shit!' she jumped up, threw her hand over her mouth and made it just made it to the bathroom before she threw up. With hands clutching the sides of the basin, she glanced in the mirror at her sweaty, pallid face and smudged mascara.

'Well, you've only got yourself to blame,' she muttered.

She wiped her mouth with her hand, swilled the basin then headed across to the window. Although it was early, the street below shimmered, indicating a hot day ahead. Few swam in the ocean, but there was a stream of joggers along the promenade. The last thing she felt like doing was joining them. She resigned herself to a few hours more rest and returned to bed.

She awoke at three, feeling washed out and drained but figured a quick dip in the ocean could be just the thing that she needed. She'd read the dangers of leaving valuables on Copacabana Beach, so she took off with only her key card placed in a small zipped pocket at the bottom of her towel, and a wide-brimmed hat. The refreshing dip had its desired effect, and she returned to her room until the worst of the heat subsided.

At seven, she stepped onto the street dressed in a short white skirt, red shirt and matching sandals, quickly looking around to see that she wasn't being cased. No one. Nevertheless, she found the thought unsettling as she headed off. Who were these men, and was she to be watched 24/7? She doubted it from what Antonio had said. She just had to behave herself, in the hope that they'd eventually back off and leave her with a measure of freedom.

She passed several cafés and bars, settling on a place that offered Spanish meals, where she tucked into a large bowl of paella. Thankfully her nausea had disappeared, and her appetite returned. Nonetheless, the inconvenience of being sick so soon after arrival irritated her. Granted, she'd had a bit to drink, but she could usually hold her alcohol well. She frowned as she watched passers-by out on the street. This bout of nausea felt different somehow. *Must have been the pizza,* she thought, as she piled some more salad on her plate. But come to think of it, she'd felt queasy when she stepped off the plane. No wonder, given the crap the airlines dished out.

Angelina gave things little more thought until the following morning when she woke up dry retching. 'Holy crap, this is all I need!' she exclaimed, pulling her legs to one side and rushing once more to the basin, where she doubled over and vomited.

Pushing the idea from mind, she busied herself with a load of washing, followed by a quick shower. She managed to keep a glass of water down but decided to stay off food for the time being. It was time to hit the gym. After a quick search of the net, she discovered one within walking distance.

This time she was being followed. A beefy, ugly man with tatts, who looked like someone not to be messed with. *Have fun waiting*, she thought as she passed through the gym's glass revolving door and into a front office that was flanked by larger-than-life photos of bronzed bodies and bulging muscles.

9

It was the six consecutive days of nausea first thing in the morning followed by bouts of fatigue that set Angelina's alarm bells ringing.

As she stood, arms crossed, in the queue at the Farmacia, she could feel her blood pressure start to soar. She fumed as the young girl at the front of the queue stood, looking helplessly at her credit card.

'But it can't have been declined,' the girl cried. 'I deposited 300 Real two days ago.'

'Try inserting it again,' another the middle-aged, female shop assistant said patiently.

Oh, for God's sake! Angelina let out an audible sigh of frustration.

Things didn't help when the same shopkeeper smiled, as she placed Angelina's purchase in a paper bag and handed it over. 'Good luck,' she said with a knowing smile. 'I hope you get the result you're after.'

Angelina glared at her, snatched the bag and headed towards the door. Outside, a man stood at a distance, leaning against a lamppost, watching her. Someone different to the one who'd followed her. 'And screw you as well,' she muttered under her breath as she swept past him.

Back in her apartment, she ripped the bag apart and took the pregnancy test. The result was instantaneous. Positive.

'Fuck you!' she cried out, dropping to her knees and unleashing a load of expletives she hadn't used since the day she fled Kilkenny.

This changed things. Big time. The first thing that came to mind was her uncle. How would he react? If she wasn't careful, she could find herself on the street. She thought for a moment, then grabbed her mobile and did a quick Google search of Brazil's abortion laws.

'Shit!' she muttered. Things were going from bad to worse. The procedure was illegal unless the mother's life was at stake, the foetus was anencephalic, or a woman had been raped. Harsh penalties were in place for those found flouting the law. Yet, it was suggested that hundreds of thousands of illegal abortions took place there each year.

Angelina slumped in the chair. Even if she was prepared to take such a risk there almost no chance of locating someone who'd carry out the procedure, or of gaining access to a banned abortion drug, given her limited knowledge of the language.

She took a few deep breaths. This changed things. Like it or not, her uncle was the only one she could turn to. He'd help out. Surely.

But she'd have to wait for the right time to come along.

9

Over the next few days, she took to eating dry biscuits that supposedly stopped nausea, according to the blog she'd read, but she'd lost her usual energy, and even a brief walk left her drained and in need of a lie-down.

Thankfully, by the time she received Antonio's text the following week her bouts of morning sickness had ceased, and she was slowly regaining her stamina. There was tenderness in her breasts and a slight swelling in her stomach. But she could deal with that. According to his instructions, she was to be ready at seven the following evening.

Early next morning she caught a taxi to the shop where she was to purchase her outfit. From the sweeping array of designer dresses and boutique garments she chose a low-cut, slinky knee-length dress in hot pink, and white high heeled sandals with fine ankle straps and a matching bag, all of which were put on her uncle's tab.

128

She caught sight of the shopkeeper's envious look as she twirled in in her outfit in front of the full-length mirror outside the fitting room. She smiled to herself. For the first time since her arrival, she felt in the mood for a bit of glamour.

Next, she found a lingerie shop and purchased a shapewear garment which she paid for herself. Up to this point she'd never considered such a thing and scoffed at women who did. If they weren't disciplined enough to keep themselves in shape, she reasoned, they should try a gym or meal replacement shakes. But she had to admit the garment was the perfect solution to her current circumstance. After wriggling into the elasticised garment in the pokey dressing room, she unzipped her new purchase and slipped it over her head. If anything, the shapewear accentuated the curves beneath the closely fitted dress.

Outside the shop, she checked to see if anyone was following. It had become a force of habit. No one. It had been the case for a few days now. Her strategy was paying off.

§

Eyes turned when Angelina walked through the main entrance of the modern hotel and through to the dining room. She noted the instant look of admiration in her uncle's eyes as he pulled out her chair and the hooded, sleazy ones of the dealer that hovered over her cleavage and slid slowly down her body. It concerned her not a bit. She'd been in this situation with her father. It would be a piece of cake — a matter of going through the motions.

'So, you in Brazil for holiday,' he said in broken English as he pulled apart a warm roll and slathered on a thick slice of butter.

'Yes, that's right.'

'For how long?'

'A few weeks then it's time to get back to work.'

'Perhaps you like someone to show you the sights?'

Angelina felt her skin crawl. 'Thanks,' she took a bite of her roll and met his eyes. 'I'll let you know if I do.'

The deal was clinched sooner than expected, and the drug dealer rose to leave at eleven. Antonio watched him go then turned to face her. 'That was quite a show,' he said with unconcealed approval.

'I said I'd earn my keep,' she responded. 'Just for interest, where do you find these creeps and what's your role in all of this?'

'None of your business,' he snapped.

She reached for her wine glass. 'Thought you'd say that,' she said sweetly, 'but worth a try. So, when's the next deal?'

§

Over the next week Angelina sat in on a further two meetings with drug dealers; both were signed without a hitch. She was an asset, and she knew it. She'd kept out of trouble, did what she was told and had no doubts Antonio would go along with her request for an abortion.

She was to be bitterly disappointed.

18

It was late at night, and Antonio was surprised to receive a text from Angelina. She'd not made contact since he'd been there.

We need to speak. When can I see you? was all it said. More curious than anything else, he responded: *I can be there in fifteen.* The response was immediate: *Okay.*

'So, what's this about?' he asked as he walked past her and sat down on the sofa.

'Would you like a drink?'

'Nope.'

Angelina stood with her arms crossed, her eyes never leaving his. 'I've got something to tell you. I'm pregnant.'

'You're what!' he lurched forward in disbelief.

'Look, it wasn't planned or anything.'

'Well, you're full of surprises, aren't you? How long have you been hiding this from me?'

She lifted her head. 'I haven't been hiding anything. I only just found out myself. Look, I'm not expecting you to believe this, but I had no symptoms. No morning sick-ness, no nothing. It's only when some of my clothes were getting a bit tight …'

'So, who's the father?' he demanded.

'Could be any number of people,' she said with a shrug.

'Christ!' he muttered in disgust. 'So where did you have sex. Here in Brazil?'

'No, just before I left.'

He did a quick calculation. 'So that would make it late October. Around five weeks, if I'm correct.'

'I s'pose so. For God's sake, cut the inquisition crap will you!' she flared. 'I need help here. I'm not expecting any-thing from you. Just a phone number.'

'You're not suggesting abortion!' his voice was incredulous.

'You're damned right I am.'

'Well, you can think again.'

'I know it's illegal in this country,' she said quickly, 'but it's the quickest and easiest solution. With your contacts –'

'I have no such contacts,' he shot back. 'You will have the child!'

'What! You expect me to lug around this thing for months? What about my figure.'

'Maybe you should have thought of that before you started screwing around.'

'Go to hell!'

'Very well then,' He went to rise. 'But let me get one thing straight. If abortion's the road you wish to take, you're on your own. Don't bother contacting me again.'

'Wait,' she said quickly. 'Don't be like that. I'm sure we can come to some sort of arrangement.'

'I very much doubt that. I'm Catholic, as are most people in this country. We protect our children, not kill them.'

Angelina's heart was racing. This wasn't turning out the way she expected.

'Okay, okay. I didn't know you felt so strongly about it. So, what if I had the baby. What then?'

Antonio sat down, his eyes never leaving hers. 'Well, that'd make things a whole lot different.'

'What'd be in it for me?'

'You'd be more than compensated for your efforts,' he said evenly.

'And once the kid arrives?'

'Your child is family. It'd want for nothing for the rest of its life. You have my word on that.'

'I was talking about me, not the kid. Will I be free to go, no strings attached?'

Antonio sat in disbelief at the cold, detached manner in which she spoke.

'If that's what you wish.'

'You'd better believe it.'

'I see,' he said coolly. 'Then don't expect me to spare more people to protect you.'

'Fine by me.'

'Perhaps you'd like time to think about it.'

'No, I'll have the kid.'

He raised an eyebrow.

'What?' she snapped.

'You expect me to take your word on that? How do I know you'll not seek out some backyard abortion place the minute I walk out the door!'

'You wanted my fucking decision, and you got it. Now lay off!'

'Very well. But as from now, you'll be under guard 24/7.'

'What!' she shrieked. 'You can't do that!'

'Watch me.'

He picked up the phone, tapped on a number and started speaking in Portuguese.

Angelina slumped in the chair, arms crossed and eyes dark.

It was a few minutes before the call ended. 'I've arranged for two guards to move into the apartment opposite yours,' he said. 'Marcos will arrive in thirty minutes to begin the night watch,' he said, 'with Fabio taking over in the morning.'

'And what if I need some exercise or to go to the shops?'

'Then the guards go with you,' he said. 'They'll just need prior notice.'

'So how long's this supposed to last?'

There was a shrug. 'Up to you. Let's say until such time you can prove yourself trustworthy.'

Angelina bristled. 'Is that all?'

'Yeah, pretty much. Unless you have further questions. I'll be on my way once Marcos arrives.'

She glared at him, picking up the TV remote and flicking through the channels.

Antonio felt a stab of guilt as he looked at what his niece had become. What would she have been like if he'd learned of her existence earlier and raised her himself? He could barely stand hearing her speak of her connections or the men she'd slept with. Every time he set eyes on her, he was reminded of his sister. But now, he thought, it would be better not to have known her at all. It was inconceivable to him that she could be so reviled by motherhood that she could simply walk away from her newborn without a second glance.

19

Angelina lay low for the next few weeks, doing what was expected in the hope it would gain back some of the freedom she'd lost. But her efforts were in vain. She heard nothing further from Antonio.

What if I'm locked up indefinitely? she began to think with unease.

Another two weeks, and she'd reach the ninth week of her pregnancy, where abortion was considered unsafe. She wasn't about to put herself at the mercy of illegal operators and seedy underworld figures, even if she did get hold of such a person. She'd heard the stories. No one would lay their hands on her body.

Medical abortion was her safest bet, a simple matter of accessing a drug like Misoprostol, considered the most effective of them all. But even this drug was known to cause severe complications after the first trimester. Time was running out. How could she lay her hands on such a drug, banned in most states yet so commonly used?

The only way she could see herself out of the mess she was in was through the guards. It was a matter of figuring out how. She could pretty much cancel out Fabio, the one with the movie star looks, honed body and tattooed biceps. Usually, a man blessed with such assets succumbed quickly to her charms, even if only to feed his ego, but he displayed no such tendencies. There was a sharpness to him, a ruthlessness.

Marcos was a different proposition altogether. A mountain of a man with a shaved head, and broad face, he possessed none of his partner's finesse and guile. She'd seen the way Marcos looked at her when she slipped off her sarong at the beach to go for a swim, and he caved in to almost any request when she fluttered her eyelashes or softened her voice. Without a doubt, having Marcos on night watch and not Fabio made things that much easier.

¶

It was Saturday night, and things were in full swing on the street below. Angelina squeezed into her shapewear, then pulled on a white low-cut, knee-length dress and sandals and picked up her mobile. 'Marcos, I'm getting so bored being locked up like this. I've just got to get out. Can we go for a walk?'

'Okay. Now?'

'Yeah.'

The look of admiration in his eyes when she opened the

door was unmistakable. The outfit had the desired effect.

Usually, Angelina walked on ahead outside, while the guards kept a distance, but this time she beckoned him to walk alongside. 'Let's forget the tailing bit from now on, huh?' she told him, 'it makes me feel so stupid. I don't know about you.'

There was the hint of a smile on the big man's face, but he hesitated.

'I could just as easily do a runner beside you as ten steps in front,' she persisted. 'In any case, I've nowhere to go. Well, come on.'

Marcos was quick to note the envious glances of male passers-by as they walked along the pavement, and he had to pinch himself to see if it was real. He'd dreamed of having a woman of such beauty alongside him. But was well aware of his lack of sex appeal and had given long ago up trying to make an impression. Growing up in the slums of Sao Paulo, he'd watched boys his age flirt with girls in the alleyways, which rendered him more self-conscious. Only when he moved to Rio and joined Antonio's gang did he finally gain a sense of fulfilment. The camaraderie of the group, coupled with the gruelling fitness regime required, replaced the need for a woman. He was glad Angelina spoke little. He wouldn't have known how to respond if she did. Perhaps she sensed it, and for that, he was grateful. It was warm and sultry. People were out in droves: chatting noisily in bars and cafés or strolling along the beach. For Marcus, the time seemed to pass way too quickly.

When they returned to her apartment, she turned to him and said, 'Thanks, Marcos. Being locked up like this has been driving me insane.'

'I'm sure it won't be for much longer.' He shuffled uneasily, averting her eyes.

'I hope so. I've done nothing to deserve this. Can we go out again?'

He paused. 'I s'pose so.'

¶

Three nights later, they set off again, further this time, and took a seat near the beach. Angelina pulled off her hair tie and shook her hair loose around her shoulders. 'Ah, that's better.' She leaned her head back and closed her eyes, taking a deep breath. 'Just to feel the wind in my hair again. It's so good.'

Marcos watched, transfixed, legs weak beneath him.

'So, tell me a bit about yourself, Marcos,' she said. 'Were you born in Rio?'

'No, Sao Paulo. I moved here when I turned eighteen.'

'Have you been back there since?'

He shook his head. 'This is my home now.'

'And when did you first meet my uncle?'

'Not long after I arrived.'

'Where?'

'The favela I'd just moved into.'

'What was he doing there?'

'He runs the joint.'

Angelina turned to him in surprise. 'Is that so? That's the first I've heard about it. How long's he been doing that?'

Antonio shifted uncomfortably. She was asking too many questions. Already he feared he'd said too much.

'Dunno.'

'So, what else does he get up to while he's over here?'

He shrugged. 'What Antonio does is his business.'

Angelina had hoped for more, something of her uncle's illicit dealings that could potentially be used as leverage. But Marcos had been well drilled. It was clear he wasn't about to divulge a thing. Probing further may arouse suspicion, so she decided to let the matter rest.

'Yeah, he's not one to talk, is he,' she concurred. 'What time is it?'

He looked at his watch. 'Just past eleven.'

'Could you do with a drink? I sure as hell could.'

'Do you think that's wise? I mean, with the baby –'

Angelina rolled her eyes. 'Give me a break, will you? You're beginning to sound like my uncle. It's early days yet. I'm only talking about one or two.'

'Well, okay. There's a bar a few streets back.'

As Angelina passed through the door, the distinctive vibrant rhythms of Brazilian music, noisy chatter, and couples gyrating on the dance floor under strobe lights in their colourful garb fired up her senses. It made her realise just how much she'd missed the nightlife. They pushed their way through the crowd and sat perched on stools at the bar while their drinks were being served, then sat by at a nearby table close to the dance floor. The baby wasn't the reason why Angelina kept her drinks to the limit. Her sole focus was on Marcos how many drinks it took for him to loosen him up. As expected for a man of his bulk, he held his drinks well.

It was as they were just about to go when she took hold of his large calloused hand and pulled him up. 'Come on, we're not leaving this place until we've had at least one dance.'

Once he realised her intentions, he stopped short and tried to pull away. 'No, no, I can't. I don't dance.'

'Bullshit. You're Brazilian, aren't you?' Angelina gave another tug. 'Come on. I'm not taking no for an answer.'

The last whisky had loosened Marcos sufficiently to accompany her without further protest. As they moved onto the cramped dance floor and joined in the swarm of bodies and waving arms, Marcos was surprised to find himself not the least bit inhibited.

'God, I enjoyed that,' Angelina said as they stepped out onto the pavement and headed towards the apartment. 'I was hanging out for a bit of nightlife.'

She paused for a moment. 'Don't mention where we went to my uncle, okay? He'd arc up. I know he would.'

'I wasn't about to.' Marcos's job was at stake as well.

'It's as if he doesn't want me to have fun at all,' she went on, with a pout. 'I had no idea I'd be tailed like this when I arrived.'

'It's for your protection, that's all.'

'Oh, for God's sake, I'm perfectly capable of looking after myself,' she shot back. 'It's not as I'd do anything to draw attention to myself. I'm not stupid.'

'It's not that simple,' he said. 'You can never be sure that the things you say to someone in a bar or on the street won't get back to the police. The authorities are on constant alert for people linked to gangs.'

'As if I've had a chance to speak to anyone,' she shot back. But the words sparked a flicker of caution. This was a different country with a different language and set of rules. She'd be even more vigilant from now on.

Marcos was barely listening. Protecting Angelina from the authorities was one thing, but rival gangs were another altogether. She had no idea what was at stake if they got hold of her. Being Antonio's niece, there'd most likely be an interrogation, perhaps a ransom attempt, in which case they'd be left empty-handed. Antonio bowed to no one.

Back at the apartment, he took her key card from his pocket and let her in, ready to resume his night watch.

'I tell you what,' she said, 'how about I book some Uber Eats tomorrow night, you organise the drinks and we eat in here.'

Marcos shook his head. 'If Antonio got wind of it –'

'How?' she said. 'He's been nowhere near the place since you two arrived.'

'There's always Fabio.'

'I thought Fabio spent his nights at his girlfriend's place.'

'He does.'

'So, what are you worried about?'

'I'spose.'

It can't do any harm, he thought.

Little did he know how wrong he was.

20

Fabio Santos was tetchy and irritable as he sat in the chair outside Angelina's room, flicking through his iPhone. Three weeks straight without a break and no end in sight was starting to get to him. Couldn't Antonio just turn a blind eye and let his niece have an abortion if that's what she wanted? To this point, she'd proved willing to play ball, so long as she had her freedom.

But his boss's strict religious beliefs were unyielding, and no one dared challenge them. The man himself was a contradiction. He'd think nothing of attending midnight mass that could last several hours, then put a bullet through the head of someone who'd crossed him a day later.

The previous night Fabio had a massive fight with his girlfriend when he arrived home at 3 a.m. blind drunk, after a bender with his mates. He'd woken up on the couch with a thumping headache and his girlfriend nowhere to be seen.

Fabio was used to charming his way out of anything.

He thought the text he'd sent would do the trick but even the offer to dine at the most expensive restaurant he could think of was met with deaf ears. Fabio's good looks ensured an endless supply of girlfriends. All with the looks and figures to feed his ego. But Adriana was different. She was smart and sassy, and he didn't want to lose her.

He could hear the flip flop of Antonio's niece's sandals on the tiles inside, and he cursed her inwardly. If not for her, he'd be back in the gang's compound with the others. From what he could make out, Antonio was onto something big, and he was itching to find out what it was.

It had come as a surprise to learn his boss had a niece, especially one as stunning. Yet, it was clear from the outset there was no love lost between them.

Initially, keeping watch over her had been easy. A matter of the occasional tag and report back. It was clear Antonio had the upper hand, and she appeared not to overstep the mark, as had been suggested she might.

Then the bitch announced she was pregnant, and everything changed. He sensed she wasn't about to take her uncle's demands so readily this time, and it was beginning to look as if he might find himself on indefinite watch. *Not if I've got anything to do with it*, he thought.

At seven Marcos stepped out of the room opposite.

'All good?' he asked.

Fabio scowled and strode off without a word.

Marcos shrugged. This was nothing unusual. Fabio's

temper and mood swings were well known amongst the gang. Truth was, Marcos was glad to have had the apartment to himself. What would Antonio's response be if he knew? he reflected.

Fabio got in his car and pulled out of the kerb. His girlfriend's apartment was on the fifth floor. The moment he stepped out of the lift; his jaw hardened as he looked up the passageway to where his clothes lay in a tangled heap outside her room. He strode angrily towards the door and thumped on it with his fist. 'Adriana?'

There was no response. 'Fuck this!' Fabio exclaimed and reached for his mobile. The number rang out, and he tried again. This time she answered.

'Adriana, what the hell's going on!' he demanded.

'I would have thought that's obvious.'

'Fuck! Give me a chance to explain, will you?'

'No need. I've seen enough.'

Fabio slammed the phone down and scooped up his belongings. 'Bitch,' he muttered. He wasn't used to being the one stood up. And now he faced being cramped up in an apartment with some insufferable dim wit for God knows how long.

Copacabana. It was late, but every available parking spot outside the apartment was taken. Hurling a barrage of expletives, he kept on driving until he found a place much further than he would have liked.

The moment Fabio stepped out of the apartment block

lift, he realised something was wrong. Where was Marcos? Why wasn't he guarding her room? Senses heightened; he strode down the passageway.

Voices came from Angelina's apartment, and Marcos's unmistakable deep drone was one of them. 'What the heck!' he muttered. Surely the big lump of lard couldn't be that stupid. He could hear little of what they were saying, even when he pressed an ear hard against the door. But it mattered little.

Thoughts of his girlfriend were long gone as he took out his key card and slipped into the apartment opposite.

¶

Angelina sat on the couch beside Marcos, legs tucked underneath. So far, things had gone according to plan. She sensed Marcos's hesitancy to talk about himself, so she'd directed the conversation to Rio Di Janeiro, its culture, its customs. Judging by what she observed the previous night, it would take a few more drinks for him to sufficiently loosen up.

An hour later and he was good to go. She considered seduction but decided against it. If Antonio got wind of it, she'd find herself out on the street. There were other ways and means.

She brushed a few loose strands of hair from her face, took a sip of her drink and lowered her eyes. 'I need your help, Marcos. I'm desperate. I've got no one else to turn to.'

'I'd like to but –'

'Please hear me out.' She placed a hand lightly on his arm, that quivered beneath her touch. 'You need to know why I can't go through with this pregnancy. Being wanted by the cops isn't the only reason I went to Antonio for protection.'

He looked at her questioningly.

'I was in a physically abusive relationship back home,' she went on. 'Coming to Rio was my one ticket out.'

Marcos looked at her and shook his head in disgust. 'I've got no time for pricks who think it's okay to beat up women. Why did you stay with him?'

'I've asked myself the same the same question many times,' she said. 'He was charming, good looking. Always said how sorry he was afterwards, that it'd never happen again.' She paused and locked her eyes on his. 'Then one night he came home drunk, beat me senseless and raped me.'

Marcos winced and squeezed his eyes tight for a few moments before turning to face her.

'I'm sorry,' his voice cracked.

'It's okay,' she said. 'I just have to learn to live with it. But I swear to God, I had no idea I was pregnant until I got here.'

'Have you told Antonio any of this?'

'Do you think he'd care?' she scoffed. 'All he cares about is the precious baby.'

Marcos didn't say a word.

She wiped an eyelid with her fingertip. 'Can you

imagine what it's like? Being forced to wait eight months to give birth to some rapist's kid? I'm younger than you, Marcus. I've got my whole life ahead of me.'

He thought about that.

Time to make her move.

'So, will you help me?' she pleaded. 'I know about the abortion laws in this place and it's fucking archaic. All I'm asking you to do is access an abortion drug for me. Misoprostol is probably the easiest to lay your hands on. I know they're illegal, but I'm sure with your contacts — '

Marcos looked at her aghast.

'Even if I could get my hands on such a thing,' he said, 'there's no way I could keep something like that from Antonio.'

'Not if I had a miscarriage.' Angelina's eyes never left his. 'On your watch in the middle of the night.'

She saw the beads of sweat forming on his brow. Heard his breaths quicken. 'I'd make it worth your while,' she said softly. 'Name the price, and we can come to an agreement.'

But before he had the chance to respond, the door burst open, and Antonio stormed in the room like a raging bull, his eyes boring into Angelina's. 'I see you're up to your usual tricks.'

'It's not what you think!' she exclaimed.

'Shut up. I'll deal with you later,' he roared.

Marcos looked around wildly, an adrenaline rush rendering him temporarily alert. His only thoughts were of a way out. Armed with a sense of bravado, he was certain Antonio could be taken down with a bout of brute strength. He went to lurch forward but stumbled, clumsy and uncoordinated.

That's when he saw the two of them lurking in the passageway, holsters on hips. The first stepped inside, and the second stood in the doorway, his bulk blocking the light from outside.

Antonio nodded, and Marcos watched, frozen in disbelief as they came at him like panthers, each taking an arm with a vice-like grip that all but cut off his circulation. Antonio quickly stepped forward, slapping Marcos several times hard on each cheek, followed by a savage blow to the big man's jaw that sent him reeling backwards, a trail of blood trickling down the side of his mouth. Still, the guards held their ground, grips tightened.

Antonio was about to inflict further damage but thought better of it. They had to get him out to the car without attracting undue attention.

Angelina watched on, eyes gleaming. She doubted that she'd ever see her uncle in action, and she was impressed by his ruthless efficiency. He had never explicitly acknowledged what he and his gang were involved in, and she knew better than to ask. Drug dealing, definitely. And he was probably up to his neck in other things as well. He wouldn't come back every year for nothing.

Antonio nodded towards the door, and the guards grabbed Marcos under both arms and heaved him upright, groaning under the weight. Getting him out of there was like hauling a concrete slab.

Outside, curious passers-by gawked as the semi-conscious man was dragged down the steps.

One of the guards shrugged with a grin. 'Tequila demais, eh.'

The onlookers walked on.

There was a dark grey van parked near the kerb, its motor running. The sliding door facing the street was open and the guards shoved Marcos in, climbing in behind him. The door slammed shut, and the van sped away.

¶

Antonio gave a few final instructions to Angelina's replacement guard, then crossed the passageway to Fabio's apartment. He entered without knocking, closing the door behind him.

'You did good,' he said. 'What's the time?'

Fabio glanced at his Fitbit watch. 'Just after three.'

'Christ!'

'Can I get you a beer?'

Antonio nodded. 'Could do with one.' He headed to the sofa and eased himself down.

'Full of surprises, my niece.'

Fabio flashed a smile of perfect teeth as he handed over a can. 'That's an understatement.'

'Has she tried anything like this on you?'

'Nope.' He pulled up a chair opposite. 'She'd be wasting her time if she did.'

'Hmm.' Antonio ripped the top off his beer and took a few swigs, wiping his mouth with the back of his hand.

'So tell me, how long have you been with us. Two years? Three?'

'A bit over three.'

'You like the job?'

'It's pissing me off right now, if you must know.'

'Why's that?'

'Thought I'd be doing something better than this by now.'

'Such as?'

Fabio's eyes locked on his boss. 'Operations.'

'Yeah, well, that doesn't just happen. First, you've got to prove yourself.'

The Operations Team comprised a select group of the gang's brightest. Amongst other things, they worked alongside Antonio and his Columbian counterparts, arranging shipments of amphetamines, cocaine and heroin from South American drop off points to European destinations. They were a small, close-knit group who kept to themselves and divulged nothing.

'Tell you what,' Antonio said, 'how about I set you a challenge. See what you come up with.'

'Like what?'

'Taking charge of my niece till she's had the baby. I'm over this shit. Better things to do with my time.'

'Reckon I could handle that,' came the cool response. 'How long's your niece got to go?'

'Another seven months.'

There was a nod. 'Just need a bit of time to come up with a plan.'

'That's no problem.'

'For starters, she needs to be pulled out of this place. The sooner, the better. She's proved she can't be trusted.'

'And where would you suggest?'

Fabio considered for a moment. 'Try Headquarters. Fifth floor.'

'What!'

'Think about it. Guards on tap, coded entrances and exits.' He paused. 'No nightlife, shops or distractions in that place.'

Antonio liked what he was hearing.

'For how long?' he asked.

'Short term at this stage. But your niece doesn't need to know that. A few weeks should bring her down to size and if not,' he gave a shrug, 'things can always be dragged out longer. I'll have come up with another plan by then anyway.'

'I'll have her out of here by tomorrow,' Antonio said.

'What time?'

'Midday. We can talk more later.'

There was a nod.

Antonio swilled the last of his beer and rose to leave. 'One more thing. You can get rid of Marcos's things. He'll no longer be needing them. Not where he's going.'

Outside, he stepped out onto the street and climbed into the car.

'Sede,' he directed.

As the driver nodded and fired up the engine, Antonio sank down in the seat with a sense of relief. At last, he'd be free to focus on the things he came here to do. The shipment of heroin about to depart from Chile, for instance. His most significant and ambitious project to date.

He was intrigued to see what Fabio would come up with next, but there was no doubt in his mind it would work. The young man already proved himself to be quick thinking, ruthless and smart, and he certainly wasn't about to place his one chance of promotion in jeopardy.

Antonio could do with another of those on his team.

Fabio packed his things, then fetched a garbage bag in which he stuffed the remains of Marcos's belongings. A black wallet in the pocket of some jeans provided an unexpected bonus; a thick wad of R$200 banknotes. He did a quick count and grinned. Not bad for a night's work. He shoved the notes into his backpack.

Maybe his luck was changing after all …

Across the hallway, Angelina paced up and down the room, furious at what had transpired. She'd almost pulled things off. She was sure of it. She had never seen Antonio so enraged, and she was edgy about what was to come. She'd caught a glimpse of the guard outside as Antonio was leaving. He, too, wore a holster and was every bit as muscled as Marcos. She wondered if he was on guard for that night only.

21

The sun was already rising. Angelina could see the early morning joggers out on the street and the beach vendors arriving. Raging like a caged lion, she cursed the day she agreed to come to Rio. She'd have figured out some way of surviving if she'd remained in Australia. But it was no use dwelling on that now. It was time to come up with a plan, and her options were quickly drying up. How long would it be before she heard from Antonio? Perhaps he was about to play mind games and keep her in suspense. She fumed. Nobody did that to her. No one!

It was eleven when she got the call. 'Pack your things and be ready to move out in an hour.'

'Where are you taking me?'

'You'll find out soon enough. And when I arrive, the place'd better be as clean as you found it.' There was a click at the other end.

'Stuff you!' Angelina cursed and stormed into the bedroom to pack her things. She'd assumed she'd be here for the remainder of her stay, and she'd been content with that. The rooms were spacious and well lit, the views beyond compare.

And now that Antonio's message had sunk in, she feared the place she was moving to shared few of the luxuries she'd enjoyed to date.

Her fears were about to be realised.

9

Antonio arrived at precisely twelve and entered the apartment without knocking. After a quick scan of the room, he gave a nod of approval. 'All right, let's go.' He picked up her things and headed towards the door. The guard was nowhere to be seen, but Fabio stepped out of the apartment opposite, returning Angelina's glare with cold indifference.

A black SUV with tinted windows was parked close to the kerb, engine running. Antonio climbed in the passenger seat, as the driver jumped out and put Angelina's luggage in the boot. Fabio opened the back door and shoved Angelina in, climbing in beside her. He produced a piece of rough material and pulled it tight around her eyes, causing her to wince.

'Shit. That hurt. Isn't this going a bit far?'

There was no response. As the car pulled away, she felt her stomach tighten. Where in the hell were they taking her?

No one spoke, but the air conditioner's continual low hum set her nerves jangling.

After what seemed an interminably long journey, the car finally came to a halt. The blindfold was unknotted and roughly removed. She wiped her cheek and glared at Fabio.

A nondescript apartment block, one of many, housed the gang's headquarters. She could see the heat shimmering off the pavement as they got out, and the air was hot and steamy. She followed Antonio into the building, with Fabio keeping a close distance behind.

Inside was a small foyer with two lifts. Antonio produced an access card, and the door to the nearest one slid open. They got in. He pressed the button to the fifth floor, where they stepped out into a long corridor with rooms leading off to either side, continuing on to the last on the right. A series of numbers, a click, and the door opened.

'Deixe-nos agor,' Antonio said. There was a nod, and Fabio left the room, closing the door behind him.

Angelina walked across to the window and surveyed the surroundings with disdain. She could see straight into the room directly across, beyond which lay a sea of high-rise, drab buildings with not a green space to be seen.

'This wasn't called for,' she said without turning.

'Well, you've only yourself to blame,' Antonio replied, 'and until you can prove you can be trusted, you'll be staying here with us.'

Angelina swung around, eyes blazing. 'You bastard!'

There was a shrug. 'It's not all that bad. You'll get used to it. Like everyone else around here, you'll have your own room key card, and you'll be pretty much free to come and go as you wish. With limitations, of course.'

'Such as?'

'You're to remain within the confines of this floor. The combined kitchen, dining and lounge is located at the far end of the passageway. Keep in mind, that there are CCTVs all through the place.'

'Why would I expect otherwise,' she shot back sarcastically.

'Except in everyone's rooms, of course,' Antonio continued as if he hadn't heard.

He smiled to himself, wondering what her reaction would be if she learned that behind the locked door across the hallway was a soundproof room with a small barred window, crude bed, table and two chairs. The housekeeper had discreetly cleaned up the blood-splattered walls and vomit many times over the years, no questions asked.

'There's a pool and gym on the tenth floor, but you'll need to let Fabio know first so that a guard can be arranged. The same goes if you wish to venture outside. Not that there's much to see. You'll find mainly apartments like this one, office blocks and a few small shops. You'll have a prepaid visa card to access online whatever you need in the way of maternity clothes. A modest amount. No visits to expensive boutiques this time around.'

'And meals?' she asked.

'We have an excellent cook, Maria, who's been with us for many years. She acts as a housekeeper as well. Not to say that she'll be cleaning your room, of course. There's a broom and whatever you need in the laundry.' He watched her look of distaste with mild amusement and continued, 'breakfast's at eight, lunch at twelve-thirty and dinner at seven. You can choose to have your meals in the dining room or your room.'

'My room,' came the surly response.

'Suit yourself. You'll need to collect your meals then and return the dirty dishes to the kitchen. Needless to say, alcohol's off-limits for the duration of your pregnancy.'

'What the hell!'

'It's for the best,' he said. 'I've no doubt you'll make up for it later on.'

He left her no time to respond. 'I'll leave you to get settled then. From now on, you'll be seeing little of me.'

'Why?'

'None of your business,' he snapped. 'You'll be answerable to Fabio and no one else. You can direct your questions to him. By the way, you'll note that nothing but Portuguese is spoken around here. You'll get used to it.'

He threw the room's key card on the table and left.

Angelina slumped on the sofa once he'd gone. She could be holed up in here for weeks, if not months. But not if she had any say in it. She just wished she knew the place's exact location. But they'd been one step ahead with the blind-fold; they probably knew that she would rat on them, given half the chance. The reality was, she was going cold on that idea after witnessing the ruthless dispatching of Marcos. They seemed to know what was going on at every turn, with connections everywhere. She would be easy to find. For now, she may as well unpack then suss the place out.

The room was large but dingy, the walls yellowing and curtains faded. The bedroom was to the side, and Angelina noted an en suite attached. The bathroom's tiled floor smelled of antiseptic, and there was a dank lingering odour reminiscent of the farmhouse she'd not long vacated. Her nose crinkled.

Antonio glanced at his surroundings as he headed down the passageway. He and the gang had occupied the premises for the last ten years without a hitch. If the owner knew of their dealings, he wasn't letting on. They were prompt with their rental payments and caused no trouble. Antonio knew they'd been fortunate to stay there as long as they had. It was only a matter of time before the authorities got wind of it, but he had a contingency plan. Finding another place would be the easy part. Finding a landlord who didn't ask questions was something else again.

The tenth-floor gym and swimming pool provided a welcome distraction for gang members from their mundane surroundings. He'd learned long ago that the carrot approach was the best way of getting the most from his workers.

The sixth floor housed the gang's operational team,

whose accommodation was luxurious compared to the one below. The entire space was freshly painted, and brightly coloured Brazilian murals hung on the walls. Individual quarters consisted of leather furnishings, flat-screen televisions that took up half a wall and self-contained kitchens.

There was no access to the sixth floor for the remaining gang members. To do so would only invite rebellion.

Antonio's quarters were at the far end of the passage-way. They comprised two spacious apartments linked by an adjoining door. The rooms were strictly off-limits to anyone except Maria, who was granted access to perform her weekly clean.

From time to time, he rented a house near the beach in the Ipanema or Lebnon regions. A bit of luxury worked wonders, he found. It was a circuit breaker from their tedious existence at headquarters in which no one, not even family, had permission to visit.

Every one of them knew their cover could be blown at any time, and at the slightest whiff of trouble, they simply vanished without a trace. Antonio and the operational group members sought refuge at his favela, while the remaining six returned to their homes and families.

Antonio dropped by the kitchen, where Maria was peeling potatoes on a bench. She looked up in surprise and said, 'I thought you'd gone out for the day.'

'Yeah, well, there was a change of plans. There's a new arrival in 507.'

Maria raised an eyebrow. It had been some time since the last. 'Who is he?'

'She,' Antonio said. 'My niece, Ava. The one I brought from Australia.'

'What!' the response was incredulous. Room 507 was explicitly allocated for prisoners. 'Why are you locking her up?'

'It's a long story. We need to talk.'

Maria nodded and wiped her hands on her apron. 'Where?'

'In the office.'

Antonio led the way to the room that stored computers and IT equipment for general access. Inside was a small table and two chairs where they sat for some time, deep in discussion.

'So you see,' he concluded, 'she's not to be trusted under any circumstances.'

'What have you told the others?'

'Not much. They heard what happened to Marcos. That's enough.'

Maria nodded. Marcos was only one of four to be dispensed with by Antonio since she'd begun work there. The others were stupid enough to think they could make a quick buck by ratting to the police. It was an unspoken fact that Antonio was not one to be messed with, and she'd been surprised to hear that Marcos had crossed the line. To that point, he'd been one of Antonio's most loyal.

'And what about Christmas?' she asked. 'Your niece. Will she be celebrating with us?'

'Shit, I'd hadn't even thought about that,' Antonio said. 'Who knows what she'll decide to do. I'll find out and let you know. Make a dinner up anyhow.'

'I'm cooking for fourteen, then?'

'Yeah.'

She nodded. 'So, is there anything else?'

'No. You're good to go. Thanks.'

Maria reflected as she headed back to the kitchen. It was the first time a woman had been housed in Room 507. She wondered how her boss's niece would take to learning the mattress she slept on had previously been used by pimps, drug lords and dealers.

Antonio remained in his seat for some time, deep in thought. Christmas was big in Brazil. It was all about family, and Antonio regarded the gang as family. It was the one time of year that he looked forward to the most, the only day when they all got together. No expense was spared, and it seemed that celebrations at headquarters were bigger and better every year than the last. Perhaps that was why the gang members chose to stay rather than return to their families in the favelas.

Maria's feast was bountiful and sumptuous. A long trestle table decorated in a festive tablecloth was covered with platters of pork, turkey, ham, salads and fresh vegetable dishes accompanied by a large bowl of rice and raisins with spoonfuls of farofa. This was washed down with copious amounts of beer and tequila. It was a stark contrast to the chicken, rice, and beans they could expect if they returned to be with their families. The gang loaded their plates to the brim, yet there were always sufficient leftovers for lunch the following day.

Panettone, rabandas, fresh fruits and ice cream were to follow, and then the gang partied into the early hours of the morning. Antonio always left for midnight mass, returning for celebratory toasts and the exchange of presents. Each member was then handed an envelope containing a "thirteenth salary", twice the monthly pay — a tradition bestowed on many Brazilian workers at Christmas.

Usually, Antonio was in high spirits this close to Christmas. But not this year. The thought of sharing festivities with his niece was the last thing he felt like doing. It's only this once, he told himself. Like it or not, she was family.

22

It was dusk when Jennifer and Cara Lorenzo headed down the cliff path for a walk.

'Isn't daylight saving the best time of year.' Jennifer remarked. 'Especially when it's warm like this.'

'Sure is. I don't know why people complain about it. Remember last year when we –' Cara stopped suddenly, letting out a small gasp.

Jennifer turned to her in alarm. 'Darling, whatever's wrong?' her eyes followed Cara's to the distant figure, seated in the sand, looking out to sea. 'Do you know that person?'

'Yeah, I do. Can you leave me for a while, Mum? I won't be long.'

'Are you sure?' Jennifer's voice was hesitant.

'I'll be fine. Honestly. I have my phone.'

Jennifer nodded, but she felt uneasy as she turned and headed back towards the house. It was five weeks since Angelina's brazen visit, but it could have been yesterday;

the pain and fear were still as raw. They'd put up a brave front, pretended things were fine. But they weren't. Every noise, every shadow made them edgy, and they no longer ventured out alone. A spectre hung over the house, with the security cameras, change of locks and police protection offering little comfort. Angelina would be back. They both knew that. It was a matter of when.

Jennifer hesitated as she neared the road. What if Angelina was out there right now and about to make a second attack? Should she go back down and check on Cara? *You've got to let go*, she told herself. *She's no longer a child.* But that did little to alleviate her anxiety. The moment she arrived home she found herself checking her phone for messages. There was nothing to do but wait.

Cara continued down the path, pausing halfway to remove her sandals, heart racing like a basketball player making an end-to-end dash. Taking a deep breath, she stepped onto the sand, warmed by the day's heat, skirting the dunes and edging closer. Five paces behind, she stopped, barely able to breathe.

'You came,' he said without turning.

Cara could feel her fingers digging into the leather of her sandals as she moved to his side.

'Mind if I join you?' the words sounded not her own.

'What do you think?' he said, looking up.

She gazed into the blue, sensitive eyes that had never

been far from her thoughts all these years and felt her legs go weak. The boy face, now a man's, was handsome and tanned, with a trace of stubble. It was framed by a dark mop of hair pulled back in a ponytail. The lanky body she remembered so well had become muscled and lean, and his olive skin contrasted starkly against his white t-shirt. He could have walked straight out of the set of a soapie.

She let go of her sandals and dropped down beside him. For a short while, they sat, side by side, looking out to sea and saying nothing. There was little wind, and the waves ebbed gently on the sand like a soothing hand. In the distance was the faint dot of a fishing boat returning home and a gull soaring across the pink horizon.

Cara was the first to speak. 'You've grown your hair. It suits you.'

There was a hint of a smile on his face. 'Aren't you going to ask what I'm doing here?'

'I was getting around to it.'

There was an awkward silence before she spoke again. 'I didn't think I'd see you again.'

'I told you I'd be back.'

She closed her eyes for a few moments, scarcely able to believe this was happening, savouring his masculine scent; an earthy mixture of sweat and musk.

'So where have you been?' she asked finally.

'All over the place. Dropped out of school in Queensland, became a carpenter and joined a building company that contracts out. That's what I'm doing down this way.'

'How long are you here for?'

'Not sure at this stage,' he said. 'Three months, maybe four.'

'And where are you staying?'

'The boss hired a house just out of town.' He turned and gave a sheepish grin. 'Four guys, coming and going at all hours. You can imagine what that's like. I wouldn't want the estate agent to drop in unexpectedly. There is one positive, I s'pose. Matty, he's the youngest, did a stint as a chef.'

She returned his smile, pulling her knees to her chest and glancing at his long fingers spread out on the sand. She could visualise him creating things with wood.

'What did your dad say?'

'About what?'

'You becoming a carpenter.'

He shrugged. 'Who knows? I just walked out one day. Never went back.'

'That bad, huh! And Maggie?'

'She shot through with the baby. The last I heard she was in a women's refuge somewhere.'

'Shit. I'm sorry.'

'Don't be. Probably the best move Maggie ever made. She texted me to say she was okay. When she settles somewhere, I'll go and see her.' He paused. 'She was good to me, even though I didn't see it at the time.'

'She was good to me as well,' Cara said. 'If not for her.'

He raised an eyebrow questioningly.

'It doesn't matter,' her voice petered out.

'Is everything okay?'

'Not really.'

'You wanna talk about it?'

Cara ran a hand across her hair. 'Yeah, no. I don't know.' She paused. 'You haven't heard about my family, then?'

'No. Should I?'

After a moment's silence, he turned to face her. 'They're all right, I hope?'

'Christ! That's an understatement.'

'Perhaps you'd better start from the beginning.'

Will listened incredulously but said little as she opened up about the years since he'd left. He remembered Cara's younger sister, Angelina, from school. Tall, willowy and beautiful — the talk of the boy's locker room. Not that he took much notice. She wasn't his type. Though she struck him as a person who knew her own mind, the thought that she'd be capable of murder was inconceivable.

'What if she comes back, Will?' the words interrupted his thoughts as the last of the night sky turned inky black.

'I'm sure they'll catch her soon, don't worry,' he said, reaching across to gently brush back a few stray locks of her hair.

The gesture brought a sudden rush of longing. She wanted him to take her in his arms, hold her close. But things had never been that way. Probably never would be.

'I'm here for a while, remember,' he added, 'just a phone call away.'

'I needed to hear that,' she said quietly.

'Come on then,' he rose, pulling her to her feet. 'Let's get you home. After what you've just told me, your mum must be worried sick by now.'

'Shit, I'd forgotten about that.' Cara reached in her pocket for her phone and sent a quick text, then activated the lamplight.

Will felt uneasy as they walked through Kilkenny's imposing front gates that resembled a macabre grin of whalebone teeth. By the time they'd passed the manicured gardens and stepped onto the porch, his stomach was a tight, hard ball. Cara lived a life of privilege and wealth — something he could never give her.

The day she'd followed him to his ramshackle house, he'd never felt such shame. Yet she'd been oblivious to the weed-choked garden, rusty doorknob and rotting windows. It was Maggie's colourful array of handmade crafts and jewellery that had captured her immediate attention. He remembered how she walked around in childish wonder, picking up bars of soap and holding them to her nose, and placing trinkets in her hand as if they were fragile birds, watching the light catch their surface.

The moment Cara's mother stepped gracefully across the room to take his hand, all sense of apprehension and inadequacy vanished. There was a naturalness about her, a warmth. She struck him as a person who'd be at ease in a cottage or a soup kitchen.

'I'm Jennifer,' she said with a smile.

'Will. I'm very pleased to meet you.'

'Maggie's Will?'

There was a nod.

'David and I are forever indebted to Maggie for what she did for Cara,' she told him. 'Can you let her know that?'

'Of course.'

Jennifer hastily wiped her eyes with the back of her hand.

'It's okay, Mum,' Cara said. 'I've told him everything.'

Jennifer looked at one and then the other. 'In that case, how about we sit for a while, and I'll make us a coffee.'

For the next hour, Will listened in disbelief as more was unravelled. 'When was the last time she came?' he asked.

'Five weeks ago, when she broke into the house.' Jennifer shivered at the memory. 'Oh, and I forgot to mention the earring she left one other time. But that's nothing in the scheme of things.'

'And the police know all of this?' Will asked.

'Yes. The local police have been nothing but supportive the whole way along. It would only take a phone call, and they'd be straight here. But the thing is, Angelina's so damned smart.' She ran a hand across her hair. 'Cara, get Will the note.'

Cara nodded and left the room, returning soon afterwards with a white envelope.

'It came this morning,' Jennifer said. 'Just what we needed at Christmas!'

Will pulled out the postcard depicting the nearby

lighthouse and flipped it over.

'It's Angelina's handwriting,' Jennifer explained.

The message read: *Happy Christmas. Thought I might pay a visit. Don't want to miss out on the presents.*

Will's blood ran cold. 'You've shown this to the police?'

Jennifer nodded. 'They're sending a patrol car around on the day, but to be honest, I don't think she'll show.'

'Neither do I,' he concurred. 'From what you've said, she prefers the element of surprise. But for peace of mind, would you like me to drop around?'

'But it's Christmas Day, Will. We couldn't impose on you like that.'

'I'm not doing anything.'

'What? You're not spending the day with family or friends?'

'I've only lived here for a few months. Haven't had a chance to know anyone much.'

'Then I insist you have Christmas lunch with us.'

Will shifted awkwardly. 'Thanks, but I couldn't do that.'

'Why not? David will be arriving from Melbourne this evening, and I know he'll be keen to meet you. Besides, we'd love you to share the day with us, wouldn't we, Cara.'

'Of course we would,' Cara replied, looking hopefully at Will.

At ten, Will checked his Fitbit. 'Geez, I didn't realise it was that late. I'd better get going,' he said, rising to his feet.

'Where are you parked?' Jennifer asked.

'Not far away. It'll only take a few minutes to jog back.'

'I hope we haven't kept you too long. Do you have to work in the morning?'

'No. We have a few days off over Christmas. The guys wanted to be here earlier to catch some waves.' He paused. 'So, if you need me anytime, I can be around in five.'

'Thanks,' Jennifer said gratefully.

'I'll see you on Christmas day then,' he said at the door. 'What time?'

'It doesn't matter, really. How about late morning.'

'Don't come too early, or she'll put you to work,' quipped Cara.

'Wouldn't worry me,' Will said with a shrug, 'just leave me out of the cooking side of things.'

'Don't worry,' Jennifer said with a smile, 'Meg, that's our housekeeper, will be handling all of that.'

Once he'd left, Jennifer bolted the door and gave Cara a hug. 'What a night you've had, young lady.'

'Do you like him, Mum?'

'Very much.'

There was an unsaid, shared feeling of relief. For the first time, they felt safer.

23

Angelina received a text: *Meet me in the dining room at three.*

What in the hell's this about? she wondered, intrigued but also apprehensive.

No one else was about as she sat in a chair by the table, glancing around the decorated room. Gold, red and green tinsel hung from the eaves and a giant Christmas tree adorned with tinsel, lights and baubles took pride of place. A traditional Presepio (nativity scene) sat at the far side of the room, resembling an item belonging to an antique shop. It all meant nothing.

Antonio arrived soon afterwards and sat down.

'So, have you settled in?'

Angelina gave a shrug of her shoulders.

'Just filling you on what goes around here at Christmas. In Brazil, we hold the main celebrations on Christmas Eve and not Christmas Day like you're used to,' he explained. 'Christmas dinner will be around 10 p.m. That's when the celebrations begin. You're free to join us if you wish. But I'm warning you, things can get a little bit wild around here. All in good fun, of course.'

'As if I've got anything to celebrate,' Angelina snapped. 'I'm staying in my room.'

'That's a pity. I thought you might have joined in the Christmas spirit.'

She glared at him. 'Is that all?'

'Yep.' He rose. 'Don't be late for Christmas dinner. You won't want to miss it. Maria serves up a feast.'

Antonio walked away, spirits suddenly high. He should have known she wouldn't join in the festivities. Now he could start looking forward to things.

¶

On Christmas Eve, Antonio gave Angelina a call. 'I'm attending the Missa do Galio tonight if you'd like to come.'

'What's that?'

'Midnight mass.'

'How long does it go for?'

'An hour, could be more.'

'How much more?'

'Who knows? in English, Misso de Galio means "Mass of the Rooster" because it's been known to go on till the rooster crows at daybreak.'

'You're kidding me!'

'Nope. As a kid I remember going when it went until five.'

'What!'

'So, you're not interested?'

'No bloody way.'

'Thought I'd ask.'

Antonio grinned as he clicked off. He hadn't had such fun in a long time.

Misso de Galio, the mass most Brazilian Catholics attended each year, was followed by a spectacular firework display. The streets were filled with Christmas lights and decorations, but perhaps most beautiful of all was the floating Christmas tree placed in the Rodrigo de Freitas Lagoon. Soaring seventy metres high, its millions of blue, silver, red and gold lights sparkled like diamonds against the night sky. It was the sight that Antonio loved the most.

¶

Angela sat on the sofa, deep in thought. Every year it had been the tradition for her and her family to celebrate mass on Christmas Eve at six, except for her grandmother, Madeleine, who drove alone to the local Catholic Church to attend midnight mass. Angelina never understood. Why stay up until that hour to go to church when you could go earlier?

She reflected on the strict Catholic upbringing that she'd come to loathe: the rituals, the pomp and ceremony, the repetition. The day she left Kilkenny she swore she'd never set foot in a church again. However, on this occasion she'd been tempted for no better reason than to escape the boredom. But six hours of it? He had to be kidding, didn't he?

The dining room was abuzz with raucous laughter and loud chatter when Angelina went to collect her dinner. Tables had been pulled together, and she noticed several men she'd never seen before seated with the others. Who were they, and where did they fit in?

She could feel all eyes on her as she walked past, and the few phrases she picked up in Portuguese made her blood boil. Since her arrival, everyone spoke nothing but Portuguese unless she addressed them directly in English. And this riled her no end. Angelina's tray was laden with food, and she snatched it angrily, striding past the mob who by now were ignoring her presence. She hadn't eaten since midday, and the smell of roasted meat and potatoes suddenly made her feel ravenous.

Back in her room, she placed the tray on the table without lifting the lid and paused for a few moments to reflect. It was hard to believe that this time last year, she'd been celebrating Christmas at home with her family. The usual traditions had taken place: late brunch on the patio followed by presents around the tree. Each year they took turns being Santa, donning the ridiculous, faded outfit that had been part of the gig for as long as she could remember. This time it had been her father, Dominic's turn to do the honours, and his eyes danced as he handed her the silver box with pink ribbon and bow. 'I chose it myself,' he said. She gasped when she lifted the lid that revealed an exquisite, hand-crafted diamond bracelet.

'That's for all the hard work you've put in this year.' he said.

'It's just beautiful, Dad. I love it.' She pulled the bracelet out of its box and held out her wrist for him to fasten it.

The three years spent alongside her father at the office, learning the ropes, had finally paid off. She'd been rewarded with a highly paid salary and was well on the way to becoming his successor.

It was a kick in the guts to Cara. She'd been all but guaranteed a management position within the company job once she'd completed her degree. But the animosity that had built up between the pair since then made that highly unlikely. Cara barely set foot in the office these days, much to Angelina's satisfaction.

If her sister was envious of her father's extravagant gesture, she didn't show it, but her mother's discomfort was evident. After a lavish Christmas spread prepared by the housekeeper, the family paid their traditional visit to the family graveyard to pay their respects to Joseph, her younger brother, who'd died tragically as a four-year-old. As usual, she remained at her father's side long after the others had gone. He'd never recovered from his son's death, and she knew her presence provided great comfort. But that wasn't the only reason why she stayed.

As Christmases came and went, Cara's enthusiasm for the

occasion waned to the point of indifference, and Angelina was quick to take advantage. She became the one who put up the Christmas lights and tinsel, chose the décor and decorated the tree. The previous year, the colour scheme was silver and aqua, and no time and expense were spared in making sure things were up to scratch. She knew it was one of her best efforts yet. Silver candles, cutlery, place-mats and trimmings sparkled on the aqua table cloth. Her grandmother commented that it was an arrangement worthy of a place in *Vogue*.

Angelina had never considered that last year's Christmas would be her last at Kilkenny. She glanced around her room with fury. How dare he lock her up like this!

One thing was for sure, Christmas would be a lavish affair next year if she had anything to do with it. New York perhaps, or Paris.

And you, my dear mother and sister, can spend Christmas lunch looking at each other over the table, she thought. *If you're still around, that is.*

24

Two weeks passed. One morning, Maria dropped off sheets and the two engaged in their longest conversation to date. After Maria had gone, Angelina reflected on the exchange and wondered if it would have a result. Probably not. She gave a shrug. It had been worth a try.

When she returned to her room, Maria immediately rang Antonio. The call was answered after three rings.

'Hi, Maria, what's up?'

'Can you talk?'

'I'm in a meeting in the board room. Give me a minute, will you?'

He directed the others to continue and stepped outside. 'Good to go now.'

'Is the bug turned on in your niece's room?'

'Yeah. Why?'

'I've just come from her there. You might like to hear what she had to say.'

'Is that so? I'll do just that.'

Maria ended the call, knowing her boss would be well pleased. She'd proven herself trustworthy many times in the past, and in return he'd confided things that he'd told no other. She was proud to be held in such high regard by the man considered a god in her favela.

Over the fifteen years he'd ruled there, he'd provided numerous jobs, albeit not legitimate, tipped in funds where there was a need and kept the place safe. The only thing he sought in return was refuge when things heated up. And there was no shortage of people willing to put him up.

Antonio wasted no time in adjourning the meeting and heading to his office. He'd inserted a new sim card in the listening device that had been hidden in her room's smoke detector. Messages were transmitted via wi-fi to his computer. He didn't have to search long to pick up Maria's voice.

'New sheets for you, lady. Where you like them put?'

'On the bed, will you?'

There was the sound of a door closing, and Angelina continued speaking. 'Look, we haven't spoken, but I need your help. I'm being held against my will.'

There was a pause. 'No understand.'

'Prisoner, yes?'

'Ah. But Antonio, he say you stay here for little while.'

'Well, he's lying. I've got no one else to turn to. Can you help me get out?'

Another pause. 'No think so. Too dangerous.'

'I pay big money. Big, big money. Think about it. Please?'

'I think.' The door closed.

Antonio closed the file and sat, fuming. It was time to give Fabio a call.

'You busy right now?'

'Nuh. Why?'

'Checking in on Ava. What's she been up to?'

'Whingeing about everything as usual. The latest thing is the food. She's insisting on takeaway of an evening.'

Antonio felt as if he was about to explode. His niece had her own money and could do as she wished, but wasting resources by collecting takeaway food was another thing.

'That's bullshit. It's time we moved her out of here. Have you thought of a place yet?'

'I have actually,' he said. 'What about your hamlet in Spain?'

'Now there's a thought.' Antonio stroked his chin slowly.

'You can't get a place more isolated than that.'

'You're not wrong there.'

'There'd still be a need for a guard, of course.'

'That could be arranged.'

Antonio's mind was racing ahead. The fifteen-acre hamlet comprised four empty farmhouses and a small cottage occupied by the caretaker and his wife. Despite their many efforts to conceive, the couple, now in their sixties, had remained childless. Filipe had accepted the fact and moved on long ago. But it was a different story for his wife, Rosa.

Antonio knew with certainty that she would adopt

Angelina's baby in a heartbeat.

'So, tell me this much,' he said to Fabio, 'would you be prepared to move to Spain to continue on as my niece's guard?'

'What's in it for me?'

'A job in Operations, if you pull things off.'

'Yeah, well that changes things.'

'So, I take it as yes?'

'So long as I'm the one calling the shots.'

'I have no problems with that.'

'There'll be no stuff-ups.'

'We'll see.' Antonio paused. 'To put such a thing in place can't just happen overnight, you understand. I'll start making enquiries, but it could take another month, perhaps two.'

'Okay.'

'I'll be in touch.' The call ended.

Fabio placed the mobile on the table with a satisfied smile. The break he'd been waiting for had finally arrived, and he was glad that Antonio had not hesitated in giving consent to his plan. The further away from headquarters she was sent, the better.

Although there was apparent animosity between his boss and his niece, it was no secret that family came above all else in his eyes. What if Antonio had a change of heart just as she was about to head home? What if he offered her a role in his gang? Operations, for instance …

Over my frigging dead body, he thought.

The woman clearly detested him, and the feeling was mutual. But right now, he had the upper hand, and he'd ensure that things were made far from easy. The hamlet, from what he'd heard, was run down and its houses abandoned years ago. By the time her four months were up, she'd be wanting nothing further to do with him, Antonio or his gang again.

¶

Once Angelina's one last chance of escape with Maria fell flat, there was no option but to behave herself in the hope that it may lead to a move to somewhere less restrictive. For the next few weeks she lay low, spending her days watching TV between visits to the gym and pool — the one thing that riled Fabio the most. She could see it in his eyes. The guards accompanying her didn't look much happier. She was probably pulling them away from a game of pool or cards with the others. But there was only so many Netflix series to be watched, and her patience was wearing thin.

Eventually, she confronted Fabio.

'I need to speak to my uncle.'

'Why?'

'None of your business.'

'I'll see what I can do,' said Fabio. 'But I can't promise anything. I haven't seen much of him lately.'

He waited till she'd gone and contacted Antonio.

'Your niece has just asked to see you,' he said.

'Did she now? You can tell her I'll drop by her room in the morning. While I'm speaking to you, the departure date for Spain is the fifth of March. We'll talk more later.'

'Okay.' Fabio ended the call.

He'd hoped it would be earlier, but seven weeks wasn't that long to wait. In the meantime, he'd quickly learned that the silent treatment was the best way to deal with Ava's ravings; it was the only way to stop himself from going completely mad.

Things should be a helluva lot easier for him once they arrived at the hamlet. Antonio would make sure her passport wasn't handed back until the baby was born, and she'd be miles from anywhere with no knowledge of the language. With her vanity and concern for her body, he doubted she'd be thinking about abortion at that late stage.

§

At 10 a.m. Antonio paid a visit to Angelina's room.

'You want to talk?' he said.

'You're fucking well right I do,' she snapped. 'I'm going stark raving mad in this place. I need to get out.'

'I've already told you that's possible with a guard.'

She waved her hand angrily towards the window. 'And what's to see for God's sake.'

'Suit yourself.' He paused. 'I tell you what, if you're that bored, you can come with me to the favela tomorrow.'

She tilted her chin. 'Okay. What time?'

'At 7 a.m.' He turned and left.

Angelina sat down on the sofa to reflect. She'd heard about the drug lords and organised crime groups that ruled the favelas and had suspected for some time he might be amongst them. With her suspicions confirmed, she looked to the next day with intrigue. Where was this place? What did he do there, and how was he regarded?

Out of interest, she conducted some web searches. Some drug lords lived in the favelas amongst those they protected, making tracing them next to impossible. She couldn't imagine her uncle living in one.

A place like this, in contrast, seemed much more his go. She thought of its access to a swimming pool, spa and sauna. It was old but comfortable, and the gang members wanted for nothing. She'd watched Antonio disappear into the lift to his living quarters on the next level and suspected that things were far more luxurious up there.

25

Just before 7 a.m. Angelina followed Antonio out to the car parked near the kerb. This time he climbed in the back seat beside her.

'O lenco?' He said to the driver, who nodded and reached in the glovebox for a scarf.

Angelina spotted what was coming. 'Oh, give me a break!' she remonstrated. 'Can't I just close my eyes or something?'

'You either wear the thing, or you travel face down on your knees.'

She pouted and lowered her chin towards her chest.

The response was swift. A fistful of hair and he pulled her head upwards, causing her eyes to smart. His face was centimetres from hers. 'Not what I asked.'

'Screw you!' She thrust her head to her knees in an exaggerated fashion, pulling her arms around her legs. 'Satisfied?'

'I haven't got time for this crap,' he said to no one in

particular and gestured to the driver to get going.

From the outset, Angelina wished she'd gone for the blindfold instead. Her neck jarred every time they hit a bump, her back hurt, and she found it hard to breathe in such an unnatural position. She could only hope that the journey would be a short one. She was wrong. The car headed in a northerly direction and continued for quite some time before halting.

With relief, she sat up, massaging her neck.

Antonio spoke a few words to the driver, then gave her the nod to get out.

On the street, she looked upwards in disbelief at the mass of makeshift, flat-roofed houses of all colours, piled haphazardly, clinging to the mountain as if their lives depended on it. She'd seen them from a distance from her Rio apartment but had taken little notice.

'How can people live like that?' she turned to him. 'I mean you'd think –'

He silenced her with a hand

'You will refer to the favelas as communities when you speak to the residents, and you'll show them nothing but respect. Is that clear?'

She gave a shrug. 'Whatever.'

Antonio's blood boiled. It took all his efforts not to slap her across the face. There were more effective means of bringing her down to size.

Ahead lay a narrow road that rose steeply. Antonio pointed halfway up. 'See that set of houses with blue roofs?'

There was a nod.

'That's where we're heading.'

He glanced down. 'Just as well you're wearing sensible shoes. Let's get going.'

Antonio's favela sat amidst Rio's most dangerous, where drug lords ruled and organised crime gangs operated. Violence was rife, and intruders quickly despatched. Bare-chested bandidos armed with machine guns guarded their turf, with others eagerly awaiting their turn. Previous police raids had proved costly, and visits were rare these days, leaving the gangs pretty much alone to do as they wished.

Antonio had no need to go to such lengths. His favela was small compared to those around it and was mainly used for minor drug deals and illegal undertakings. He looked after those who lived there, and in return, they provided refuge. He posed only a minor threat to rival gangs, and that being the case, his territory had remained relatively unscathed. Nonetheless, if his patch was threatened, he'd be up for the fight.

The favelas covering the hills to the south of Rio were safe in comparison. Crime gangs that once dominated the area were long gone, driven out by UPP (Police Pacifying Units,) who patrolled the streets and kept order. Most boasted outstanding views of Rio's best landmarks and the Atlantic Ocean. It was only a matter of time before the inhabitants were forced out and their illegally built, makeshift houses bulldozed and sold as prime real estate.

For the time being, life would continue on as always.

There was nowhere for the inhabitants to go. Meanwhile, bars and eating places were springing up, and vibrant street parties a tourist drawcard.

He couldn't see that happening in his favela. Not in his lifetime, at least.

9

Angelina felt a sense of unease as they walked up the uneven, narrow street. Antonio looked straight ahead in silence, and the unwelcome glances cast her way only heightened her trepidation. She was glad to have Antonio alongside.

The moment they turned the corner into his block of favelas, it was as if a switch flicked on. Antonio seemed taller somehow, a commanding presence, tough and uncompromising. Those passing received a cursory nod, and no one approached unless spoken to. A few houses down, he put up a hand. 'You're to stay put until I return, understood?' he told her. Without awaiting a response, he headed across the road to the thickset man with tatts standing in a doorway. She wasn't about to disobey his order. There was nowhere to go.

Antonio was the one doing most of the talking. The man produced an envelope and handed it over. It quickly disappeared into Antonio's pocket.

'Do any of them speak English?' she asked when he returned.

'Not many.'

'They don't like me, do they,' she pressed.

'You're a foreigner.'

'They're not curious to know who I am?'

'They already do.' He caught her eye. 'Just as well for you.'

Angelina looked around at the jumble of brick and concrete dwellings barely a metre apart. Most had small windows and flat, corrugated iron roofs with large, blue tanks used for storing water. Some were in far worse condition than others, and she wondered how long they'd been there. Antennas stuck out from walls and electric cables dangled.

'Do they have wi-fi around here?' she asked.

'Is that all you can think of?'

'Well?'

'Most places do.'

Nearby was a dark alleyway with graffiti on the walls and concrete stairways leading to the second and third floors. He stopped and pointed. 'See that green door third one down?'

She nodded.

'That's where the backyard abortionist works. Think about it.' He strode on.

Angelina felt her stomach tighten into a hard knot as she followed.

Further along, people sat chatting on orange plastic

chairs outside a small café, and she could hear the squeals of children as they chased each other up and down a nearby concrete stairwell. Antonio glanced up a side street where a group of teenage boys rap danced to music blaring from a boom box. Any one of them could find himself his next recruit.

Up ahead, he crossed the road and knocked on a faded red door.

'Who lives here?' she asked.

'Renata, Maria's sister. I'm dropping off these clothes.'

The door was opened by a small woman in her late fifties with an olive complexion, and grey hair pulled back in a tight bun. She appeared worn and tired, bearing little resemblance to her thickset, lively sister whose eyes missed nothing.

Angelina followed them into the dimly lit house that was basic but neat and clean. The woman thanked him for the parcel and gestured to a small table with red plastic chairs.

The moment they were seated, Antonio struck up a conversation in Portuguese.

'So, how have you been, Renata?'

'Fine. And you?'

'Can't complain.'

'She's beautiful, your niece. But she looks trouble.'

He gave a wry smile. 'She's been a handful, to stay the least.'

'You should leave her with me for a week or two.'

'God forbid, I wouldn't put you through it.'

'What's she saying?' Angelina snapped.

'She's asking about Maria, that's all.'

'Bullshit.'

Antonio gave her a quick, menacing look and resumed the conversation.

'Is there anything you need?' he asked. 'Money? Food?'

A wave of gratitude swept over her. Antonio never failed to enquire.

'No, thanks for asking.' Renata glanced across at Angelina. 'Does she ever smile?'

'No.'

'Pity. You'll join me for lunch, I hope?'

He turned to Angelina and translated into English.

'I'm not hungry.'

He gave a shrug. 'You can sit there then. You don't know what you're missing out on.'

As Renata busied herself in the kitchen, Angelina glanced around the small room with distaste, wondering how anyone could live like this. Music blared through the paper-thin walls that separated Renata's house from the next, and the room was excessively hot under the corrugated iron roof. She wiped her brow with one hand and sank sullenly into the old chair, reaching into her pocket for her mobile. Antonio moved quickly and snatched it from her hand. 'Not while you're a guest in this house.' His voice was low and angry.

He turned to Renata and resumed the conversation in Portuguese. 'She's only with me for a short time.'

'Just as well, eh?'

They exchanged grins.

The smell of meat frying caused Angelina's stomach to rumble, and when the large platter of meat, rice and assorted vegetables was placed on the table before her, she regretted her decision not to eat. Lunch was Brazil's most important meal of the day, with always more than enough to go around, and this one was no exception.

'Come. Don't let it get cold,' Renata said, drying her hands on a tea towel before joining him. Antonio gave a broad smile and reached for a plate, piling it high with food. The pair took their time eating, pausing now and then to speak.

All the while, Angelina sat with her arms folded, look-ing totally bored. 'How much longer do we have to stay here?' she asked.

The comment was ignored, but the look was enough. *Probably just added another hour, you idiot,* she told herself.

After the dishes had been cleared, Renata returned with two coffees. Antonio tried to remain focused on what she was saying, but his mind was elsewhere. The community had become his family, and Angelina's blatant disrespect towards Renata was the ultimate insult. He vowed that she would pay.

The music stopped next door, and a conversation took

place. Although Angelina understood none of it, every word was distinctly audible. Little would go on around here that the neighbours weren't aware of. Through an open window she could even see someone walking around just metres from where she sat.

It was three by the time Antonio rose, thanked Renata, and they left. Instead of heading back to the car as Angelina had hoped, they continued on down the street. This time she dared not say a word. In the distance came the sound of hammering and sawing. As they drew closer, she noticed a small, yellow house where a group of people appeared to be engaged in its renovation. Some were engaged in carpentry and others pushed wheelbarrows full of bricks, while women mixed concrete by hand, small children playing at their heels. Antonio explained that a young widow's friends, relatives and neighbours had gathered to build another storey. Once complete it would be rented out, providing her with a much-needed income. It was favela way.

As they passed by, a young woman carrying a young baby and a toddler alongside motioned them to stop. She disappeared inside the house to return soon afterwards with a box of vegetables that she handed to Antonio.

'What was that all about?' Angelina said as they moved on.

'Some vegetables for Maria.'

She wasn't to know that it was a gesture of thanks for covering the cost of the building materials.

The afternoon sun was searing, and the back of her t-shirt

was damp with sweat, but the humidity seemed to have little effect on Antonio, who strode on regardless. She was in desperate need of a drink, but she wasn't about to ask, having refused one earlier at Renata's house.

It was another half hour's wait before Antonio stepped into a small shop and returned with two water bottles and a brown paper bag of sandwiches.

'You've got the baby to think of,' he said.

Angelina was too tired to think of a comeback. Ripping open the bag, she wolfed down its contents in between gulps of water.

'So can we go now?' she said, wiping her mouth with the back of her hand.

'Not quite. There's a few things to be said first.' He took the empty bottle, screwed up the bag and threw them into a nearby bin.

'I saw the look on your face as we walked around today,' he said with undisguised fury. 'You forget that your mother and I lived in a place just like this for ten years before we left for Australia. You're an ungrateful, stuck-up bitch. Don't be so quick to judge. If me and the gang have to get out at short notice, these are the people who'll save our arses.'

He pressed on ruthlessly. 'And make no mistake, you'll be right alongside us, staying at any one of the places you've just turned your nose up at. And that could be for a week, even a month. Then you'll find out what it's like to go without.'

She didn't respond.

'I know all about the bribe you made to Maria,' his eyes bored into hers. 'Try something like that again, and you will find yourself on the street.' He turned on his heels and headed back towards the car. She followed, again not saying a word.

The Lexus was parked in the same spot as before. It was sweltering as she climbed inside, its interior reeking of cigarettes.

'Get him to open the windows for Christ's sake!' she snapped at Antonio as he climbed in beside her. 'And give me the fucking blindfold. I'll put in on myself.'

Antonio smiled to himself and reached for the scarf on the front seat.

The day had gone just as planned.

26

It was another three days before Angelina heard from Antonio.

'I've got a proposition to put to you,' he said.

'What?'

'I'll be down in fifteen minutes.'

The line went dead.

Angelina placed her mobile on the bench and chewed her lip. *What's he on about this time,* she wondered.

When Antonio arrived, he closed the door behind him and stood with his arms crossed.

'How would you feel about moving to Spain until the baby is born?'

'What!' she exclaimed in disbelief.

'I own some land there. The caretaker's wife heard about the baby. She asked if they could adopt, and I agreed. So, you can either stay here to have the baby or move to Spain, to be closer to them. What will it be?'

'Spain.' The response was quick.

'You're quite sure about that?'

'Anything'd be better than this dump,' she retorted.

'Is that so? Well, I think I have all I need for now.'

'Wait.' She grabbed hold of his arm as he turned to leave. 'Where is this place? When can I go?'

'I'll let you know soon enough.'

'And the caretaker couple?' she pressed.

'What about them?'

'Do they speak anything apart from Spanish?'

'They're not Spanish. They come from my favela.'

'So, they speak Portuguese.'

'Correct. But they have a good understanding of Spanish as well. Either way, there's no need to worry. Fabio will be there to translate.'

'What the fuck!' she said furiously, digging her nails into his arm. 'You never mentioned anything about that!'

'You never asked.'

'Screw you,' she muttered furiously.

Antonio was unperturbed, calmly extricating her hand from his arm as if she was a woman in a bar who'd paid him an unwanted advance. 'Surely you didn't think I'd leave you alone to your own devices.'

'And what did you expect I'd do? Clear out or something?'

'I wouldn't put it past you.'

'In this state?' Angelina laid her palms on her prominent bump in an exaggerated fashion. 'You've got to be kidding me.'

There was a shrug. 'Just being cautious. As I've already

told you, once the baby's born, you're free to do as you wish.' He paused for a brief moment. 'Well, I've got things to attend to. Expect to hear from me soon.'

Angelina scowled as Antonio pulled the door closed behind him. She wasn't about to ask Fabio's help on anything. He could go to hell as far as she was concerned. Antonio smiled to himself as he headed along the passageway. The day she left couldn't come quickly enough. On the way to the lift, he stopped and texted Fabio:

She agreed to go.

Have you told her what it's like there? Came the quick response.

Not yet. Don't want her pulling out on us.

Fabio grinned as he hit the emoji thumbs up symbol.

❡

Antonio returned to his room, made himself a coffee and switched on his computer. There were so many things to arrange in such a short amount of time. He'd first learned of Spain's 'ghost villages' a few years back. There were over three thousand dotted around the countryside, mainly to the north.

Dating back to the fifteenth century the abandoned hamlets, comprising generally around four to six stone houses, had been deserted by their owners as subsistence farming became unsustainable. Most moved to larger towns to find work, while others headed to South

America or parts of Europe in search of a better life. As the remaining few eventually died out, buildings crumbled, and properties became overgrown with weeds.

Hamlets were being snapped up at bargain prices. Thirty were sold by the same estate agent the previous year, primarily to foreign buyers like Antonio. It was only a matter of time before the remaining ones were snapped up for holiday retreats or retirement places for wealthy Europeans.

Antonio had been quick to act. It mattered little how run-down the hamlets were. To him, they were ideal for concealing illegal goods and arranging clandestine meetings. If he'd been twenty years younger, he might well have tapped into Galicia's lucrative drug trafficking trade as well.

He'd flown to Spain to begin his search and found what he was looking for within the first five days. Situated in the Galicia region in the north of Spain, his fifteen-acre hamlet was set inland, not far from Viveiro, its nearest town. From what he'd been told, the place had lain idle for the past thirty years after the last remaining couple moved to Switzerland. They hadn't returned since and only recently decided to sell.

Antonio found it hard to believe he'd acquired an entire medieval village for just under three-hundred-thousand euros.

Unseen from the main road, the property sat nestled into the hill of a lush valley of oak and chestnut woodlands.

Alongside the caretaker's cottage and four stone slate farmhouses were a granary built on stone stilts, a bakery, a cattle barn and a water-well, all in varying states of disrepair.

A forgotten orchard sloped down to a pristine stream that flowed over smooth rocks and granite boulders before winding out of sight. Wild boar fossicked for acorns, and brown bears were not uncommon in the region. Also, what Antonio had been told, the place became a proliferation of wildflowers in springtime.

There was a certain old-world charm about the place which was he chose it above a number of others.

Two houses lay in ruins, but the two still standing were salvageable at considerable cost. Not that Antonio was bothered by this. Renovations would take place in due course. His immediate priority was restoring and refurbishing the caretaker's cottage and clearing the property of weeds and brambles. He also ensured that electricity, telephone and mains water were connected, the dirt track leading to the main road flattened and cleared of potholes. By then he'd secured the services of a live-in caretaker couple from his favela.

He couldn't think of a better pair to run things in his absence than Filipe and Rosa Cardoso. The two met when Filipe came to the favela in search of work when the farm he'd been working on fell on hard times. They'd married not long afterwards.

Filipe never adjusted to living in confined spaces, despite his many years in the favela. When the offer was made to relocate, he and Rosa jumped at the chance. The couple had proved their worth over the years, and Antonio knew they could be trusted to keep their mouths shut on matters concerning the gang. Filipe had been at his side when he'd stored the consignment of drugs in the hamlet's granary a year ago, and it was Filipe who'd dug the graves of the three bodies buried in the orchard.

In retrospect, Antonio was glad to have employed a couple who spoke his native tongue. It made things much easier. Nonetheless, the traditional Galician language was a mixture of Portuguese and Spanish, not too difficult to decipher. It would be a different story for Angelina, however. Some locals spoke Spanish only, with little or no understanding of English.

Antonio drank the last of his coffee and got down to business, making a quick call to Filipe to confirm Angelina's arrival. Next, he emailed the contractor that Filipe recommended, seeking a quote to bring the two remaining farmhouses up to an acceptable standard. Ava would be placed in the one closest to Rosa's in case of complications and Fabio, the house to her left.

 g

The contractor's response arrived came five days later, with two quotes attached. The first covered window, door and roof replacements, along with and basic refurbishments. The second factored in additional costs to inner walls, floors, kitchen and staircases. Antonio chose the first option. He'd see that she was comfortable enough, but he wasn't about to outlay unnecessary expenses.

He didn't particularly care about the uneven stone walls, ancient iron stove in the kitchen and antique chestnut furniture that by now was likely to have rotted or be inhabited by an infestation of contented woodworms. His niece had been surrounded by luxury all her life. It wouldn't hurt her to see how the other half lived. Not for the first time, he wondered how she'd cope living under such conditions, but one thing was for sure: she'd let everyone around her know.

The caretakers had been warned of Angelina's surly, rude demeanour, yet they seemed unfazed. If anything, Antonio detected a note of amusement in Filipe's voice.

'Sounds like a spoiled brat to me, Boss,' was his reaction.

'You're not wrong there.'

Antonio's mind turned once more to the farmhouse in which Angelina would stay. Although she'd be arriving before the onset of winter, it could be cold and rainy in March. He had visions of her shivering and wrapped in blankets, huddled around the small, open fireplace. And he could not allow that to happen, for his sister's sake. There'd need to be adequate heating, ample bedding and an electric blanket.

Antonio had returned to the hamlet just three times, but each visit had left him feeling more attached. Perhaps it was the stillness of the place; its ancient stone buildings, old well and even the abandoned tractor at the foot of the orchard.

Filipe had planted a vegetable garden, purchased some sheep and cows to keep the grass down, revitalised the orchard and fixed broken fences. The place was barely recognisable. It was during Antonio's most recent visit that he made the decision to retire there.

If I make it that far, he thought with a rueful smile.

27

It was another three weeks before Antonio met with Angelina and Fabio to discuss arrangements for Spain.

'So, when are we going?' Angelina had barely sat down before she fired the question.

'Wednesday, March 5th.'

'Thank Christ for that,' she said. It was not that much longer to wait. 'So, whereabouts in Spain is your property?'

'To the north. The Galicia region.'

'Near the beach, I hope.'

'You could say that.'

There was an enthusiastic nod. 'Great. I'll be needing bathers and some more summer clothes then. Most of mine no longer fit.'

Antonio exchanged glances with Fabio and remarked, 'You haven't told her about the weather yet?'

'No, I was getting around to it.'

Antonio turned to her to explain. 'Where my hamlet is located, it can rain up to fourteen days a month.'

Her shoulders dropped visibly. 'I thought Spain was supposed to be warm and sunny.'

'In most parts, it is. We get those days as well. But that's in summer, and by then you'll be just about to leave. Expect temperatures of between fourteen and eighteen degrees for most of your stay, with cold nights.'

Fabio leaned against the door frame, thoroughly enjoying himself. It was not often he'd seen Ava lost for words.

Antonio pulled out his iPhone and clicked on images taken during his last visit to the hamlet.

'This'll give you a bit of an idea of what the place looks like,' he said as he handed over the phone. 'It dates back to the sixteenth century, actually. The buildings are beautiful but in varying states of repair, as you will see.'

Angelina gasped with disbelief as she scrolled through. 'You're not expecting me to stay holed up in one of those!'

'Just look at it this way,' Antonio continued on smoothly, 'it's a chance to get away from it all. Get in touch with nature.'

'Shit, now I've heard it all!'

'Eventually, I'll get around to fully restoring the buildings, but for now, a builder's working on bringing both farmhouses up to an acceptable standard. You'll find things comfortable enough. You're there for only four months, remember.'

'Any more surprises?' she shot back at him.

'No, I think that's just about it. The rest, you can work out with Fabio once you arrive.' He paused for a moment.

'You did say you needed more clothes, but I suggest you wait and let Rosa take you shopping when you get there. You'll be able to purchase clothes that best suit the weather conditions. Now, if that's it, I'll get going.'

¶

Angelina sat by the window, looking out at the heat shimmering off the ugly apartments opposite and wondering what the temperature was outside. She had air conditioning. That was one thing. There were just two weeks before the flight to Spain, and the time couldn't come soon enough.

The second letter that Theo sent would be arriving at Kilkenny any day now. "Missing you. Not," it said. "Planning a visit home soon. PS. Do you really think the security cameras will make a difference?"

Angelina twirled a lock of hair absent-mindedly in her fingers. She smiled. The bikie gang contact had come in handy. Theo might just be the one she'd need when she returned to Australia. He seemed happy enough with her more than generous payment. Had been quick to say he was available if she needed him again.

¶

The flight to Spain departed Rio Janeiro at 10 a.m. and Angelina was packed, ready to go early.

Maria was the last person she passed when they left the building. 'Bitch,' Angelina muttered, loud enough to be heard, and kept walking. Maria gave a shrug of her shoulders, glad to see the end of this petulant, disagreeable woman.

Antonio walked some way behind, deep in conversation with Fabio.

'Do you want her blindfolded from the airport to the hamlet?' asked Fabio, as they stepped outside and watched the driver place their things in the back.

'No need. Tell her the place is an investment property only and currently on the market.'

There was a nod. 'I've covered everything else. Does Ava know you're not accompanying us to the airport?'

'Nope. You can let her know. I've got a business arrangement to attend to.'

'Okay.'

'I'll be in touch. Good luck.' He gave Fabio's shoulder a pat, turned on his heels and strode back inside.

28

The Air Europa flight to Spain took close to seventeen hours, much to Angelina's displeasure. She'd expected an eight hour to ten hour's journey at the most, not having factored in stopovers, of which there were three.

'Well, you could have checked the flight details before we left,' Fabio responded to her barrage of complaints as they headed towards Departures.

She scowled and ignored the comment.

Once they'd cleared customs and fetched their bags, they collected the pre-booked hire car and headed off.

The Citroen's GPS estimated the distance between Santiago de Compostela airport and the coastal town of Viveiro at a hundred and forty-eight kilometres, an hour and fifty minutes' drive.

They travelled just thirty minutes when Angelina turned to him. 'We need to talk.'

'Do we? I was quite enjoying the peace and quiet, actually.'

'Look, I realise you don't want to be here anymore than I do, but we may as well make things as easy as we can for each other.'

'What are you getting at?'

'Just cut me some slack, and I'll stay out of your hair. Simple as that.'

'Let's get things straight,' he said frostily. 'My instructions are to keep guard 24/7, and that's what I intend to do.'

'Yeah, I know, I know. That's not what I meant.'

'So, what exactly did you mean?'

'All I ask is to be left alone to do my own thing. I'm sick of being watched every minute of the day.'

'Well, you've only yourself to blame.'

'Geez, I've only been trying to find a way out of this nightmare!' she shot back. 'What do you expect?'

He said nothing. If she had arrived in Brazil unaware of her pregnancy, as she claimed, the ordeal that Antonio put her through would be enough to make any woman hostile.

'I'm hardly in a position to do a runner now, am I?' she persisted.

She had a point, he found himself thinking. She'd passed the stage of safe abortion, her passport and papers were to be locked in his safe, and she knew little, if any Spanish. He could hardly see her risking her cover to go to the authorities. She was probably just as worn down as he was by the whole thing as he was. Still, he'd seen firsthand what she was capable of and wouldn't put anything past her.

'Well?' she said.

'I'm not committing to anything. You prove you can be trusted, and then we can talk.'

'Fair enough.'

It looked as if it was about to rain as they pulled into the supermarket in Viveiro.

'We're stopping here for supplies,' he said, 'and then we'll look around for a place to buy some warm clothes.'

She nodded. 'Sounds good to me. My place has a fully contained kitchen, right?'

'Yeah. But you don't have to worry about meals. Rosa will be cooking for us.'

She shook her head. 'I want to do my own cooking.'

'Have it your way then. But remember this: Rosa and Filipe have bent over backwards to make us welcome. Joining us for dinner every now and then isn't too much to ask, is it?'

'If I must.'

He gave her a stony glare. 'It wouldn't be a good look if you didn't, put it that way.'

'Listen,' she snapped, 'before we arrive at this godforsaken place, we need to get one thing clear. I wish to see as little as possible of the pair of them until the baby arrives. Is that understood? Especially her. The last thing I need is some gushy old woman fussing over me.'

'That's a bit harsh, isn't it? After all, Rosa's about to be the baby's adoptive mother.'

She waved her hand dismissively. 'I don't care a shit. I'm perfectly able to take care of myself.'

'I'm not saying you're not.'

'What she does once I've left is fine be me.'

Fabio made no comment. It was early days yet. He was sure that she'd come to appreciate Rosa's expertise in midwifery as she neared full term. For the moment, she appeared strong and healthy enough, with a clean bill of health from doctors before their departure. He just hoped that no complications arose in the meantime. He glanced at the temperature before cutting the engine. 'Thirteen degrees. You'd better put on your jacket.'

The late afternoon air wind salt stung their cheeks as they headed towards the main door, and she zipped her jacket up to her chin. 'Geez, it's like being in frigging Melbourne,' she complained.

Fabio shook his head. The silence had been good while it lasted.

Once they were inside, she took a trolley and headed off on her own, leaving him to complete purchases sent through by Filipe.

After Fabio had loaded their bags into the car, he produced a debit card from his pocket and handed it to her. 'Use this for anything you might need for the baby over the next few months,' he said. 'And that includes your clothes and personal expenses.'

'Thanks,' she said, taking it and slipping it into her purse. 'So, where's this shop you told me about?'

'In the main street, five minutes' walk from here, according to Filipe. We can drive if you like.'

She arched her back, hands on hips. 'No, I'm over sitting down. I could do with a walk.'

Half an hour later, they returned to the car armed with bags of warm clothes. 'Geez, you told me the place was old,' she said, 'but I didn't think it'd be *that* old.'

'I told you it was originally a medieval fishing village,' he said, loading the last of the bags in the back. This part of town is the historic quarter. The stone buildings we passed probably date as far back as the sixteenth century.'

'I was expecting to see more people,' she remarked.

He shook his head. 'We've come at the quietest time of the year. It'll be a different story in summer when the tourists arrive.'

'Well, I'd go nuts living here. Where's the nearest night-life and decent shopping?'

'You mean the nearest city?'

'Yeah.'

'Madrid, I s'pose.'

'And how far away's that?'

'Hundreds of kilometres. You can forget that idea.'

She gave a shrug. 'No harm in asking.'

Fabio shook his head and opened the passenger door for her.

They'd no sooner pulled out of the car park when a few spatters of rain fell onto the dusty windscreen, followed by a sudden, heavy downpour.

'Welcome to Viveiro,' he said, reaching for the wipers.

Angelina made no response, and she sank into the seat, eyes dark. Things were looking grimmer by the minute, and they were yet to set foot on the place. *Four months and you'll be out of here,* she told herself. But it did little to lift her spirits.

The European Development funds had helped better connect the hamlets to the main towns through a series of main roads recently built to the latest standards. Fabio had not yet set eyes on the hamlet, but he envisaged it to be in the middle of nowhere from Antonio's description. He was surprised to discover that it was close to the main road and only a twenty-minute drive from Viveiro.

The dirt track leading down to the property appeared to have been recently graded, and its roadside foliage was well cut back. Apart from that, it was hard to make out anything much at all. The rain had well and truly set in. The wind shook the trees, and the buildings looked like odd-shaped blurs in the distance.

They'd barely pulled up in front of the caretaker's cottage when Angelina remarked, 'You said there's a TV, right?'

He gave a nod.

'And wi-fi?'

'I'm not sure about that one.'

She swung around quickly to face him. 'What do you mean you're not sure? Everyone has wi-fi these days.'

'Not around these parts,' he said. 'From what I've been told, there's 4G Internet service in some places, but they're few and far between.'

'Great,' she muttered angrily as she flung open the door. 'What other surprises am I about to be hit with?'

Moments later, the front door opened, and the couple came forward to greet them. They appeared younger than their sixties at first glance. Although both had grey hair and lined faces, their movements were quick and decisive. Filipe was of average height, with the robust build of a man of the land and his handshake was firm and strong. He wore thick pants, boots and a red flannelette jacket. Rosa was small, plump and business-like with a sharp eye and no-nonsense air, wearing a thick, maroon cardigan and black pants.

She headed straight to Angelina with a customary kiss on each cheek that was met with undisguised contempt. She frowned. Fabio was quick to note and glared at Angelina as they followed the couple inside.

As they entered the main room, flames licked a thick log in the open fireplace, and the place exuded a welcoming ambience. Fabio glanced around in appreciation of the hours it must have taken to bring such an ancient building to its current state. The interior stone had been retained, wooded doors stripped back and rehung, and the ceilings newly painted. Polished wooden furniture gleamed in the firelight like burnished amber, and the kitchen had an old-world charm with its ancient iron oven and large sideboard upon which sat pieces of an old pink and white crockery set.

He turned to Filipe in admiration and struck up a conversation in Portuguese, much to Angelina's annoyance.

'Antonio tells me you did all this yourself, Filipe.'

He nodded. 'A bit hit and miss, but we got there. I'm a farmer by trade. Not a carpenter.'

'Well, you've done an amazing job. I'm impressed.'

'Thanks.'

At that point, Angelina cut in rudely. 'Ask him if there's wi-fi.'

Fabio shot her a stern look and addressed the question to him in Portuguese.

Filipe shook his head. 'Not yet, but it's coming soon, from what I've been told.'

'A fat lot of good that is,' she pouted when he translated the response.

He shrugged. 'People lived without it once, remember.'

'Oh, shut up,' she snapped.

Filipe and Rosa exchanged glances.

Fabio was quick to notice and resumed the conversation in Portuguese. 'You'll get used to it, believe me.'

Filipe grinned. 'Yeah. Antonio told us what to expect.'

Angelina bristled. She knew they were talking about her and wished she'd taken the time to get a handle on the language while she was holed up in the bunker.

'Can I see my place now?' she asked.

Rosa nodded. 'Soon, yes? Dinner first.'

Angelina was about to say she wasn't hungry, but one icy glare from Fabio and she stopped herself short.

'Come,' Rosa beckoned with an enthusiastic nod, 'you sit next to me at table near fire.'

Angelina muttered under her breath but removed her jacket and did what she was told.

She hadn't realised how hungry she was after hours of plastic-wrapped food on the plane, most of which she had barely touched. The pungent aroma of garlic and tomatoes wafted from the kitchen as Rosa pulled out a large pie from the oven with gloved hands and carried it across to the table. 'Empanada,' she said proudly, placing it before them. 'Galician dish. Traditional, yes?'

Angelina tucked into her oversized meal, savouring each bite with relish. To follow was a *filloas* — a sweet-savoury pancake — covered with sugar and cinnamon. She was glad she'd made the decision not to eat alone.

As Rosa cleared the last of the dishes, Angelina sat, arms crossed, bored as Fabio sat, deep in conversation in Portuguese. Rosa was quick to take note. 'You tired. Yes?'

She nodded.

Rosa silenced her husband with her hand and said a few words Angelina couldn't understand. The two men rose, and Fabio said, 'They'll show you over your house now.'

'Thank Christ for that,' she muttered, rising and rubbing her aching shoulders.

Filipe picked up a torch and led the way. The night chill had settled in, making Angelina's teeth chatter, as they made their way along the uneven path towards the old two-storey, stone farmhouse that sat not far from theirs.

An unpleasant odour of dampness, moss and mould hung in the air like an unwelcome guest, evoking unpleasant memories of the farmhouse she'd all but erased from memory. *It had better be nothing like that dump inside,* she thought with gritted teeth.

But the place was not as run-down as she'd expected, and as neat as a pin, thanks to Rosa. Filipe had lit a fire in the main living area's old fireplace and closed both doors to stop the heat from escaping. Two well-worn woollen rugs covered the concrete floor, and she noted two of the windows had new timber frames. *At least a bit of an effort's been made,* she thought. Like the caretaker's cottage, the interior walls were predominantly stone, and the remainder neglected, with paint peeling off in large sections. Ancient wooden beams that could have been hand cut originals crisscrossed the ceilings. The furniture was made of wood and well beyond repair, but she could live with that. An old iron stove lay in the kitchen, beside a brand new one, although the taps and benchtops looked as if they hadn't been replaced for decades.

The wooden stairs leading to the second floor creaked, but the steps, no longer safe, had been newly replaced, along with the banister. Upstairs contained two bedrooms, one with a small bathroom and a ladder leading up to an attic.

Rosa said something to Fabio in Portuguese, and he turned to face Angelina. 'She apologises that there was little time left to touch anything upstairs apart from your bedroom.'

'Tell her I don't care. I'll be out of here soon anyway.'

Angelina could see the muscles of his jaw clench as he turned to the couple and switched to Portuguese once more. 'She says it doesn't bother her and to thank you for all you've done.'

Rosa beamed, and Filipe nodded.

'Look, I think it best we leave her to settle, now,' Fabio continued, doubting his ability to stay calm for much longer. 'It's been a long day.'

'Of course,' Filipe said.

'Look, how about you two head for my cottage and I'll meet you there once I've fetched Ava's bags.'

There was a nod, and the pair walked ahead of him down the stairs.

Soon afterwards, Fabio returned with Angelina's things then walked past her without so much as a goodbye.

And good riddance to you, she thought, slamming the door behind him.

Fabio's house was smaller than Angelina's, but similar improvements had been made. After the pair had shown him around and left, he headed straight to his room. It was time for a shower and a much-needed sleep.

Angelina was relieved to discover that the bed had an electric blanket. She sat down and tested the mattress, nodding with approval. It appeared brand new, a far cry from the bumpy one at the farmhouse. The bright patchwork quilt looked as out of place on the old iron bed as did the thick towels hung on the bathroom's rickety towel rail.

The shower was barely the size of a cupboard, but at least the water was piping hot.

Once she changed into her pyjamas and climbed into bed, her head hit the pillow and she remembered little else.

29

As Fabio made his way to the caretaker's cottage for breakfast, a large black puppy with a shaggy coat and feet way too big for its body came bounding around the corner, almost bowling him over.

'Hello there,' he said in surprise 'where did you come from?'

The dog gave a silly grin, its tail wagging furiously, then proceeded to jump up on Fabio's chest.

'Manuel, get down.' Filipe rushed up to restrain the dog. 'Sit.'

'It's okay. I'm good with dogs,' Fabio said. 'I didn't know you had one, that's all. There was no sign of him when we arrived.'

'No, he was outside, asleep in his kennel. We're just minding him for a few days while my nephew's away on holiday. Talk about a ball of energy. Makes me feel old.'

Fabio laughed. 'Well, running around this place should wear him out.'

'Yeah. I can't keep up with him. Loves people, as you can see. Don't be surprised if he follows you all over the place.'

Fabio nodded, ruffled the dog's ears and followed Filipe into the house.

'Is she still asleep?' Filipe asked after they'd washed their hands and sat down at the table.

'Appears to be.'

'Let me know when she wakes, and I'll get her fire started.'

'Listen, I need to explain a few things,' Fabio said. 'Ava wishes to be left alone for the remainder of her stay.'

'Why?' Rosa was baffled. 'Did we say something wrong last night?'

'No, not at all. It's just her being difficult. You'll get used to it.'

'But I so want her to see the nursery. It's just been painted. There's a new cot and bassinet and –'

'I'd wait for a while, okay?'

'All right then,' she said in disappointment, 'but what about her washing and cooking? I told Antonio –'

Fabio shook his head. 'She wants to handle all that herself.'

The couple exchanged perplexed looks, and Fabio could understand why. They'd spent years in the favela where families and friends dined together and looked out for each other.

'What about shopping?' Rosa asked.

'She can head to town with you when you do your

shopping and get what she wants then.'

'Okay.' Rosa looked far from convinced.

'Look, maybe she'll come around over time,' Fabio remarked, 'but I'm not holding my breath.'

'What on earth has made her this way?' Rosa asked.

He gave a shrug. 'I've asked myself that many times.'

'Do you know anything of her background?' Filipe enquired.

'Not really. Except that she's on the run. But I expect that you know that already.'

There was a nod. 'I have to admit, we were expecting Antonio's niece to be tough and feisty but definitely not as beautiful.'

'Yeah, well, she knows how to use her looks to her advantage. You can't afford to let your guard down for one moment.'

Filipe met his eyes as he reached for another piece of toast. 'We've been around a long time, my boy. She'll soon learn it's a waste of time trying anything on us.'

'Good.'

For another hour the three sat, discussing the favela and the work that Filipe was about to begin on the property.

'Well, yell out if you need a hand,' Fabio said. 'I've got nothing else to do. Besides, some physical work will do me good.'

'I might just hold you to that.'

'Well, thanks for breakfast.' Fabio rose from the table. 'I

thought I might take a look around before the rain sets in. It looks pretty bleak out there.'

Filipe nodded. 'It's what you'll get at this time of year. Do you want me to go with you?'

'No, thanks anyway. I'm sure you've things to attend to.'

'Well, make sure you wear a coat and boots.'

'I've come prepared.'

Fabio glanced up at Angelina's window as he headed towards the track that led down through the orchard, the dog at his side. The curtains were still drawn. He wondered whether he would catch sight of her at all that day. *Not my problem*, he thought, as his feet crunched over the wet gravel. It would be interesting to see how things eventually panned out. One thing was for sure, if she wanted to play things this way, it'd make his job a helluva lot easier.

The fog looked like it had set in, and he found himself blowing on his hands to warm them. Next time, he'd have gloves at the ready. He could hear the faint lowing of cattle in the distance, and close to the brook, a bunch of grazing goats looked up with childlike curiosity.

He looked forward to seeing the property when visibility was better, especially the brook that Filipe said wound around to a small waterfall. He wondered if it contained fish. For now, he'd head back to the farm buildings — the part he most wanted to see. As a boy, he loved to explore and play make-believe amongst the alleyways and staircases of the favela where he was raised. Sometimes, he'd climb up the hills to where the houses ended and the terrain became wild and tangled, imagining he was a policeman in pursuit of some fugitive.

Fabio had never seen houses or buildings this old and was itching to see what was behind the ancient facades and stone fences. From what Filipe had said, four families and their descendants had occupied the houses for the last hundred and twenty years.

He stopped to get his torch and looked around, lost in time for the next hour, crouching down through old door-ways and stepping inside darkened buildings, gagging on the thick dust and stepping over fallen beams and boul-ders. Only the downpour that looked like having no sign of abating called a halt to his efforts. The old cowshed and granary on stilts would have to wait until next time.

¶

Angelina awoke, disoriented and confused in the darkness of a room blackened out by heavy, drawn curtains. The orange fluoro numbers of the clock on the bedside table registered she'd slept for twelve hours straight.

'Shit,' she muttered. Swinging her legs to the floor, she fumbled for the lamp switch, then padded across to the window to pull aside the drapes. It was raining outside as she half expected, with no signs of letting up. The view over the orchard was marred by thick fog. It looked as gloomy as she felt.

She had no intentions of venturing outside. She would spend the remainder of the day familiarising herself with her immediate surroundings and unpacking her things. It was too late to light the fire, so she switched on the small heater in the main living area, closing both doors to trap in the heat. After a light dinner, she kicked off her shoes and sat in the old winged armchair, pulling the cushion behind her back and turning on the television to see what stations were available. As expected, there was no Sky Digital access. And to her dismay, the choice of free-to-air channels was limited to just three: a twenty-four-hour news channel and two international ones: Galicia Television Europa and Galicia Television America. 'Oh my God! You can't be serious,' she cried out in disbelief. The months ahead didn't bear thinking about.

¶

Over the next four days, steady rain hampered Angelina's attempts to step outside, and she began to feel like a cooped-up homing pigeon. Rain splashed against the outside walls and onto the path below. And in the blackened chimney, the wind howled like an angry banshee. The only thing that stopped her from going mad was the trip to town with Filipe and Rosa for weekly supplies.

¶

The second week showed more promise. The weather held up, and the sight of the sun peeping through the clouds lifted her spirits. Her baby bump was now prominent, much to her annoyance, but she used it as an incentive to resume exercising, determined to see her figure return to normal as soon as possible post-birth. With new resolve, she set up a daily routine, beginning with lighting the fire followed by breakfast and an hour's walk down the path alongside the river, looping back up through the orchard. This she continued, regardless of the weather.

It was during one of these walks that the thought first entered her mind. 'Shit, that's it!' She yelled, causing a nearby bird to take off in alarm, and wondered why she hadn't thought of it before.

Finally, she had the means to turn the birth to her advantage.

With a renewed sense of purpose, she set about using the remaining few months to formulate a plan. Little did she know that a chance meeting would bring a twist of fate that would move her life in yet another direction.

Fabio and Filipe were fixing a fence on the orchard's perimeter when Angelina appeared in the distance.

'Good to see her out walking,' Filipe remarked.

'Yeah, and she's actually responding instead of grunting.' Filipe grinned.

'Might as well put it to her now, eh?'

There was a nod.

As she approached, Fabio beckoned her across with a wave.

'How've you been?' he asked.

'Okay,' she said warily. 'You?'

'All good. Anything you need?'

'No, nothing I can think of.'

'Filipe's just been telling me about an internet café in town. Thought you might be interested.'

His words caused a rush of excitement. 'Really?'

He gave a nod. 'Would you like me to take you there?'

'You bet I would. When?'

'Would tomorrow do?'

'Hell yeah!' she flashed a winning smile that left both men gaping in astonishment.

'Be out at the car at one, then.'

'Thanks.' There was a spring in her step as she headed off, reminding Fabio of a young girl about to choose her first puppy.

'She should smile like that more often,' Filipe remarked.

'Yeah, she should,' Fabio concurred as they resumed work. His mind turned to the coming months. Things had worked out well so far. But he feared that stormy times were ahead, given what Rosa had told him to expect with the final stages of Angelina's pregnancy. He could only hope that there'd be no complications.

He felt comforted that Rosa would be close at hand.

❡

Fabio looked twice when Angelina stepped out of the farmhouse and walked towards the car. Her shoulder-length, dark hair was freshly washed and blow-dried, her face impeccably made up, and she wore the stylish red cashmere jacket and black woollen pants outfit purchased in Viveiro that could have belonged to any model. She certainly had the trademark glide of one as she approached, despite her prominent bump. He was surprised he'd never noticed that before.

'You're only spending a few hours on a computer,' he remarked as he opened her door.

'Maybe, but do you know how long it's been since I've been out anywhere?'

Her words had him thinking. Truth was, probably not since she accompanied Antonio to the restaurant to meet with the drug dealer. If getting dressed up made her happy, then why not, he thought. Ava had not much else to look forward to over the next few months.

'You didn't have to tell me about the internet café,' she said, clicking her seat belt in place. 'Could've left me holed up in that dump. So why did you?'

'I told you I'd rethink things if you proved you could be trusted.'

'So you think I can be, now?'

'No, not at all.'

Angelina's face flushed in anger. 'I suppose you're going to sit beside me all afternoon.'

'I wouldn't go as far as to say that, but I won't be far away.'

'Of course, you won't.'

Angelina crossed her arms and glared out of the window, not uttering a word until they arrived.

The icy wind swirled as they cut through an ancient, stone-paved walkway, now an undercover mall, and headed to the small group of shops of which the internet café was one. Elena Perez stood behind the counter, inspecting her chipped nails. No one was in the café except a thin backpacker near the back wall, with scraggly long hair under a beanie, eyes glued to the screen. At this time of the year, the days passed painfully slowly. Just the odd traveller passing through, or regulars from the countryside with no wi-fi access, spending a few hours getting square-eyed when they came to town for supplies. Summertime was different altogether. The place was jam-packed with tourists, with every computer station occupied. It was the time of year the owner made most of his money and put on extra staff.

Elena had arrived recently from Puenete de Vallecas, one of the poorest parts of Madrid, desperately in need of work and a place of refuge from her alcoholic father and controlling two brothers. She remembered little of her mother, who'd walked out when she was a young child, and she'd not heard from since.

Things hadn't always been bad. Her father had done his best to hold the family together, working long hours on a low wage to pay the rent on the shabby flat she'd spent most of her life in, and bills and food. But when he injured his back at work and was laid off indefinitely, he took out a debt that he had no hope of repaying, and things quickly got out of hand. He took to drinking, and his two teen-age sons were quick to take advantage, wagging school and running amok. By the time Elena fled, they'd become heavily entrenched in a local criminal gang and behaved violently towards her.

If not for her father, she would have cleared out long ago. He'd done his best, and she felt the least she could do was bring some money in for food and other essentials. Her brothers' efforts to contribute were spasmodic, depending on how much they made, or as time wore on, whether they chose to or not.

At sixteen, she dropped out of school and began searching for work. It wasn't easy. Jobs were hard to come by, and those available were usually short-term prospects. Elena had held six different positions as kitchen hand and cleaner by the time she was nineteen, all for little pay. Her father's money had all but dried up, and she could no longer cover the costs of his drinking. As time went on, he became morose, bitter and filled with self-hatred.

The day she approached her oldest brother for more money to help out and was met with a brutal smash across the face was when she decided to leave.

She glanced at the clock on the wall. Another six hours to go. She had almost forgotten what it was like not to work. She'd quit her previous job as a dishwasher on the spot and had landed the internet café job within a day of her arrival. The few nights she spent clubbing in Madrid were now a long distant memory.

She wistfully recalled the day she sat alongside her closest friend, Damita, experimenting with make-up and hairstyles as thirteen-year-olds. They had such plans: good jobs, money, boyfriends and travel. She flicked on her phone's camera roll and scrolled through the selfies they'd taken, photos she was glad she'd not deleted.

She'd lost track of Damita long ago and found herself wondering if she'd any more luck in fulfilling her dreams. Probably not. Damita lived in a small, shabby flat not dissimilar to her own, alongside five siblings. Her parents worked long hours with little pay, and the chance of a decent education for any of them was next to nil. More than likely, Damita would be working in a lowly paid job as she had. Elena could only hope that she wasn't struggling somewhere as a single mother — an all-too-familiar fate in these parts.

She was about to pour a pack of coffee beans into the grinder when something caught her eye. A young couple was crossing the street and heading her way. They oozed class; the man, tall with Chris Hemsworth looks and the woman equally as stunning in her stylish, red jacket. It was rare to see people of their ilk in town.

As they neared, Elena's eyes were drawn to the woman's face and perfect make-up. *Are those lashes natural or extensions,* she found herself wondering. It was only after the woman's partner departed that Elena noted the bump under her red jacket.

Angelina caught the look of admiration on the girl's face the moment she stepped inside the café and thought with accustomed arrogance, *I've still got what it takes.*

The girl appeared to be a year or so younger than she, with long hair that needed a wash, pulled tightly back in a ponytail. She wore black as expected for a café worker, but her black leggings and short, tight top accentuated the extra weight she carried. *Why do they let themselves go like this?* Angelina wondered with disdain.

'What time do you close?' she asked.

'Five-thirty,' came the response.

'Good.'

There was a pause. 'Was that your husband outside?'

'No, it was not.' Angelina snapped. 'Any more questions?'

The girl flushed and quickly shook her head.

'Good. I'll let you know when I'm in need of a coffee.' Angelina strode to a computer station at the far wall and unzipped her laptop bag.

Her eyes barely moved from the screen until the time she rose to leave and paid for the time. Elena wondered whether she would see her again.

Fabio noted a distinct change in Angelina's demeanour when they met outside the café at five. The anger had vanished and, in its place, purpose and focus. On the walk back to the car, he found himself wondering whom she'd emailed, which websites she'd accessed.

¶

There was a marked improvement in Angelina's behaviour in the days that followed, and Fabio could see no reason not to allow more internet café visits if that's what kept her happy. He knew she would be getting in touch with contacts and making arrangements for the future, whatever they might be. It didn't worry him. In fact, he was looking forward to spending more time in town, if the first visit was anything to go by — lunch at the local, followed by an afternoon unwinding in a leather chair with a beer, watching the soccer and getting some welcome wi-fi access himself.

The sooner Ava was out of the country, the better. His initial fears of her becoming part of the gang and a threat to his future were now long gone. The look of utter contempt she shot Antonio the day she left the gang's headquarters was all Fabio needed. Even better, the look was reciprocated.

30

Fabio was tying up his runners when his mobile rang.

'Hi, Boss. What's up?'

'Nothing. Just checking in. Everything okay?'

'Yep. Just about to head out for a run.'

'I should start up again myself. What's the weather like?'

'Shit.'

'Bit different from Rio, eh,' Antonio said with a laugh. 'So, how's the girl? Still up to her tricks?'

'Let's say we've come to an agreement.'

'Oh?'

'She behaves herself, and in return she gets wi-fi access three days a week.'

There was a roar of laughter.

'Ingenious. How do you manage that?'

'Filipe put me onto an internet café in town.'

'Do you stay there with her?'

'Nah, that'd be pushing things.'

'You're not worried about her doing a runner?'

'Where would she go?'

'You've got a point.'

'I'm never far away, don't worry.'

'You know what you're doing. So, what does she do all day at the hamlet?'

'God knows. We hardly see her.'

'Still? I thought she'd have joined you for meals by now.'

'Nope. Keeps to herself. Have you spoken to her since we arrived?'

'No. I might get around to it.'

Fabio made no comment.

'Well, I'll let you get on with your run,' Antonio said. 'Let me know if you need anything.'

There was a click at the other end.

As Fabio jogged down the track, he wondered whether Antonio would visit his niece before she left for Australia. He doubted it.

§

It was 6 p.m. when Filipe's nephew came to pick up the dog.

'Sorry, I'm late,' he said as he entered the house. 'Got stuck in traffic.'

'Not a problem,' Filipe said, taking his coat. 'As long as you're okay.'

'So, how's the boy been? Not too much trouble, I hope. I've missed him.'

There was a pause.

'He's all right, isn't he?'

'Yes, yes, he's fine, it's just — well, Rosa and I have had some concerns over the last few days. He hasn't appeared quite himself.'

Filipe made no mention of the dog's guardedness, the way it cowered when approached. Rosa was slowly coaxing it around, and it was gaining back some of its appetite. He could only think that it had been kicked or chased by the less than friendly gander, or a cow perhaps?

'He's probably missing you, that's all,' he concluded, hoping that he was right.

To his relief, the dog pricked up its ears at the sound of his nephew's voice and rushed across to greet him.

9

The moment Angelina entered the internet café, her eyes fixed on the hair of the girl who'd worked there three days prior. It was cleanly washed, blow-dried, in the same style as her own. A bit shorter, but even the parting was the same. The girl shifted uneasily, her eyes averted.

'I didn't think you'd be back,' she said.

Angelina said nothing and proceeded to a nearby table.

It was the first time in her life that Elena had come across someone so glamorous, and she found herself wondering where the woman was from, what she was doing there. A mixture of awe and curiosity had led to the question about her relationship with the man outside. The

240

sharp response had come as little surprise. It was naïve to think she'd disclose anything about her life. But it had been worth a try, all the same.

Angelina paid the girl scant attention for the remainder of the afternoon except to order a coffee and give a perfunctory glance as she headed off at the end of the day.

⁊

Over the next month, Angelina appeared at the café three days a week. Elena became accustomed to her surly demeanour, which she simply shrugged aside. Meanwhile, she watched intently and began mimicking Angelina's mannerisms, taking note of her make-up, her choice of clothes. The only way she saw herself getting somewhere in life was to become sophisticated like the woman before her. Nonetheless, the intrigue of Angelina's identity and what she was doing there was never far from Elena's mind, as was the man who accompanied her there. Was she free to come and go at will? Elena had her doubts. One thing was clear: there was no love lost between them.

Another thing of intrigue was the content of the sites the woman accessed during her visits. Elena dared to peek one day when curiosity got the better of her. She noted that Angelina appeared unusually unsettled and agitated as she worked, fingers tapping the keys impatiently and eyes never leaving the screen.

The café was near to total capacity as Elena weaved

between the tables, delivering coffee and cleaning work-spaces while hovering and observing. Angelina was feverishly typing in one Google search after another on the breaking news story concerning the latest global police sting bringing hundreds of drug lords and organised criminal gangs to their knees. When Elena first heard of it, her immediate thoughts turned to her brothers.

She continued to watch. There had to be a correlation between the sting and those she mixed with. Her troubled expression attested to that.

Interesting, Elena thought, as she gathered the last of the cups.

¶

Angelina sat at the old kitchen table, cold dinner before her. It seemed incredible that the encrypted communication devices commonly used by the criminal underworld to freely exchange messages undetected were, in fact, traps planted by the police.

Years of recorded conversations had been stored and decrypted, with hundreds of raids and arrests made globally over the past twenty-four hours alone. It came as some comfort that there was no mention of anyone she'd been involved with. But it was early days yet …

Beads of sweat formed on her brow. What would happen if Antonio was nabbed, she found herself wondering. Would he rat on her? She wouldn't put it past him. You're probably worrying over nothing, she reassured herself. He's been in the game for too long to get nailed.

Little did she know that at that very moment, Antonio was scrambling for cover after having just returned from Columbia, where he'd signed off on the biggest cocaine deal of his life.

It came as no surprise that the big gangs had been targeted first. Her mind turned to Isaac's gang in Nigeria. She may well have taken up his offer to join him there had Antonio not appeared on the scene. She'd simply run out of places to hide.

Angelina shivered. Where would she have been then? Perhaps embroiled in the biggest shake-up that the country's underworld had ever faced; holed up somewhere with Isaac in some squalid high-rise, in fear of her life. He'd promised she'd be free to return home if things didn't work out. But upon reflection, she doubted he would have kept his word. No one in the criminal world was to be trusted. The past few months on the run had taught her that. But like it or not, she needed her contacts a while longer. Especially with what she had in mind.

As a child, her random attacks carried out on people's pets had emboldened her with a sense of daring and invincibility that had only strengthened as the years wore on. Killing had been easy — until the failed attempt on her sister's life. She'd come so close to losing it all ... so close. A sobering reminder that killing was best left to the professionals because they did the job right.

Rodriguez was a testament to that. His masterminding of Dominic's hit job was clinical. No loose ends; nothing to link her at all. She didn't mind paying for the best when it came to her contacts. It put their lives on the line, not hers.

31

'**H**ave you seen Mum?' Cara asked Will.

'She's gone to check the mail box,' he said, looking up from the decking, where he was crouched, nail gun in hand. 'What do you think?' he asked.

'It looks amazing. Mum's so grateful for all you've done.'

'Too easy. I should only be a few more days on this then I'll start on the kitchen cupboards.'

'Are you sure? You've only got a week left of your holidays. Why don't you give things a break?'

'Keeps me busy. Only happy to help out,' he said. 'I'm quite enjoying it actually. Have you two chosen the cupboards you want?'

'No, we're getting round to it. I can tell you one thing though, I can't wait to get rid of the old ones. They're so ugly.'

He nodded with a grin. 'I've seen better.'

'Mum doesn't think much of them either. I don't know how she put up with them as long as she has.'

Will raised an eyebrow.

'Dad was a tightarse when it came to anything that needed to be done around the house,' she paused. 'A different matter when it came to his women.'

'I'm sorry.'

'Don't be. That's all over now.'

Will's thoughts strayed to his own father, who was stingy in his own right. But much as Will hated to admit it, his father had good reason. To begin with, at least. There hadn't been much left after a bitter divorce. Corners were cut and sacrifices made to keep a roof over their heads and put food on the table. *But you weren't so stingy with your bloody alcohol, were you Dad*, he thought scathingly.

'Will? You okay?'

'Yeah, just thinking.'

'About your dad?'

He nodded.

'It's a shit, isn't it, growing up with dads like ours; stepdad in my case.'

He held her eyes. *Perhaps it's why we came together in the first place, Cara Lorenzo*, he thought. He always knew he'd come back to her. He'd never stopped caring, daring to dream that she'd one day feel the same. And when the truth came out about her sister, his very existence became about protecting her.

Cara, still waiting for a response to her remark, reddened and averted her eyes. 'I wonder why Mum's taking so long,' her voice sounding shrill in her ears. 'I think I'll go check.'

'I'll go with you, if you like. I'm about done for the day.'

'That'd be good.'

The morning winter's sun was just beginning to peep through the grey clouds as they headed towards the driveway.

'So, how's your mum's birthday preparations going?'

'Good. The cake's been ordered and I've asked the guests to arrive a bit earlier. The plan is for them to be seated when she walks in.'

'Where are we taking her?'

'The local Thai restaurant. Her favourite.'

He nodded. 'She still has no idea?'

'None whatsoever.'

'I wanted to make sure things were special. Her last birthday was a complete write- off.'

'Why's that?'

'There were no birthday celebrations. Nothing to celebrate. I'd had a massive row with Dad over taking a break from uni and Gran's dog was found with its throat cut, causing her a massive heart attack.'

'Geez.'

'It was touch and go whether she'd live and she died not long afterwards.' Cara paused. 'It hit Mum pretty hard. Those two were close. Then Dad cracked it and went back to town — something to do with Gran's will, I think.' She ran a hand through her hair. 'God, I don't know how Mum managed to keep herself together.'

They passed the sweeping curve of the driveway and

Jennifer came into view, at the letterbox.

'What's been keeping her?' Cara said.

'Perhaps she's only just got there.' Will suggested, 'Perhaps she's been sent some birthday cards.'

Cara looked at him. 'Oh shit!' She tore off down the driveway without another word.

Will, bewildered, took off after her.

Cara held out her hand. 'Show me, Mum.' The words were gentle.

Jennifer passed over the card with trembling hands.

"Happy birthday Mum," the message read, "I'm thinking of you. Sorry I couldn't be there to share it with you but I'll be back soon. I've got a present for you. The biggest surprise ever. Your loving daughter, Angelina."

'Christ!' Will said, looking over Cara's shoulder. 'We need to get on to the police about this.'

'You don't think, she'll come this time, do you?' Jennifer said to him.

He shook his head. 'She's way too smart for that.' But deep down, Will feared she would be back, at a time least expected.

'Shit, is this never going to end!' Cara cried out angrily. 'Why can't she leave us alone?'

'It's exactly the reaction she'd want from you,' Will said calmly. 'It's your mother's birthday and we're going to make it a good one. Come on, let's get back to the house. I wouldn't mind a coffee right now.'

Once they were inside, Jennifer headed upstairs to call

the police. Cara sat perched on a stool, beside Will, behind the bench as the coffee machine warmed up.

'She'll never feel like going out tonight after this,' Cara said despondently.

'Yes she will. I'll take you both for a drive to look at some kitchen places. That'll keep her mind off things. By the time we have a bite to eat along the way and get back, it'll be time to go.'

'Thanks.' Cara touched his arm lightly and his heart skipped a beat.

'No probs.'

'David's coming, isn't he?'

'Of course. He's driving down from Melbourne. He's been spending a few days with his mother. She's not been well.'

'Not serious, I hope.'

'Just old age, I think.'

'Do you think he'll ever get back together with your mum?'

'I'm not sure,' Cara said with a sigh. 'I'd give anything for that to happen. I think they still love each other but you know what –' she paused, 'I think that it's probably all a bit late.'

It's never too late. He kept the comment to himself.

32

The wind was icy as Angelina and Fabio headed along the cobbled street towards the internet café, and she welcomed the rush of warm air that met her as she stepped inside.

'I thought you might be in today so I turned up the heat,' Elena remarked, as if reading her mind.

Angelina was about to respond when a woman in her thirties with spiked, dyed blonde hair came through the door behind her. She glanced at each in turn. 'Are you two sisters?' she asked.

'No, we're not.' Angelina's response was curt.

'Oh, well, you sure look alike. Can I sit anywhere?'

Elena nodded.

'I'm only here for an hour. Got to pick my kid up at two,' said the blonde, as she headed to a nearby computer.

Angelina ordered a latte, removed her coat and settled at a station near the window. When the coffee arrived, she gave a brief nod and watched the girl as she walked away.

There were similarities between them, she found herself thinking. The same heart-shaped face and olive complexion. *Her features are not as prominent as mine, though. And she's not as tall. But that's nothing a pair of heels couldn't fix.* The girl's eyes were not as dark and dramatic but her hair had the same glossy texture, although lighter.

She stirred a spoonful of sugar into her cup and took a sip thoughtfully. The germ of an idea was forming in her mind in which the girl could prove herself useful.

Angelina barely focused on her computer for the next few hours, and before she realised it was time to leave. She placed the laptop in its bag and headed across to pay the bill.

'What's your name?' she asked as she tapped her credit card.

'Elena.'

Angelina nodded. Reaching into her laptop bag, she pulled out two fashion magazines she'd purchased at the airport; *Harper's Bazaar* and *Elle*.

'I'm finished with them. You can have them if you want.'

'Really?' the girl said excitedly. 'Thanks.'

'Do you work here every day?'

'Yeah, except Sundays.'

'I might be in on Thursday.'

Elena watched Angelina leave, her pulse racing. Moments later she picked up the first magazine and began flipping through. Pages of sophisticated, beautiful women like the one who'd just left. She would give anything to look that way.

She'd hoped that she'd one day get to travel the world; get a taste of the high life. She glanced around at her shabby surroundings. The owner had made few improvements since he'd taken over. It was almost as if he was waiting for the opportunity to sell. Wi-fi was about to become widely accessible in the region, and once that happened, the café and her job would be obsolete.

§

Thursday was busy in the café, and Elena only got to speak to Angelina as she was leaving.

'Thanks for the magazines,' she said. 'You're just like one of the models. I wish l could look like you.'

'Well, if you had some decent make-up, you could make yourself quite attractive.'

'But that's expensive.'

'If I remember, I'll bring in some that I no longer use.' She headed to her usual spot and pulled out a chair. 'Get me some coffee, would you?' she said over her shoulder. 'And make it a double shot.'

§

It was Jennifer's birthday, May 12th, and Angelina sat drinking a cup of tea before the open fire. The card would have arrived by now. She reflected on the words she'd penned about dropping by for a birthday surprise, and a smile came to her lips. *Not yet Mum*, she thought, moving a finger slowly around the rim of the teacup, *not yet …*

A storm was approaching, and the wind screamed. Windows rattled, the old house groaned and the afternoon clouds morphed from dark grey to black. Reaching into the old crate, she took hold of a log and threw it on the fire, prodding with the rusty poker until there was an explosion of orange. She sat, curled up on the sofa, pillow pulled to her chest, watching the fire sizzle and dance. Content.

At closing time, the following day, Angelina produced a small make-up bag and placed it on the counter.

'Experiment with this and let's see what you come up with,' she told Elena and left without saying another word.

ʃ

'What the hell!' Angelina exclaimed the moment set her eyes on Elena three days later. 'You look like a hooker. Is that how you want to come across?'

'Of course not,' Elena stammered.

'Well, you could have fooled me.'

Elena's heart sank. She'd never used make-up much except for the rare times clubbing with friends. There'd been no point in wearing it to work. There was no one to impress in a steamy kitchen or an apartment about to be cleaned.

She'd spent the past two nights experimenting with the make-up Angelina had given her, flipping through the magazines and trying out one look then the next.

'I just don't know how to look like you,' she said, looking down.

'I can show you if you wish.'

'Really?'

'Is there a back room we can use?'

'Yes,' Elena nodded towards a nearby door, heart racing. 'It's the staff room.'

'If I remember, I'll bring in some make-up next time I come.'

'Great. Thanks.'

Long after Angelina left, Elena found herself wondering why the woman was paying her attention like this.

9

Three days later, Elena ushered Angelina into the small staffroom that served as a storeroom. Angelina removed her coat, tossed it over one of the two plastic chairs on either side of the coffee-stained table, and pointed to the other.

'Take it over to the mirror and sit down,' she ordered. 'If the bell rings, I'll deal with it.'

She closed the door and headed across to Elena with a striped make-up bag, spreading its contents on the small ledge below the mirror.

'What are your favourite lipsticks?' Elena asked out of curiosity, surprised that her question wasn't met by a cutting remark.

'I particularly like this shade of pink,' Angelina pointed to a lipstick, 'with this nail polish to match. You'll find that coral and poppy colours best suit olive skins like ours.'

'And reds?'

'Reds have to be chosen with care. As do eyeliner and mascara. They're not to be slapped on thickly like I saw you do yesterday.'

The words stung, but they only hardened Elena's resolve. This was her one chance to learn.

'You must choose your make-up to suit the occasion,' Angelina began as she reached for a primer. 'Certain circumstances call for a dramatic look, but you don't have to overstate things to make an impression. Keep things subtle, okay?'

Elena nodded, soaking up every word.

'It's simply a matter of practice.' Angelina continued. 'Get into the habit of applying your make-up and doing your hair every day before you leave for work. You never know who might walk through the door.'

For the next hour, Elena watched as Angelina reached for one product and then another, applying each with expert precision and explaining each process as she went.

'There' Angelina finished with a flourish. She smiled to herself as she glanced at their reflections in the mirror. There was a resemblance all right.

Elena stared in the mirror, barely able to comprehend what she was seeing. The peach gloss lipstick made her lips fuller; the mascara, eyeliner and muted eye shadow gave her eyes a sensual allure and the subtly applied blush accentuated cheekbones she never knew she had.

'I can't believe it's really me. Thanks so much.'

A girl just like Elena sprung to Angelina's mind. A girl at school with long, mousy hair who'd idolised her; did what she was told to do. Took the wrap if need be. It hadn't taken much.

'Now stand up and let me look at you.'

When Elena did so, Angelina looked her up and down with a frown. 'You need to lose some weight. You know that, don't you.'

Elena's face reddened. 'Yeah, I know.' She quickly looked down. 'I've tried before, but I can't.'

'That's crap,' Angelina snapped. 'Look at me.'

Elena slowly raised her head.

'You said you wanted to be like me, didn't you?'

There was a nod.

'Well, make-up alone won't cut it. You need to be slim as well, so that you can wear whatever you wish, knowing you look damned good in it. And that comes with a healthy diet and regular fitness routine.'

Elena bristled. She felt like shouting 'You think I don't know that? You think I haven't gone on every diet there is?' But she remained silent.

'It takes self-discipline, commitment.' Angelina pushed on relentlessly. 'There's no such word as can't.'

'Okay.'

'Take me, for instance. You've got no idea how much I

hate lugging this baby around. I've never been fat in my life, and I'm used to pushing my fitness levels to the limit. I just want life to return to normal.'

'So the baby wasn't planned then –' the words spilled out before Elena had time to stop them.

'That's none of your concern!' Angelina snapped.

'I didn't mean –'

'Now, let's just get one thing straight. What happens in my life is my business. If I want your opinion, I'll ask for it. Understood?'

Elena nodded, hands squeezed in tight balls against her thighs.

'Good. Now that's clear, let's get back to your weight. Are you willing to take some advice?'

Elena's hand unconsciously went to her neck. 'Yeah, I could do with some help.'

'All right then. Let's go out to the café, where we can sit and talk. While I'm finishing up here, you can make us a coffee.'

The café was quiet, and they sat until closing time.

Long after Angelina had left, Elena sat alone in the darkness, reflecting on the discussion that had just taken place. If only things were that easy. Elena thought of the block of chocolate at home she'd yet to open and the tray of lasagne in the fridge: that night's dinner. Just how she liked it — double quantity of cheese and an extra layer of pasta. The generous portion she dished up usually ended up as two, with leftovers, if any, heated up as snacks the next day.

As for the exercise Angelina insisted on … she groaned inwardly at the thought. It was one thing to get up early to go for a walk, but jogging? She'd tried before. Each step had left her gasping for breath, her legs feeling like they'd been weighed down by lead, and with her thighs chafed and red. Weight sessions at the gym held more appeal, but the cost made that impractical.

She'd lied to Angelina when she said she'd never been more motivated about losing weight, made a commitment she had no idea how she'd keep. She slumped in her chair and ran her hands down her face. 'Christ, what have I got myself into,' she muttered. What was it? Twenty kilos she had to lose? She glanced across at the glass cabinet that contained leftover cakes and slices about to be replaced. Usually, they went home with her.

That evening, with gritted teeth, she tossed the entire tray of lasagne in the bin and assembled a salad with ingredients purchased on the way home. Without the dressing, it might as well have been a bowl of crunched up leaves. The meagre portion of chicken was hardly satisfying, and she wished there was a fresh roll with lashings of butter to follow. By 3 a.m. she was wide awake, stomach rumbling like a freight train. She cursed and rolled over to the other side. Every diet blog she'd read told her that hunger pangs never lasted long, but it took every ounce of willpower not to swing her legs off the bed and make her way to the pantry.

❡

Angelina didn't show the next day, and the café was busier than usual. Before Elena knew it, it was closing time. As she cleaned up, she took time to reflect. The weight loss steps she'd taken so far were clearly not sustainable: an apple for breakfast, a repeat of last night's salad for lunch, black coffee instead of full cream milk. She was starving, and her legs felt weak. The jog she'd attempted that morning had ended up as a walk. There had to be a better way, on her terms and in her own time.

The next day, Angelina placed a bag on the counter when she walked in.

'See what you think,' she said, watching as Elena pulled out a set of size six running pants and a matching top. 'A few sizes too small, I know, but I thought you could use them as inspiration. Always works for me,' she said ingratiatingly. 'They're Lulu Lemon — one of Australia's best-selling brands. I've only worn them a few times.'

Rage burned deep within Elena like an angry beast, and it took all her self-control to keep her voice neutral. 'Thanks, but you didn't have to.'

'Why not? The colour will look good on you,' she said with a shrug. 'By the way, you've done a good job on your make-up. You obviously took a selfie like I suggested.'

There was a nod.

'For all my troubles, you can do me a favour.'

So that's what all this has been leading up to, Elena thought. 'Oh? What's that?'

'I'd like a bottle of alcohol now and then. Can you do that for me?'

'Yeah. That's no problem.'

'Good. I'll transfer the money in advance once I get your bank details.'

'Okay.'

'Just one bottle at a time will do. Make it vodka for starters.'

'When do you want it by?'

'I'll be in tomorrow.'

Elena nodded. 'I'll call by the bottle shop on the way home.'

As Angelina headed to her usual spot, Elena wondered what was stopping her from getting it herself.

A few hours later, two women arrived at the café and walked over to the counter. One was in her seventies and the other around fiftyish, a younger version of her companion, with dark eyes and short black hair streaked with grey.

'Do you speak Italian?' the younger asked in a thick accent.

'Si,' Elena answered. 'Che cosa vorresti sapere?'

Angelina swung around on her chair in surprise.

The conversation continued in Italian for a minute, and Elena pointed down the street and said a few more words.

'Grazie,' each said in turn and left.

'I thought you were Spanish,' Angelina remarked.

'I am. But I'm fluent in Italian. We learned it in school, as well as English.'

Angelina leaned forward. 'Is that so? Do you speak other languages as well?'

'About four. Enough to get by, anyway. You have to in this business, especially in the summer.'

Angelina nodded and turned back to what she'd been doing, eyes thoughtful. This put a totally different slant on things.

The mention of school and languages brought up memories that Elena had forced from her mind since she'd arrived in Viveiro. Languages came easy to her, and her Italian class was the one she looked forward to the most. By year eight, she'd won an interschool Italian recital competition, and her teacher had recommended that she continue to higher studies. 'You could make a career as an interpreter,' she'd said.

Yeah, right, Elena thought bitterly. She would have liked to go further in school. Learning came easily, and with good results.

But it became a matter of putting food on the table.

33

Elena turned up as promised the following day with a bottle of vodka inside a brown bag.

'Good girl,' Angelina gave her one of her inimitable smiles and Elena's jaw dropped.

'Any time.'

Angelina took the bottle and shoved it in her laptop case, glad Elena purchased the bigger one. 'You can call me Ava if you wish.'

'Okay,' the response was wary.

'Perhaps we could have another chat later.'

Elena hesitated, wondering where all this was heading. 'If you want.'

Just after four, Angelina logged off and called Elena across. 'I'm finished now,' she said. 'How about you make us a coffee, and we can have that chat.'

Elena nodded and headed back to the counter.

Angelina gave a nod of approval to the cup of black coffee placed opposite hers. Elena pretended not to notice as she pulled out a chair. *You'd better not start about my weight,* she thought. *If so, your little chat won't go for long.*

There was a sudden loud pit-a-pat on the tin roof, and Angelina glanced up with a scowl.

'Don't you get sick of it?' she asked.

'I'm used to it, I s'pose. It'll become dry soon, once summer hits. You'll love it. The days are warm and sunny, and things really liven up around here.'

Angelina pursed her lips. *Yeah, just as I'm about to leave,* she thought. 'So, what does the temperature get to?'

'Around 23-26 degrees most days — nothing like the heat you'd be used to.' She paused. 'You are from Australia, right?'

'What's it to you?' Angelina shot back.

'Oh nothing.' Elena had expected such a response. She'd been angling for an opening into Ava's background, what she was doing there. It had been worth a try. 'I just like to guess where people come from by their accents,' she said with a shrug. 'Australians aren't hard to pick.'

Elena had been captivated by Australia since she saw a documentary as a child, in awe of its stunning scenery, wide-open spaces, amazing wildlife and cosmopolitan cities. The beautiful, long stretches of coastline left Galicia's beaches for dead. *One day, I'll make it there,* she thought. *If only it wasn't so damned far away.*

'So, tell me a bit about yourself, Elena,' the words interrupted her thoughts. 'Do you come from around here?'

'No, I'm from Madrid. I've only been here a year.'

'Are your family with you?'

'No, I left without telling them.' It felt good to be opening like this. Elena supposed it couldn't do any harm. 'Things weren't good at home.'

'I see,' Angelina's eyes never left hers. 'So, any intentions of returning?'

'My family are dead to me,' Elena looked down, rolling the ends of the serviette tightly between her fingers.

'I know the feeling.'

Elena gave her a look.

'So, do you live by yourself?' Angelina continued.

There was a nod. 'Why are you asking me all this?'

'Just curious.' she took a sip of coffee. 'Tell me something, Elena, what do you plan to do with your life?'

'Huh? What do you mean?'

'Well, are you intending to settle here, start a family perhaps?'

'No way.' The response was instant. 'I plan to see the world. It's all I've ever wanted.'

Angelina took another sip. 'That'll take a while, won't it? The pay can't be much in this place.'

'That's for sure,' Elena said with a sigh. 'I'm only staying 'til something better comes along.'

Angelina said nothing and glanced at her Fitbit. 'It's almost time. I'd better get going,' she said, downing the last of her coffee and gathering her things. Elena watched Angelina's graceful exit with a pang of envy.

Late that night, Elena was up at all hours, imitating what

she'd observed: head erect, shoulders back, pretending she was ten kilos lighter, practising the glide.

¶

Fabio was curious to know why Ava was adding a selection of drinks to her shopping trolley before they headed to the café. Bottles of orange, tomato and cranberry juice and a six-pack of lemon bitters. Unseen, he slipped into the next aisle.

Later, as he sat perched on a bar stool, beer in hand, he reflected further. She was getting her hands on some alcohol — had to be. But from where? Unbeknown to Angelina, he'd given up making random daily checks at the café. She'd kept her promise not to leave the premises, and he doubted she'd start now. One word from him, and she'd be locked up before she had time to blink.

Things were turning out better than expected. Ava kept to herself, leaving him pretty much free to come and go as he wished. However, he was careful not to make a habit of it. Antonio and Filipe kept in regular contact.

Viveiro was a world away from Rio's fast-paced, vibrant buzz, yet he was surprised to find he didn't miss the latter as much as he'd expected. In fact, he was quite enjoying the peace and solitude of the hamlet. An ancient farmhouse that came to feel like home, a blazing open fire, the mouth-watering aromas wafting from Rosa's kitchen, the bleat of distant goats and warble of birds outside his window at dawn. He didn't mind the wet seeping through his runners as he jogged in a morning, with rain slapping his face, or the aching muscles from a hard day's work in the fields with Filipe.

At the same time, he was looking forward to resuming life at gang headquarters. He missed the dangers that came with the job, the drinking and gambling sessions in between. And now dangled the tantalising prospect of being part of the team in Operations. There was an undeniable camaraderie amongst the group that he was itching to be part of. Lurks and perks he'd yet to discover. And of course, the money …

As he swirled the ice around in his glass, his mind once again turned to Ava. If his hunch proved to be correct, he could hardly blame her for getting hold of some alcohol. Antonio's demand for abstinence during her pregnancy had been harsh and unrealistic. A drink here and there surely couldn't hurt. After all, she was no alcoholic — his days of tailing her attested to that. But she'd never disguised the fact that she enjoyed a drink or two. What young woman her age didn't? None that he knew of anyway. It was a wonder she'd left things this long.

Well, he wasn't about to inform on her, and she sure as hell would be keeping things discreet. However, a cold trickle ran down his back. He was walking a fine line, and he knew it. One slip up …

Angelina was in a particularly good mood when they

met at the end of the day. He noticed the bulge in her lap-top case.

'Looks as though we're in for another downpour, so I brought the umbrella,' he said. 'How about you put it up ready, and I'll take your laptop.' He reached across to take it.

'No,' she quickly pulled away. 'I don't need your help.'

'Suit yourself,' he said with a shrug, grinning to himself.

They hurried towards the car, collars up, pushing against the wind, water swishing against their ankles. They only just made it back to the car when it bucketed down. Fabio opened the umbrella just in time to save them a soaking, and they jumped inside.

'Shit, that was close,' he said, turning over the engine and flicking the wipers on to full. 'I forgot to mention, Filipe asked me to pick up a part for the tractor on the way back.'

'Whatever.'

'It's in a warehouse on the other side of town.'

Fabio was glad to have his GPS as the rain pelted down. He could barely make out the road.

It was right on closing time, and the manager had just left, leaving the young assistant who had little clue where to start looking. Ten minutes turned into twenty, but Fabio wasn't particularly worried. Filipe rarely asked for favours. It would be a different story with Ava, however. She wasn't one to be kept waiting. *Do you good*, he thought.

Darkness had fallen, and a thick fog had settled as they

drove along the last stretch of road towards the hamlet. Filipe was already waiting when they arrived and struck up a conversation in Portuguese with Fabio.

'I've been worried,' he said. 'I was expecting you back an hour ago.'

'Everything's fine. We were delayed a bit at the warehouse, that's all.'

'I forgot about that. The part was in, then?'

'Yep.'

'Thanks. Saved me a trip.'

'No problem.'

'It's turned cold this last hour,' he said. 'Would you both like to come inside to warm up?'

Fabio glanced at Angelina. 'I think she's had enough for one day.'

'Well, ask her if she wants me to get the fire going. It'll only take a minute.'

Fabio translated and was surprised when she agreed.

Filipe helped Fabio bring in the groceries, then headed outside, returning with an armful of wood. Moments later, the first flame exploded into a ball of orange, and Angelina watched, arms crossed, transfixed.

'Don't you love fire?' she turned to Fabio, 'I do.' She paused. 'Love watching things burn.' Her voice was dreamy, yet somehow disturbing, as she gazed into the flames. 'I had this boyfriend once,' she went on, 'said he worked in a crematorium. Would you believe that?' she said. 'I asked him to take me there once. Wow, was that something else.'

Where in the hell did that come from, she thought, quite impressed with herself.

Fabio was too stunned to speak.

'What did she say?' Filipe asked him in Portuguese.

'I'll tell you later.'

An uncomfortable silence hung in the air. 'We'll leave you to it then,' Fabio said, nodding to the door to Filipe.

It was edging towards seven. Angelina headed to the kitchen, unpacked the groceries and made herself a sandwich. She'd considered having a vodka, but the day's events had left her exhausted and barely able to think straight. Best to leave things until the following evening when she'd be able to appreciate it. God knows, it had been hard enough getting her hands on the stuff. Right now, sleep couldn't come soon enough.

❡

Ribbons of bright sunshine streamed through the window, awakening Angelina and lifting her spirits. It had been some time since she'd not woken to rain. She rose and stretched, energised by a long, uninterrupted sleep.

After breakfast, she decided to take a walk down through the orchard. The welcoming sun's warmth seeped into her bones and she was glad she'd made the effort. Pregnancy was taking its toll. She was fed up with her lack of stamina, swollen ankles, blotchy skin and restrictive diet.

The day passed surprisingly quickly, and by seven she'd finished dinner, topped up the fire and settled in, drink in hand, watching the flickering shadows from the fire bounce around the darkened room.

This is more like it, she thought, straining to think of the last time she'd had a drink.

She was on her second vodka and orange when there was a knock on the door.

'Shit!' she lurched forward, knocking the drink flying. 'Who is it?' she called out.

'Rosa.'

'Just a minute.'

Angelina jumped up and turned on the light, then rushed to the kitchen for a dishcloth to mop up the quickly spreading puddle. She hastily screwed the lids back on the bottles and took them to the kitchen and shoved them into the pantry. Wiping her mouth with the back of her hand, she headed towards the door.

Rosa was standing on the porch with an esky in hand. 'Filipe call at market today. He buy you fish.'

'Thanks,' Angelina reached across to take the esky, heart racing.

'No, you no carry,' Rosa said, pushing past and heading towards the kitchen, giving Angelina little time to think.

As Rosa lifted the esky onto the bench and unpacked it, Angelina's attention was caught by something else, causing her to stop dead in her tracks. Her hand flew to her mouth. 'Oh shit!'

'What is it?' Rosa swung around in alarm.

'Oh, nothing. I just forgot to take the washing out.'

'I help.'

'No, no. It can wait.'

Rosa shrugged and resumed what she was doing.

Angelina's eyes swung from the pantry door behind Rosa that she'd forgotten to close, to the wine glass laying on its side. *Stupid, stupid,* she berated herself, moving quickly to Rosa's side and shoving closed the pantry door shut behind her as she did so. Then under the pretence of stoking the fire, she headed for the living area, pushing the wine glass under a chair with a foot as she passed.

Rosa had barely opened the freezer lid when there was a loud crack from above that made them jump, followed by a dazzling display of lightning outside the window.

'Quick, you'd better get going,' Angelina said, rushing over to take the fish from Rosa's hand. 'I'll finish here. We'll catch up soon, okay?'

Rosa nodded and followed her to the door. As Angelina reached for the brass doorknob, Rosa placed a hand on her arm. 'You eating well, I hope?'

'Yeah, yeah.'

Rosa's sharp brown eyes never left hers. 'Not long to go now. You okay?'

'I'm fine, but –' the words spilled out before Angelina could stop herself.

Rosa raised an eyebrow.

'To tell you the truth, I'm feeling shit. That bloating you told me about, the fucking bad back and swollen ankles –'

There was a sympathetic nod. 'Last five weeks never good.'

Angelina felt her spirits drop. 'I know, I know. You've said all that before.'

'I only next door,' Rosa said. 'You call any time, yes?'

And she was gone.

Angelina closed the door and leaned against it. Tears stung her eyes. Tears of anger and frustration. What she'd really wanted to say was, 'I'm scared, Rosa. I'm scared shitless.'

Wiping her eyes with her sleeve, she returned to the kitchen. 'God, that was close,' she muttered as she opened the pantry door to retrieve the vodka.

She threw another log on the fire, turned on the TV and poured herself a drink, double strength this time, followed by another.

It was 5 a.m. when she awoke, sprawled out on the carpet, empty bottle at her side, television still blaring, fireplace a pile of ash. 'Oh, shit,' she rubbed her temples, rose, stumbled across to the sink and threw up.

34

It had been three weeks since Elena began dieting, and her resolve was already paying off, with Angelina's words her mantra: "there's no such word as can't." Her face was thinner, her bra straps were no longer digging into her ribs, and her jeans showed the first signs of bagginess.

Late one night, she pulled out the activewear from its bag and held it up against her body. Ava was right. The aqua, pink and black design did complement her skin tone. 'It won't be long before I'm in you bloody things,' she muttered determinedly, stuffing them back in the bag that she tossed in the corner. She'd no idea how many kilos she'd lost and wasn't about to find out. Past weigh-ins only led to failure, with life becoming a perpetual cycle of satisfaction or self-loathing — depending on the numbers on the scales — intermingled with alternate bouts of fasting and bingeing. She'd let her clothes and the mirror tell the story.

Another week with more success only strengthened Elena's resolve. Leftover cakes and slices from the café were discreetly passed on to the needy family who lived nearby, and meals were replaced by weight loss shakes. They were filling enough but soon proved repetitive and boring. Once she could trust herself to stay on track, they'd be the first thing to be ditched.

§

Early morning walks turned into power walks, interspersed with jogging and if she wasn't too tired at night, she did a session on weights that had been picked up at an op shop.

§

'Rosa's been asking when you'll join us for dinner,' Fabio remarked as he accompanied Angelina to the supermarket. 'About time, don't you think?'

There was an indifferent shrug. 'I guess so.'

'Good, I'll let her know.'

§

Smoke curled from the caretaker cottage chimney as Angelina headed along the path. She gave the old door-knock a rap, and the door soon opened.

'Come,' Rosa beamed, beckoning her inside. 'I take coat.' The living room was toasty warm and Filipe and Fabio stood, backs to the fire, deep in conversation.

'I keep food plain, don't worry,' Rosa told her as they took their seats.

Chapter 34

Angelina nodded. 'Thanks.' She'd abandoned rich, spicy food some time ago; the stabbing heartburn that came with it made it hardly worth her while.

Rosa's meal was surprisingly delicious despite the simple ingredients, and Angelina reflected on her own miserable attempts. Joining them for dinner wasn't such a bad idea. Dessert was a colourful array of fresh fruit and cheeses that she tucked into readily.

Rosa looked on in approval.

After dinner, the two men remained at the table, sharing a whisky, and Rosa nodded towards the two chairs close to the fire. 'We sit. More comfortable. Yes?'

Angelina nodded, her back aching already from the wooden kitchen bench.

'So, how you been feeling?' Rosa wasted no time in asking once they were seated.

'Okay.'

Rosa arched a brow.

There was a moment's silence. 'Everything's shit if you must know.'

'I think it time we talk, yes?'

§

Angelina was tetchy and irritable. She felt sluggish and heavy, and her commitment to maintaining her fitness was long gone. Even her daily yoga routine had slipped by the wayside. She was fed up with having to run to the toilet umpteen times a day, sleeping on her side, pillow between her legs and a constantly aching back. And there were still six weeks to go. At least, thanks to Rosa, she knew what to expect.

She poured herself another glass of red and looked out into the darkness, her face grim. A drink at night was all she'd looked forward to, but even those days were numbered. She barely had the energy to get out of bed, let alone go to the café to order more. In any case, it wasn't long before she'd be under Rosa's watchful eye. She glanced at the bottle of untouched Omega-3 supplements on the kitchen bench. 'You must take,' Rosa had insisted. 'Important for baby's brain.'

Yeah right …

She put down her glass and leaned down to rub her aching feet and ankles, wondering why in the hell women would go through it all a second time … let alone a third.

One thing was for sure, the moment the whole thing was over, she'd be back in the gym. There'd be no wasted time getting back in shape. There would also be an appointment with a qualified beautician. So much for the "glow" that supposedly accompanied motherhood. Her skin had never been as blotchy and lifeless; brown patches were appearing on her cheeks and forehead, and the fine lines and dark rings under her eyes made her feel years older. Rosa assured her that the face's shininess was due to increased blood supply that would dissipate with delivery, but that came as little comfort. She'd tried a selection of lotions with little success, so she set about covering things up the best she could with make-up. But now, she'd reached a point where it no longer mattered.

It seemed an eternity since her last visit to a beauty salon. Images flashed through her mind of white fluffy robes, heated beds in treatment rooms and thick, fresh towels. The scents and feeling of luxurious masks and creams being rubbed into her skin were what she loved the most. *Not long to go,* she thought dreamily, as the alcohol kicked in. A facial first up, then a salt scrub followed by a spa, sauna and massage. Absent-mindedly, she twirled a lock of hair in her fingers. The pedicure and manicure would come later.

There were no beauty salons near the café as far as she could tell, but there had to be some in the busier part of town to accommodate the flood of tourists soon to arrive. That could be the next Google search.

God, to think I had a beauty appointment every few weeks in Melbourne, she thought.

35

The café was busy all day, and Angelina waited until the last of the customers were gone before she called Elena across.

'I'd like you to double my wine order today.'

'Okay.'

'Good girl.' Angelina paused. 'Would you get other things for me if I asked?'

'What kind of things?'

'Cigarettes?'

Elena looked surprised. 'I didn't know you smoked.'

'I don't.' There was a pause. 'Drugs?'

Elena started, but her eyes never wavered. 'I'd need time.'

Angelina nodded. Not that she did drugs. Health and fitness was her thing. Besides, she'd seen first-hand the damage they could do. Drugs were the means to a buck as far as she was concerned. What she'd really been probing was Elena's willingness to put up and shut up. So far, so good.

She smiled and said, 'I'll let you know.'

Elena's mind was in turmoil as she headed back to the counter.

¶

Angelina thanked Elena for the wine and wrapped each bottle separately in a handtowel, shoving them into her empty laptop case.

'I want to speak with you later,' she said. 'There's something I wish to discuss.'

'I can come now, while it's quiet –'

'No, I've got things to do.'

Elena bit a thumbnail, heart pumping, as she watched Angelina head to a nearby table. *God, I hope it's nothing to do with drugs,* she thought.

It was 4 p.m. by the time Angelina indicated she was ready to talk. Elena nodded, overcome by a rush of anxiety. 'Can I get you another coffee?'

'No, not at the moment.'

'So, what did you want to see me about?' Elena did her best to appear nonchalant as she pulled up a chair.

'Today's my last day at the café.'

'What do you mean!' Elena looked at her in alarm.

'I've been feeling crap for weeks now, and it's only getting worse. I'm staying put now till I have the kid, and then I'm out of here.'

'You're leaving Viveiro? But I thought –'

'Thought what? That I'd stay in this dump any longer than I had to?'

Elena's mouth went dry. 'Where are you going?'

'Back home to Australia. I've some unfinished business to attend to.'

'When?'

'You're full of questions, aren't you?'

Elena looked at her hands. 'It's none of my business, I know.'

'You're damned right it isn't.'

There was a short silence.

'I said I had something to discuss,' Angelina said, looking at her. 'You said you wanted to travel abroad.'

There was a nod.

'I could just be of help.'

'What do you mean?'

'I might need someone to work alongside me. Someone willing to learn, who would do what I say and knows how to keep their mouth shut. There would be a generous clothing allowance. Knowledge of languages would give you an advantage. Would you be interested?'

'Yeah, of course I would!' Elena jumped with excitement. 'What sort of job?'

'None of your business,' Angelina snapped. 'You'd just be there to do as I ask.'

There was a quick nod. 'So, where is this job?'

Angelina shrugged. 'Could be anywhere. Europe, South America the Caribbean –'

Chapter 35

'You're kidding!' Elena stared at her in stunned disbelief.

'Listen, don't go getting your hopes up. I said I was considering someone, that's all. Everything may well fall through yet.'

'I don't understand.' Elena's fingers dug hard into the sides of the chair as she looked at her.

There was a shrug. 'Depends on what happens when I get back home. And that's the last thing on my mind right now. I've got three weeks more of this shit, and as soon as possible after I give birth I'm out of here.'

'Won't that be a bit soon for the baby to be travelling?'

'You don't think I'm taking the kid with me?'

Elena's jaw dropped.

'How old are you, Elena?'

'Twenty-two. Why?'

'Not that much younger than me. Would you be prepared to give up everything right now just to have a kid?'

'No.'

'Thought not. Maybe you should think next time before you speak.'

Elena's cheeks burned, and she nodded.

'It's not as if I'm dumping it on the street,' Angelina continued, as if she was referring to a cat or a dog. 'It wasn't hard finding a Spanish couple wanting to adopt.'

Elena made to respond but thought it best to say nothing.

'Well, that's about it, then.' Angelina reached in her bag for her iPhone. 'So, what's your number?'

Elena waited until Angelina had punched in the

numbers and dipped into her pocket for her own phone.

'Hang on, I'll get your number as well.'

'What for?'

'In case I need to contact you.'

'No need,' Angelina's eyes flashed at her, 'you'll know soon enough if things work out.' She paused. 'But if you make mention this to anyone, you won't be hearing from me again. Understood?'

Elena nodded quickly, swallowing hard.

Without another word, Angelina rose, picked up her laptop bag and left.

Elena stood motionless for quite some time, too gutted to think straight. Put-downs and threats and were one thing, but to leave her dangling like this …

But now was not the time for self-pity. She had just one chance to break free, and she wasn't about to let it slip.

There was silence except for the intermittent, slow plops of the tap she'd forgotten to turn off. She glanced at her watch. Later than she thought. Rising, she headed across to clean the coffee machine.

Darkness had fallen by the time she stepped out onto the cobbled back street, the only illumination a distant, dull streetlamp. She'd left this late on other occasions and had never felt threatened, unlike the dark alleyways back home, where drug dealers and pimps lurked in doorways and stairwells. No one paid attention to her as she exited the connecting laneway to the main road. Her shabby flat sat further along at the back of an old brick cottage which was occupied by a retired fisherman and his wife.

All was quiet as she walked past the cottage. It was probably dinner time. The fisherman spent most nights drinking and his wife, hard of hearing, had the television up full blast until all hours of the night. But Elena learned to live with it. As she did, the stench from two bins wafted not far from her back door.

The front door light bulb had blown long ago, and she fumbled in her bag for her keys. It was damp and cramped inside the low ceilinged flat, but the rent was cheap. It was colder than usual, and she immediately turned on the old three-bar heater, holding her hands in front of it as the circulation crept back into her fingers. A faint smell of the previous night's dinner hung in the air, reminding her to take out another to thaw. But after the day's turmoil, the last thing she felt like was eating.

The long shower left her sleepy, and it wasn't long till she drifted off, dreaming of Venetian gondolas and Parisian cafés.

❡

The café was empty. Elena leaned against the counter and surveyed the drab surroundings, wondering how she'd fill in the coming hours, or the weeks and months to come, for that matter. It seemed more than a month since Ava's departure, and she missed the glamour, the intrigue. But her mind was focused on other things now. So much to be done, and time was running out. Weight loss remained at the back of her mind, a niggling, unwelcome companion.

She'd stuck to her diet, apart from a slip up here or there. Had rarely missed an exercise session, yet there'd been little to show for it all these past few weeks. She'd been hoping to be wearing Ava's activewear by now.

I need to exercise more, that's all, she thought, *skip some meals …*

36

'**A**ntonio say you must have complete rest till baby come,' Rosa told Angelina.

'Oh really?' Angelina shot back sarcastically. 'Since when does my uncle get to say what I can or can't do?'

Rosa shrugged. 'He say I wash for you, clean your house. Okay?'

'Yeah, you can do that,' Angelina said, wondering why she hadn't taken advantage of Rosa before — especially in the last few weeks where every movement proved such an effort. She'd grown up with a housekeeper and the only times she'd attended to such duties was on the housekeeper's days off. And only because she had to ... *that's what you pay people for*, she'd thought, never dreaming that things would one day come to this.

The places she'd been forced to clean while on the run came to mind: the dilapidated kitchens that always appeared dirty no matter how much they were wiped down, the smoke-stained walls and threadbare furniture.

At least some effort had gone into making her current surroundings more liveable. Nonetheless, the place was still far from ideal. There was the smelly carpet, the shower's thick, stubborn film she was yet to get rid of and the dust from the ash-filled fireplace that, when swept out, permeated her clothes and clogged up her lungs.

Her airy apartment in Rio was a palace in comparison.

'So, when I start?' Rosa asked.

'Tomorrow will do. Make it at ten.'

❡

Angelina sat, feet up on the sofa, watching Rosa as she scrubbed and cleaned the kitchen and vacuumed the floor. The ancient washing machine banged and clattered as if it was about to topple over, and she wondered why she'd never noticed before. Many a time, it had stopped midcycle, and the spin cycle barely worked, forcing Angelina to lift a few articles out to dry at a time if she wasn't to do herself an injury. She placed her hands behind her head and smiled. *Your problem from now on, Rosa,* she thought.

Angelina had nodded off by the time Rosa climbed the stairs, armed with a stack of fresh linen and towels. It would take a few visits to get things as she would have liked them. Most of the recent improvements had been made downstairs, and the rooms above had been left largely untouched, except Angelina's bedroom, where she headed to first.

Half an hour later, she stood, arms on hips and surveyed her work with satisfaction. She didn't hear Angelina come up from behind.

'What's taken you so long?' the words were sharp.

Rosa swung around in alarm, hand to her chest. 'You scare me,' she said. 'Lots to clean.'

'Hm, well, don't forget, the washing needs taking out.'

'Me no forget.' Rosa grabbed the pile of used bedlinen from the floor and followed her out of the room.

¶

Rosa moved up to Ava's bedroom the next day, heart pumping. If Ava knew what she was up to …

She quickly made the bed, straightened things on the bedside table and turned on the vacuum cleaner on, leaving it running while she took a quick look around. This may well be the last opportunity to learn something of the woman whose child she was about to adopt. She was used to knowing everyone's business — that was the favela way. But Ava was secretive and tight-lipped about her past, and Antonio divulged little.

It came as a windfall to get to clean Ava's house. There'd be no way of her getting in otherwise. Part of the agreement was that she be left alone, with her own key. Her passport and papers were in Fabio's possession, but Rosa knew they'd been forged. She noted a small safe in the bottom of the wardrobe, but as she expected, it was locked.

She was about to give up when things took an unexpected turn … something she almost missed under a tangle of underwear in the top drawer. With a satisfied nod, she took it out, and studied it for a moment before reaching in her pocket for her phone.

And photographed both sides …

Rosa only began using a mobile phone when a nephew handed down his old one and showed her the basics. It took her a while to master, but now she was grateful that she'd persevered.

¶

Fabio was watching TV when Antonio rang.

'Hi Boss,' he said, pressing the remote's mute button. 'What's up?'

'Just checking in on Ava. How is she?'

'So far, so good, but things are starting to take their toll.'

'Thought so. She's got what, three weeks to go?'

'Yep. She's due on July 28th.'

'Okay. Contact the hospital and confirm the date.'

'Has Ava mentioned anything to you about a hotel?'

'No. I haven't spoken to her.'

'She insists on staying in one the moment she has the all-clear to leave the hospital.'

'Is that so? For how long?'

'Around a week, from what she tells me, until she flies out.'

'Go ahead and organise things, then. I can't deny her that much. Come to think of it, book two rooms for the week leading up to the birth — one for my niece and the other for Rosa. It might make things easier all round.'

'Good move. Rosa could do with a break. She's gone beyond what's expected.'

'Without much thanks, I expect.'

'Not wrong there. Even offered to move in with Ava these last few weeks, but she'd have none of it.'

'I'd expect as much,' Antonio's voice was tight. 'But that could well change. Has she been for a check-up?'

'Yeah, the ultrasound showed everything's good. I felt a bit sorry for Rosa, though. Ava didn't want to know the sex of the baby.'

'That'd be right,' Antonio said, in annoyance, hoping to hear the word of a boy. 'Well, if there's anything she needs, put it on the card.'

'Will do, Boss. So, any further word on the police sting?'

'No, it appears we're safe. I'm about to give the boys the all-clear to return.'

'Good.'

'Things should be pretty much back to normal at head-quarters by the time you return.'

Fabio considered pressing him further on Operations but thought it prudent to remain silent.

Antonio clicked the end button and lay on the old iron bed, arms behind his head, looking up at the paint peeling off the ceiling in Renata's spare bedroom. *Need to add that to the list to be done*, he thought, listening to the heated argument between the young couple next door. It had been a scorching day, and he couldn't deny that he missed the air-conditioned comfort of his apartment in Rio.

Usually, a week or two spent in the favela came as a welcome break. It felt like coming home somehow. A place to switch off and relax. But not this time.

It had been three weeks since he'd got wind of the global police sting that was bringing organised crime groups to their knees. Within twenty-four hours, the gang's Rio headquarters had been evacuated, computers removed, with not a shred of incriminating evidence to be found. The place could be just another apartment block.

It was only as details of the sting unfolded that he knew that it would be safe to return. He may even rent out a house for them all first, somewhere near the coast. But things could well have been different if he'd followed the lead of those using encrypted communication devices to plan crimes, keep messages safe and the authorities at bay. He'd been close to securing one himself at the suggestion of Operations but never got around to it. And right now, that made him a very relieved man.

He'd dodged a bullet this time but was not out of the woods yet.

For some time, he'd considered amalgamating with other drug cartels and transactional syndicates. Under the illusion that encrypted phone apps allowed them to conduct their illicit dealings from afar without fear of detection, their operations were rapidly becoming more daring and sophisticated. Gangs shared supply routes and resources pooled. There was big money to be made. Antonio knew only too well the risks of dealing with those he didn't know, and perhaps that's why he'd held off as long as he had.

If only he hadn't given in this once. Beads of sweat formed on his brow that he wiped with the back of his hand.

Before he left for Rio, he'd been approached by a member of an Australian cartel who'd forged business with a Chinese triad involved in importing large amounts of drugs from Columbia into Australia. The cartel had a network of corrupt insiders who were willing to wave the drugs through at Australian seaports and airports. Others were planted amongst law enforcement authorities and government officials, to provide advanced tip-offs.

Antonio knew he was of interest because of his gang's Australian connections to South American drug dealers and crime figures. Initially, he'd been wary of entering into discussions, citing his preference for doing things alone. But when the cartel approached with the offer of a multi-million-dollar cocaine deal, Antonio found himself thinking, why not? All he had to do was develop close links with a well-known Columbian drugs lord to secure supplies and pave the way for future offers.

He'd spent five days in Columbia finalising the arrangement in the back room of an abandoned warehouse, watched on by a tattooed hulk of a creature with a shaved head and piercings. The scale of the operation exceeded expectations: a shipment of 1.4 tonnes of cocaine worth 320 million dollars smuggled from a port on the Columbian Ecuador border, bound for Australia via the Pacific Islands.

It all seemed too easy. There was no shortage of users on the Australian streets willing to pay big money for their fix and the Columbian drug lord had the ways and means to supply it. The sky was the limit.

He'd only just returned when news of the police sting broke out. None of his contacts had been nabbed, to his relief, but the deal he'd just signed was front and foremost on his mind. So many involved. What if one of them had been caught up in the sting and implicated him?

He'd spent the last week working on a contingency plan just in case. The gang were used to dispersing at short notice. But depending on the circumstances, this could mean starting all over again, perhaps in another country.

¶

It was another three weeks before he got word that the Columbian drug lord was safely bunkered down until things settled and the shipment of cocaine stockpiled in a secret warehouse, ready to go.

When that would be, was anyone's guess. His cut would be worth the wait. It would take just one phone call to participate in future deals, but the more Antonio thought about things, the more he found himself backing off. There were too many what-ifs and uncertainties. Over the past few years massive quantities of cocaine had been seized from small boats off the coast of Australia, authorities were tightening their act at ports and airports, and the police sting had been a "wake up." Next time he mightn't be so lucky …

Best to stick with what he knew. Better to be safe. The more comprehensive his criminal network, the more he laid himself open to threats and extortion.

And kidnapping …

A cold shiver ripped through him.

He'd not yet stopped to consider the safety of Angelina's baby. It was not uncommon for family members of drug lords to be seized and held to ransom for substantial amounts by rival gangs or disgruntled drug runners. Victims faced extreme violence and torture if the needs of the kidnappers were not met.

Angelina's baby should be safe in the hamlet short-term, but it would not be long before word of the birth leaked out. Despite Filipe and Rosa's good intentions, Antonio knew that he could never be at peace while the place remained unguarded.

He imagined a dark van pulling up outside the caretaker's cottage in the middle of the night. Could envisage Filipe being dragged out of bed by a balaclava-clad figure, beaten senseless, and left lying in a pool of blood. Could taste Rosa's terror as she was gagged and tied by the wrists to the bedposts as the baby was whisked away before her eyes. To what God forbidden, remote location would be anyone's guess.

His blood ran cold.

He'd have to come up with another location until he moved there himself, which could be some time yet. Not that he'd tell Filipe and Rosa yet, especially Filipe, who'd poured his heart and soul into the place over the last few years. He thought of photos that Rosa had sent through of the nursery she'd spent months setting up. A freshly painted room with nursery rhyme curtains, a large bassinet, hand-crocheted rugs, embroidered bunny pillowcases, and rows of stuffed toys and animals of all shapes and sizes.

He'd felt pangs of pain deep within his chest, regretting his decision not to settle and have a child of his own. But there was no changing the past. He'd thrown his entire life into the gang, and had been constantly on the move, in a world fraught with danger. It wouldn't have been fair to subject a wife and family to that.

News of Angelina's baby came as a turning point in his life. Someone of his own flesh and blood but to whom he could hand down his legacy. He'd felt a new lease of life, a sense of purpose. Nothing would jeopardise the safety and wellbeing of the child. Rosa and Filipe were yet to learn that the infant they would spend years nurturing and raising would become infiltrated into the gang as soon as

Antonio deemed it fit to do so. Growing up, the youngster would have nothing but the best.

When Angelina first walked into his life, he hoped there'd be some way of bonding. He would have given whatever it took to connect with his sister's child. The sister he loved above everything and whose life had been so cruelly ripped away.

It didn't take long to rationalise that such hopes were way out of reach. It had been shattering to discover that his niece bore none of his sister's kindness and sensitivity. He found her selfish, cruel and heartless. It had not been hard to impose restrictions that placed her in the shoes of those she treated with derision. Yet she was family. Nothing he could do or say would change that. His jaw hardened. Angelina would forfeit her right to the baby from the moment she walked out of the hospital. If she thought she could simply return later on to reclaim it, she had a surprise coming.

No one would snatch the child from his grasp.

Little did he know that ultimately, this would not be the case.

37

As the birth drew nearer, Rosa gave Angelina's house a final clean up, noting the size of Angelina's packed luggage. 'Why you not pack small bag for hospital? Come back later for rest.'

'Shit, no. I never want to set foot in this place again.'

Angelina agreed to have dinner with them on the final night. As Fabio escorted her back to her house afterwards, she paused on the doorstep and remarked, 'Will my uncle come to Spain to see me before I fly out?'

'No, he told me he'll be elsewhere. Does that bother you?'

Angelina shrugged. 'I couldn't care a stuff.' She unlocked the door and swept past without another word, shutting the door behind her with a bang.

As she sat on the edge of the bed to take off her shoes, reflecting on what Fabio had just told her, she was annoyed but hardly surprised. Annoyed because Antonio had been the one with the upper hand the whole way along, and she didn't like not being in control. But it was hardly surprising. Their relationship had been fractured from the outset. She pursed her lips. It was time to move on. Antonio had served his purpose, and she had no intention of contacting him again unless he was of use.

But that didn't stop the anger welling up inside her as she reflected on the wasted last six months. Antonio knew how much it meant to her to discover her roots. Yet he'd not so much as shown where her mother had been raised. Moreover, he'd denied her the things she'd looked forward to the most. The chance to participate in Rio's New Year's Eve celebrations and, above all, Carnaval. Well, she'd be back soon enough to check things out. Perhaps with Elena in tow as interpreter.

The following day, Filipe drove them to A Coruna, a thriving, historic coastal city on the Atlantic coast, where Angelina was booked to give birth at a large hospital. Antonio had arranged a week's stay beforehand at a budget, five-storey hotel in the heart of the CBD. The rooms were basic and clean, with white walls, curtains and bedspread contrasted by a purple feature wall, cushions and furnishings.

'Ah, that's more like it,' Angelina said to Rosa and Filipe as she scanned her surroundings and kicked her shoes off, curling her toes in the thick shagpile rug. The porter arrived soon afterwards with her luggage after dropping off Rosa's in the adjoining room.

'You settle, yes? I come see you later.' Rosa followed the porter with Filipe behind her.

Rosa looked around her room with awe. The only time she'd been in such a place was when she did a two-month cleaning stint at a large hotel in Rio. She walked around, running her hands over the smooth wooden surfaces, feeling the textures of the bedspread, holding the fresh white towels to her nose.

'Why don't you stay a few days, Filipe.' she said. 'I know you've got things to do at the hamlet, but –'

He shook his head.

The truth was that Filipe felt out of place already. He'd worry about leaving a grubby mark on the furnishings, for instance, and being deprived of fresh air and the chance to light up a smoke would send him stir-crazy. He could, however, cope quite nicely with the room's large flat TV screen. He envisaged lying on the bed, head propped against the pillows, beer in hand and watching the soccer till the early hours.

'I'd only be in the way,' he told her. 'Maybe I'll join you the night before we pick up the baby.'

'That'd be good.'

'Well, I'll get going then.' He kissed the top of her head. 'Make sure you have plenty of rest and call me if you need anything.'

'I will.'

'You have Antonio's credit card for meals and expenses?'

There was a nod. 'I might get used to not cleaning and cooking. Watch out.'

Filipe grinned as he headed for the door.

Rosa listened to the familiar steps receding down the hallway and then crossed to the window to pull apart the drapes. The expanse of indistinguishable, high-rise buildings that lay beyond caused her to shake her head. She couldn't imagine why anyone would choose to live here. At least her favela had character. And the people there knew and looked out for each other.

❡

The next few days went off without a hitch. Angelina and Rosa spent most of the time in their rooms. Angelina was too sluggish to walk far, meeting up only for breakfast in the dining room or to venture out to the nearby cafés for meals. As was expected, Angelina found food less appealing, and Rosa had a challenge on her hands to get her to eat at all.

'You must eat. Must have strength, yes?' Rosa urged.

'Food just makes me feel sick. I've told you that. Or gives me frigging heartburn — one or the other.'

'Then you eat little and often like I say before.'

'Yeah, yeah.' Angelina stabbed at another forkful of red meat.

Rosa looked at her. She doubted the hints she'd dropped along the way of what to expect had been given much attention. It had been liked addressing a belligerent teenager. Meanwhile, she was bracing for the storm to come, knowing only too well the ordeal Angelina was yet to face. But she was in no way about to put the fear of God into the girl and could only hope that there'd be no complications in the meantime. With a shudder, her mind turned to some of the precarious situations she'd faced as a midwife in the favela. But this was different, she reminded herself. Angelina was a fit young woman giving birth in one of the region's finest private hospitals.

¶

Two days before Angelina was to give birth, Rosa received a frantic phone call in the middle of the night.

'You've got to get in here fast. I don't know what to do.'

Rosa threw the bedcovers and aside and swung her legs to the floor.

'I coming.'

She fumbled for the light switch, hurriedly threw on some pants and a sweater, and rushed into the next room.

'Hurry!' Angelina screamed, wringing her hands together.

'You tell me everything, yes?'

'The baby's coming!' the voice became even more shrill.

'How you know that?'

'I can feel it. I'm in pain.'

'That normal,' Rosa soothed. 'Contractions, yes? Remember, I tell you before. Many more yet.'

'What?' Angelina shrieked. 'How many?'

There was a shrug. 'Each person different. You have while to go.'

Angelina planted her hands on her hips, eyes flashing. 'Well, I'm not about to take any chances. Call a taxi. I need to go to the hospital, now!'

Rosa sighed inwardly. It was no use arguing. Things could become ugly if she didn't comply.

'Okay, you pack things. I go get bag, call hospital.'

Back in the room, Rosa spoke to the nurse in charge, explaining the situation with a muttered apology of what was to come. But Antonio had already been in contact, warning of Angelina's antics. Making clear his distaste of hospitals' early discharge of new mothers and their babies, he'd donated a generous amount in return for an extended stay after the baby's birth.

¶

The maternity ward was on the fifth floor, overlooking the vast car park. They were met at the nurses' station by a short stature, middle-aged charge nurse, whose warm greeting was met with a scowl by Angelina. Rosa blushed with embarrassment as they followed her to the room directly opposite, wondering if being so close to the nurses' station was wise.

When they entered the room Angelina became sullen and demanding, insisting that she immediately see a doctor.

'The doctor is currently doing his rounds and will see you shortly,' the nurse said in English with accustomed patience. 'Now I suggest you settle yourself in and try and get some sleep.'

Angelina gestured to the nurses' desk opposite where a buzzer was going off, and the phone rang. 'And how do you propose I do that?'

Rosa cringed. She could only hope that Angelina would become more compliant as the birth drew nearer, but she very much doubted it. Angelina did not deal well with not being in control.

Rosa placed the small case on the bed and said, 'Me help unpack, then come back tomorrow. You in good hands.'

'No!' Angelina shrieked, grabbing her arm. 'You're to stay here with me.'

The nurse shot Rosa a concerned look.

'It's all right; I'm used to it.' Rosa began a conversation in Spanish. 'This was to be expected.'

'Has she any idea how long she could be in labour for?'

Rosa shook her head. 'Best you don't tell her.'

9

As the hours wore on and Angelina's pain intensified, she became more insistent, pressing the button to the nurses' station at any opportunity, despite Rosa's protestations and coming out with volleys of profanities loud enough to be heard halfway down the passageway. Despite the angry outbursts, Rosa could see the fear in her eyes, and there was nothing she could do to help.

At one point, Rosa waited until Angelina was dozing to leave the room for a much-needed coffee from the cafeteria, two floors below.

Later, she watched in concern as Angelina thrashed in a tangle of wet sheets muttering incoherently and dreaming of her room in Kilkenny. All Rosa could do was fetch a cold washer to wipe her brow.

'Go away!' Angelina screamed at her, and when she turned to leave, there was another order. 'No, don't you dare leave me. Not for one minute. You understand?'

The commotion caused a nurse to come rushing in, and Rosa gestured with a nod of her head that she was not needed.

It was eight hours later when the contractions intensified and began coming at four-to-five-minute intervals. Angelina screamed with pain, leaving deep scratch marks in Rosa's arm as she clung on like a vice.

By the time Angelina's water broke, she was screeching. Eyes squeezed shut. She hadn't noticed Rosa being ushered out of the room by expert staff, who took over and wheeled her down the passageway to the delivery room.

In the waiting room, Rosa sank in the leather chair, eyes closed, exhausted. It had been twenty hours with no sleep, and her back was stiff from the plastic chair on which she'd sat by Angelina's side. Soon afterwards, a nurse shook her shoulder gently, placing a tray laden with coffee, sandwiches and cake on the small table beside her. 'You must eat, Rosa. We'll call you when there's news.'

'Thank you,' Rosa said gratefully. 'You don't think I should be there during the birth?'

'I think you've done enough.' The response was firm.

In only a matter of hours, Angelina gave birth to a 7lb baby girl after a relatively uncomplicated birth. She gave the nurses a dismissive wave in the recovery room when they placed the baby against her chest for regular face-to-face contact.

'How about you give things a try, just for a little while,' the midwife soothed.

'Just leave me alone, will you?' she said, and turned away.

The response had not been unexpected.

A nurse quickly removed the baby and took it to the neonatal intensive care unit until it was safe for transfer to the special care nursery. Under Angelina's instructions, there was to be no breastfeeding.

After the birth, she sank into her bed, limp with exhaustion and slept for hours. Things were quiet again at the nurses' station. For a while, at least.

Once the grogginess wore off, the sharp pains to Angelina's stomach felt like a boxer's jabs and she called impatiently for painkillers. The two nurses seated at the desk opposite exchanged a look of resignation.

'Here we go again,' one muttered.

Every time Rosa brought the baby into the room, Angelina looked away, saying she was tired and in need of sleep. And in the ensuing days, Rosa found herself tiptoeing around Angelina's bed as if she was housemaid to a movie star. It was Rosa who had borne the full brunt of Angelina's fury when she found her pyjama top drenched with milk after the fourth day. 'Christ! This whole damned thing has gone on for long enough. Do something, will you?'

'Will stop soon. You'll see.'

'Argh!' Angelina slumped against the pillows and turned her face away.

In contrast, the nursing staff would have none of her tantrums or demands from the outset.

'She's just a patient like everyone else,' the head nurse told her staff. 'Answer her bell only when you think it is necessary.'

¶

Rosa carried the sleeping baby, swaddled in pale lemon, into Angelina's room, with Filipe by her side. 'We come to say goodbye,' she said.

Angelina was squashing last of the things into a bag. 'Yeah, well, I hope it all works out. I'm glad you got what you wanted.'

A sad smile crossed Rosa's face, but she held her composure. 'Baby's name Talita. Mean "reborn child." You like?'

Angelina shrugged. 'Whatever.'

Filipe felt a surge of rage surge that he hadn't felt since he'd seen an innocent child caught up in gun fire between rival gangs in Rio. He put his arm around Rosa and said in Portuguese, 'Let's get out of here before I do or say something I might regret.'

'But aren't you going to offer her a lift back to the hotel?'

'She can walk for all I care.' He guided Rosa and the baby out into the hallway.

Angelina gave another shrug and zipped the bag.

Rosa felt a pang of uneasiness as they left the hospital. She knew there was little chance of Angelina having a change of mind, but what was stopping her from returning for the baby in the future? *Well, she'll have me to deal with, she thought grimly.* And Antonio …

Filipe secured the baby into its capsule in the car park. Closing the door, he climbed into the front seat beside Rosa. It had been a long time since he'd seen her looking so radiant and excited. He turned to her and smiled.

'Well, here's to our new family, Rosa. A bit late but worth the wait, eh?'

Rosa smiled and placed a hand over his.

'It would be interesting to know who the father of our baby really is, though,' Filipe added.

'I think I may already have the answer to that.'

'What do you mean?'

'I found a photo of a young man in her drawer when I was cleaning, with a hand-written name and contact details, with an Australian address. I took a photo with my phone. There's a printout in the filing cabinet, with my papers. It's worth chasing up, should you ever need to make contact with Talita's father.'

¶

Fabio's phone rang as he was finishing the last of a late breakfast. He took one look at the number and picked up quickly.

'Just checking in. Everything go to plan this morning?'

'Yeah, I'm expecting them back from the hospital at any moment.'

'And Ava?'

'She's returning to the hotel for another week, from what Filipe said. Not sure when she's flying out.'

'Hm. Well that's it, then. You're free to leave. Good job, by the way. Operations are expecting you.'

Fabio grinned as he pressed the end button, glad to know it was the last of his dealings with Angelina.

38

Angelina caught a taxi to the hotel where she collected the remainder of her luggage from storage and proceeded to her room. She still had another week's stay, courtesy of Antonio, before her flight home. It had never occurred to her that she wouldn't be able to bounce back within a day or two of giving birth, with some rest. Rosa had been right. Things weren't to be that easy. She'd found herself with barely enough energy to pack her bags at the hospital.

After three days, she still felt exhausted and drained, and by the fourth, she'd cancelled her flight and rescheduled it in a month. Once she arrived home, what she had in mind would require every bit of stamina she could muster. Meanwhile, she searched the net for a list of the city's five-star hotels. With another three weeks remaining till her flight, she figured she may as well do things in style.

She settled on an impressive hotel on the harbour front, focused on fitness and wellbeing and within walking distance of the shops, restaurants and eating places. Boasting three heated outdoor pools, two gyms and several massage rooms, saunas and spas, the hotel's adjoining sports centre provided just what she needed to replenish her energy levels and rejuvenate.

ⰻ

There was a knock on the door. Angelina frowned and put down the mobile she was about to give a last-minute charge. It couldn't be the porter already. The taxi wasn't due for another hour.

She crossed the room to the door and opened it.

It took just one look and Elena realised she'd made a big mistake in turning up.

'What in the hell are you doing here?' Angelina demanded furiously, hands on hips.

Elena's heart was pounding, her hands in tight balls at her sides. 'I wanted to see you before you left.'

'How did you find me?'

'I rang the hospital. They told me you were here.'

'Well, this'd better not take long. I've got a plane to catch,' Angelina lied, stepping aside to let her in.

Elena noted the bulging suitcase alongside the two bags of designer clothes in the corner. Another day, and she'd have missed her chance.

'So, what's this about?' Angelina said as she closed the door. 'I'm sure you didn't come all this way to see how I was.'

'I needed to speak to you about the job.'

'There's nothing to discuss.' The response was cold. 'I told you I'd be in contact if things worked out.'

'I know that, but –'

Angelina bristled. The girl was beginning to sound like the dog that belonged to Filipe's nephew. The dog that constantly whined. The dog that could be silenced by a kick to its guts.

'But what?'

'Can you at least give me some idea of when that might be?'

'Who knows. Look, I can't give you any more information at the moment,' Angelina said dismissively. 'I think it's time you got going.'

'I see.' Elena felt like an actor who'd failed an audition but was determined not to let Angelina see it. She squared her shoulders and said, 'I won't waste any more of your time then.'

Angelina nodded. 'You can let yourself out. And I'll get back to my packing.'

Elena had barely made it to the door when the words came from behind.

'You're doing well with your weight, by the way. I'm impressed. Still a way to go yet, though. Keep in mind, you'll need to get down to a size 6-8 if you get the job. We'll be sharing clothes, remember.'

Elena stood, frozen in her tracks, fingers clenched around the doorknob.

'You don't have to remind me,' she said without turning.

She could barely remember leaving the room and stepping into the lift at the end of the passageway.

The street was busy outside. People scurried past, office workers perhaps, returning from their lunch breaks, and intermittent bouts of loud chatter came from the patrons in a nearby, crammed café. All of a sudden, she felt light-headed. It had been hours since she'd last eaten, but a quick glance at her mobile told her that there was little time to grab something now. The bus was scheduled to depart from the terminal in twenty minutes. Across the road, two taxis were lined up at the rank. *Thank God*, she thought, stepping hurriedly out on the road and narrowly avoiding being hit by an approaching car. The driver slammed the horn with a volley of abuse that caused her to flinch.

The bus to Viveiro arrived right on time, and she clambered aboard, making her way down the crowded aisle to one of the few remaining seats at the back. Few spoke. Some stared out the window, eyes distant, while others sat, had heads bent, some with earphones, scrolling through their devices. The slightly built man in his thirties alongside her was asleep, mouth slightly open, head propped against the window.

As the bus pulled out onto the road to begin its three-hour journey back, Elena closed her eyes and reflected on the day. It had been a wasted trip, but that came as no surprise. She'd clung onto the hope that Angelina might have softened post-birth — shown at least some sign of being pleased to see her. But her face bore the austerity of a lawyer, matched by the dark hair pulled back in a tight bun, black pants and scarlet lipstick matching her silk shirt.

Who was she really? What made her like this? What was she doing here in the first place? Questions tumbled in her head like autumn leaves, questions she was never likely to receive answers to.

As the bus slowly emptied, Elena moved to another seat to stretch her legs and try to rest. But the engine's whir and constant reverberation from beneath kept her wide awake.

Once she finally alighted from the bus the bus in Viveiro, she found herself heading to the nearest takeaway shop. Dark clouds were rolling in from the sea when she stepped outside twenty minutes later, armed with a family-size pizza, large garlic bread and a two-litre bottle of coke. She could feel the temperature plummet as she made away along the final stretch of road to her flat, and she'd barely made it inside when it bucketed down. Rain lashed the windows, the tin roof shook, and the main light flickered precariously.

Chilled to the bone and exhausted, she headed to the bathroom for a hot shower. The hot steamy jets rejuvenated her, washing away the barrage of negative thoughts that had consumed her on the return journey.

Ten minutes later, she was seated, cross-legged on the floor in her flannelette pyjamas, flicking on the movie channel and devouring thick slabs of pizza as if she'd not eaten for days.

'Shit, that was good!' She gave her mouth a quick wipe with the serviette and snapped shut the pizza box.

It wasn't the first binge she'd had since Angelina left, and it wouldn't be the last. Progress might be slower, but Elena had learned the hard way that an all or nothing approach only led to disaster. She'd be back on track in the morning; increase the intensity of her workouts perhaps, or fast for a day or two. She had no doubts about reaching her target weight on time. Too much was at stake. Nonetheless, the thought of swapping clothes with Angelina made her uneasy. It didn't feel right somehow.

You can always walk out, remember, she told herself.

Little did she know how far from the truth that would be.

9

Angelina stepped out of the taxi at the hotel, waiting as the driver unloaded her bags from the back. A quick glance of her surroundings told her she'd made the right choice. The hotel sat directly in front of the harbour and promenade that stretched away into the distance. After months of being cooped up and being tailed, she couldn't wait to get out and explore.

Her room, on the sixth floor, offered sweeping views of the ocean and she nodded her approval to the porter as he awaited instructions of where to place her bags. Once he'd received his tip and left, she took a look around. Her quarters were spacious and airy and the furnishings stylish, in subtle tones of cream, pale blue, with an olive tinge.

Wasting no time, she kicked off her shoes, pulled out a pair of denim shorts, t-shirt and sandals from her case and did a quick change. Grabbing her keys and bag, she set out to gain her bearings. There was a large restaurant on the first floor and several small shops, including a hairdresser, boutique and café. But it was the sports complex that she most wanted to investigate.

Making her way through the lobby and out into the sunshine, she followed the signpost to the expanse of buildings set amongst tree-lined paths. The complex didn't disappoint. With three swimming pools, gyms, workout studios and treatment rooms, she could see herself spending most of her time there, without venturing outside the hotel, as she'd planned. Not that she had the slightest interest in exploring the old historical part of the city with its Roman and Baroque architecture, monuments and churches.

Every day began with early morning yoga stretches followed by a leisurely breakfast at the hotel's restaurant. It didn't take long for her appetite to return to normal, with the days of incessant heartburn and bland food now a distant memory. A series of non-stop activities followed, be it laps in the pool, cardio and weight sessions or spin classes in the cycling studio. Late afternoons were reserved for beauty treatments or a massage. Money was no issue. Thousands of dollars had been transferred from offshore accounts to her debit cards.

Nights were spent drink in hand, dressed in her thick, white bathrobe and curled up on the couch against the pillows, watching in-house movies. There was little inclination to go out on the town as planned. Time for the high life would come soon enough. In any case, there was no shortage of admirers at the hotel. The lanky, twenty-something-year-old gym instructor whose face flushed whenever she approached, the admiring eyes of the concierge, the lascivious glances of the bald-headed diner at breakfast, all served to feed her ego.

¶

The warm, salty air caressed Angelina's bare legs as she walked along the harbour front, and she smiled. It was a welcome relief from Viveiro that always seemed cold, even when the sun was out. A faint aroma of seaweed intermingled with fish wafted from off shore, reminding her of her hometown. She gave a toss of her head and tried not to think about it. Destinations more exotic and exciting awaited.

It seemed like an eternity since she'd not been followed or guarded. Yet, she still felt the need to watch the moves of those around her. Subsequently, she changed her hairstyle every day and wore baseball caps or a sunhat and oversized, dark sunglasses whenever she set foot outside. Yet she realised that may not be enough when she arrived back home. One morning she went to a hairdressing salon and had her long dark hair cut to shoulder length, making it easier to pile up under a wig. Finding a shop that stocked them was another matter.

Eventually, she found the small shop she'd sourced online that sold wigs and accessories. It was in the older part of town in a narrow, cobbled street, next to a barbershop. The middle-aged, thickset woman behind the counter watched as she walked in. Angelina knew that look of envy only too well.

'What can I do for you today?' the woman said in a thick English accent, curious as to why Angelina was there in the first place. Few customers were blessed with the luxurious, thick locks she possessed.

'Cancer,' came the response. 'I'm in for months of chemo.'

The woman gasped and put her hand to her mouth. 'Oh, I'm so sorry,' she said, 'here, let me help.'

Not long afterwards Angelina, walked out carrying a bag that contained three wigs of different colours, textures and lengths.

Three days before she was to leave, Angelina texted Theo to say that she would be in Melbourne and there could be another job he may well be interested in. There was an affirmative response not long afterwards, with details of an encrypted app to download before they next spoke.

She spent her last night seated on the harbour front's

stone wall, legs dangling, watching the orange sun slowly dipping beneath the pastel-streaked clouds.

39

Angelina's flight touched down in Melbourne at 11 a.m. to heavy grey skies with the threat of rain. She planned two nights in Melbourne to recover from her jet lag before contacting Nic. But staying at a well-known hotel could be unnecessarily risky. Instead, she'd secured a one-bedroom rental apartment not far from Nic's, at Docklands.

It was busy at customs and close to midday by the time she'd collected her luggage and made her way outside. Despite the stream of taxis lining the pavement, she headed for the zebra crossing that led towards the bus bay. Better to travel on public transport than risk being identified. The distinctive red double-decker Sky Bus sat some way ahead, and she knew she'd be cutting things fine to make its midday departure. A quick sprint, and she arrived just as the bus driver was closing the underneath luggage compartment.

The bus was close to total capacity, and she was directed

to one of the few remaining seats on the top level. The traffic thinned as they left the airport, past the endless stretch of parked cars that resembled child's toys from her vantage point, and onto the ring road leading to the city. It took just a little over twenty minutes before the bus pulled into Harbour Town, and she wheeled her luggage along the esplanade to her accommodation, in a modern apartment block, one of many, overlooking the water.

She was exhausted and drained from the long flight, which had been already delayed prior to departure, with sleep the only thing on her mind. After check-in and a quick shower, she changed into her pyjamas, yanked the curtain shut and fell into bed. It was another twenty-four hours before she stirred.

❡

For several days, Angelina watched the comings and goings of those entering the apartment block where Nic lived, but there was no sign of him. There'd be no way of entering the building without a key card or code, so she had no choice but to wait.

At first, she assumed he was away on a job and that never lasted more than a few weeks, from what he'd said. It didn't matter. Gave her more time to rest up and prepare for what was to come. But as time passed, she became more on edge. What if he no longer lived here? Maybe he'd shacked up with some woman.

She was not to know that he was in North Queensland, staying with his brother and family.

40

David Zielinski sat in the bedroom of his ailing mother, holding her hand as she slept, gazing down on the garden he had loved to explore as a child. Branches of once trimmed bushes spilled over moss covered concrete paths, and trees that had been left untended for years were towering giants, letting in little light. The gardener that Helena Zielinski had employed for the past thirty years did the best he could, but his eyesight was failing and fingers arthritic.

David glanced up at the ceiling, where large cracks were beginning to appear. Window frames were splintered and needed replacing, and the carpet faded and worn. The place had an old people smell about it. Of dark rooms and damp and cupboards. In truth, the house was deteriorating. Rapidly.

He no longer had the attachment he once had to the place. His whole world now centred around being close to Jennifer and Cara. He'd done his grieving for his mother, who'd just days to live. Made his peace with her before she slipped into a coma. Revealed to her the grandchild she thought she'd never have. Filled her with that much happiness, at least.

Once she'd gone, he'd set about selling the place. It wouldn't take long. The inner-city double-storey brick residence was in prime position and would likely be bull-dozed for development. But first, he'd find comfortable accommodation close to public transport and amenities for Alice, the family's long-term, live-in housekeeper and Ben, the gardener, per his mother's wishes, permanently funded by a trust set up in both names.

Five days later, David was making arrangements for his mother's funeral.

⁋

The day after Helena Zielinski's funeral, David returned home to be near Jennifer and Cara. He'd spent the last four weeks of his mother's life by her side, and was putting in place arrangements to settle her estate.

It was close to dark as he walked down the dirt track towards Kilkenny, the familiar salt-laden wind whipping his cheeks. As he approached the main gates, he realised it was no longer possible to go along like this, feigning noth-ing more than deep, platonic affection towards Jennifer.

He'd been naïve to think she'd always be within a stone's throw from his house, waiting for him to arrive to give Cara

322

her next piano lesson. Perhaps it was the photo he spotted in the society pages of the Melbourne newspaper, showing Jennifer dressed in an elegant, emerald satin dress alongside two men, not much older than she, at a charity concert held for her mother-in-law's trust. He didn't recognise either. Perhaps they were just acquaintances.

But there'd be others ...

David's mouth went dry as he rang the bell and listened to Jennifer's light footsteps approach.

'At last,' she reached up to kiss his cheek and put her arm through his. 'Cara's been hanging out for you to get here.'

He managed a smile and accompanied her to the living room where Cara stood, back to them, sorting through some sheet music.

At his voice, she turned and rushed over to greet him with a tight hug as if he'd been away for years. His mother's funeral had been neither the time nor place to reconnect. He felt his heart squeeze as he pressed his face into her hair. No matter what eventuated between him and Jennifer, there remained a shared, profound bond — their daughter's love.

As Cara played, David found his eyes drawn towards Jennifer, who seemed lost in thought, absorbed in the music. Wanted her even more. But she'd indicated no such sentiment. If anything, David sensed a contentment in the knowledge that he'd never willingly walked away from her all those years ago. That he'd loved her once as she'd loved him. It seemed enough. As they reconnected and she confided little-by-little what she'd suffered at the hands of Dominic, he wondered if she'd ever find it in her heart to truly love again.

In the middle of the third movement of a Beethoven Sonata, he gestured for Cara to stop playing.

'Did I not play that correctly?'

'No,' he said. 'There's something I need to say to your mother. Something that should have been said a long time ago.'

He turned to face Jennifer. 'I'd like you to become my wife, Jennifer. Will you marry me?'

Cara gasped and swung around towards her mother, too overwhelmed to respond.

There was an awkward few moments' silence. 'I don't know what to say,' Jennifer said. 'This is all so unexpected.'

'I know, and I shouldn't have sprung it on you like this. Perhaps you need time to think about it.'

She shook her head. 'No, I already have my answer, David. The answer's yes.'

'Oh my God!' Cara jumped up and threw her arms around Jennifer's neck.

David's eyes never left Jennifer's as he stepped across to wrap his arms around the two of them, his heart soaring.

A simple ceremony was held after five days, attended only by the couple and Cara and Will, with Cara giving her mother away. It took place in Kilkenny's gardens under the pergola, given a last-minute paint job by Will and adorned with a profusion of pink and white flowers. Jennifer wore the same green emerald dress that David noted in the society pages, and he was in an open-necked white shirt and grey pants. Dinner followed at an exclusive Italian restaurant that had just opened, thirty kilometres from town.

The honeymoon was placed on hold until after David had settled his mother's estate. Meanwhile, they returned to Kilkenny as husband and wife, with plans for his neighbouring house to undergo significant renovations and then be placed on the market.

Will wiped his brow at the end of the shift and arched his back. It had been a particularly long day, with a worker short, returning home to Queensland to be close to his family. Will didn't blame him. It was only a matter of days before the building contract expired, and the novelty of their beach bum existence had long worn off for the remaining housemates.

Things had come to a head at breakfast that morning.

'If we work an extra few hours each day, we can get out of here by Thursday,' Matty, the youngest, said as they tucked into a stack of bacon and eggs. 'What do you reckon, Will?' he asked.

'Depends on you, Liam,' Will turned to the third member. 'Are you okay with heading back a few days earlier?'

'Wouldn't mind, actually.'

'Well, that looks like it then,' Will remarked, masking his true feelings.

'Beaudy,' Matty said with a mouthful of toast, 'let's have

a party on Wednesday night to celebrate. Go to the pub the night before to latch onto some chicks.'

Will gave a wry grin. 'Maybe the night after that. We've got to clean the place first, remember. Get rid of all the shit.'

There was a groan in response and a grin from Liam.

¶

Will reached for his water bottle on the newly sanded bench, swilling the last of its warm contents and wiping his mouth with the back of his hand. He'd been upfront with Cara from the outset. Told her he'd be in town for only a few months, and they hadn't discussed it since. Surely, the news would come as little surprise.

But the fact was, time had passed way too quickly. For the first time in Will's life, he'd felt wanted, needed, by Jennifer and Cara. He was prepared to go above and beyond to protect them from the menace of Angelina. But it was more than that. He felt as if he belonged, was part of a family. Laughing with them, sharing their fears, doing what was needed around the house.

But things had changed now that David and Jennifer were married.

Not that he wasn't happy for them, particularly Jennifer. She deserved happiness after what she'd endured over the past few years. And Cara was positively glowing. She had her life ahead of her, with David arranging music lessons in the city with a recently retired concert pianist.

'He's by far a better teacher than I could ever be,' David had quipped.

There was nothing here for him now. It was time to leave.

Maybe it wasn't such a good idea to return to Cara in the first place, he thought. But he'd always known that he would. There was something about Cara Lorenzo, something he was yet to put the finger on. He had the choice of women at his fingertips. His good looks and easy-going manner ensured that. There'd been several flings and a long-term relationship. Yet Cara sat at the back of his mind all this time. Elusive. Out of reach.

He had no idea what to expect when he returned. She seemed happy enough to see him, didn't she? A hand in his when they walked, an occasional head on his shoulder. But was it just the protection from her sister that Cara so badly needed? Will had searched for a spark of affection. He could find none. Perhaps it was for the best that he left earlier than planned. Each day spent with Cara only made things that much harder.

9

Cara opened the door with surprise. 'Hi. I thought you said you were working late today.'

'Yeah. We knocked off not long ago,' Will said. 'I need to speak to you about something. Is that okay?'

'Sure.' she said, 'come in. Mum and Dad are over at his place, sorting through a few things. They shouldn't be long.'

He nodded and followed her towards the living room. 'Why don't you stay for dinner?' Cara said over her shoulder. 'I'm about to get it ready.'

Will stopped her with a hand on her shoulder and stepped around to face her. 'I've come to say I'm leaving in three days, Cara. The boss has a big job starting up in Brisbane.'

'Oh?'

'Earlier than expected, I know, but –'

'You don't have to explain yourself.'

'You don't mind?'

'Does it matter what I think? You need to go where the work is.'

Will's felt his spirits plummet.

'I'll drop by, of course, to say goodbye.'

'Mum will be sorry to see you go.'

And you? he thought. 'There are always jobs down this way,' he said all too quickly. 'I'm sure I'll be back some time.'

Cara raised an eyebrow.

This was turning out worse than he thought.

'Thanks for the offer of dinner, but best I get going.'

Will bent down, cupped her face in his fingers, gently brushed her lips, and said, 'I'll miss you, Cara. I'm glad everything worked out for you.'

She watched him walk away.

9

Will looked on as Matt and Liam loaded the last of the rubbish to be taken to the tip, then headed back inside. Hands on hips, he scanned the room. It would have to do. The place was as clean as they were going to get it. Will was the only one for order and cleanliness. The past few months had driven him nuts. Dirty cups and plates in the sink when he got up, a fridge that reeked of cheese, garlic and salami and a toilet bowl that would have resembled one at a run-down sports ground if he'd not cleaned it daily with what remained of a toilet brush.

Luckily, there'd been no broken windows or beer stains from the previous night's wild party. Not that he could remember much. His flatmates had watched him with considerable amusement. It wasn't like Will to wipe himself out on whatever he could lay his hands on.

It was close to midday. Will had woken with a thumping head and downed a few strong coffees before dragging the other two out of bed. He knew he'd made a big mistake not organising the final clean up earlier. He was about to head to the shower when he heard a knock on the door. Looking up in surprise, he crossed the room to answer it.

Cara stood on the front porch. 'I'm sorry to drop in unannounced, Will, but I thought you might be in need of this.' She pulled out a red tape measure from the pocket of her jeans. 'I found it on the decking.'

Will grinned broadly. 'I've been looking for that bloody thing all over the place.'

Cara looked down at the floor and then met his eyes. 'That's not the real reason I'm here, Will.' She hesitated for a moment. 'You said you'd miss me. How much?'

'What's that supposed to mean?'

'Were you saying that just to make me feel better?'

'Feel better? Shit, Cara. Why do you think I came back in the first place?' He said, eyes flashing. 'What's all this about, anyway?'

'I don't want to lose you a second time, if you must know,' she fired back. 'I'm asking you to stay. Is that good enough for you?'

Will stared at her, barely able to take in what he'd heard. 'Yeah,' he said, after a few moments. 'That's good enough. And in answer to your question, I'll stay.'

Cara tilted her head and said, 'In that case, would you move in with me?'

'I reckon I could handle that.' He pulled her into his arms.

42

Nic Drakos was making himself a protein shake at his Docklands apartment after a late afternoon run when his phone rang. A quick glance at the number, and he jumped with a start, sending the glass and its half-filled contents flying.

Heart hammering, he fumbled for the reply button. 'Christ, Ava, what do you want?'

'I'm back in Australia, Nic. I need to see you.'

'Why?'

'I can't discuss it over the phone.'

'Where are you?'

'Below your apartment. In the park.'

Nic's eyes whipped to the window, and with legs suddenly weak, he hurried across, forehead pressed against the cold glass.

'I'll be down.'

He turned and headed to the door, grabbing his key card, his mind a whirl of conflicting emotions. Fury that she'd dare show up after what she'd put him through, and a longing for her so intense it took his breath away. *There'd better be a damned good reason for this*, he thought as he strode through the main entrance and crossed the path to the park, oblivious of the wind that bit through his lightweight t-shirt.

Steeling himself, he strode across and stopped before her, jaw set hard and eyes cold on hers.

'You look good.' She lay a hand on a muscled bicep. He pulled away.

'Aren't you cold?' she said.

'How did you find me?' he demanded.

'The photo of us taken by the hotel waiter. Remember? You scribbled your address on the back before you left for Bangkok.'

'Yeah. I remember.' The words were frosty. 'Thought you'd be here when I got back.'

'Don't be like that,' she pleaded. 'I explained why I had to get the hell out of the country.'

There was no response.

'I missed you, Nic,' she said.

He stiffened. 'I've moved on, Ava.'

There was silence except for the intermittent faint shrieks of children from a distant playground.

'I see. I can hardly blame you.'

'So what is it you wanted to see me about?'

She looked around. 'I'd rather not discuss things here. Plus, it's bloody freezing.'

He didn't return her smile.

'All right then. You can come up to my apartment.'

Not another word was spoken as they headed towards the building opposite, and Angelina took a deep, inward breath as they entered the lift. This was far from the reaction she'd been expecting.

As they entered the apartment, Angelina's eyes fixed on the packing boxes lining the walls.

'You're leaving?' she turned to him.

'Yeah, sold the place three months ago. Have to be out by the end of the week.'

'Where are you going?'

'Queensland, probably. I've got family up there. Buy some land, perhaps.' He shrugged. 'Who knows.'

Her eyes swept the modern, tastefully decorated apartment, and she headed over the window to take a look at the view. 'I really like this place,' she said, turning to face Nic. 'Aren't you going to miss it?'

Another shrug. 'Haven't spent much time here, to be honest.' He turned on the heating and reached for the jacket that had been slung over a nearby chair. 'Coffee?'

'Yeah. That'd be good.'

'Take a seat.'

Nic headed to the kitchen, hastily mopping up the remains of the protein shake before attending to the coffee. Not long afterwards, he placed two expressos on the coffee table and sat opposite on the matching leather two-seater.

'All right then' he said, wasting no time, 'so what's up?'

'I gave birth, two weeks ago, in Spain, Nic. To a baby girl. You're the father.'

'What!' he shot bolt upright. 'You expect me to believe that?'

Angelina pulled out her iPhone and scrolled through her camera roll, clicking on a photo of the baby in the hospital nursery.

'It could be anyone's baby.' he said quickly, mouth dry and heart racing.

'It's yours, don't worry. A DNA test will prove that.'

'Fuck, Ava! Why did you wait all this time to tell me?'

'You were so angry when I called you from Doha,' she said. 'It was clear you wanted to move on. I could understand that. I didn't know I was pregnant then, I swear.'

Nic sat in stunned disbelief, barely able to take in what she was saying.

'Where is she now?' he demanded.

'She's in safe hands, don't worry.'

'I'm her father. I want to see her.'

Angelina breathed deeply. 'I was hoping you'd say that. I considered abortion. I can't lie.'

His stomach clenched. 'And why didn't you?'

'I missed you when I was away, Nic. Realised I needed you. Had to know if you felt the same about starting up as a family as I did. In the end, it was a risk I had to take.'

'Christ, Ava.' He ran a hand through his hair. 'I wished you'd told me all this before. When can we go and get her?'

'I'll get to that. First, I've a favour to ask.'
'What sort of favour?' His voice was wary.
'I want you to do one last job before we leave.'

Who is the girl in the background and
what does she know that others don't?

THE GIRL
IN THE
BACKGROUND

The culmination of the chilling
Dark Illusion Trilogy